WHEN SHE'S GONE

WHEN SHE'S GONE

A THRILLER

JANE PALMER

CROOKED
LANE

NEW YORK

Copyright © 2016 by The Quick Brown Fox & Company LLC.

All rights reserved.

Published in the United States by Crooked Lane Books, an imprint of The Quick Brown Fox & Company LLC.

Crooked Lane Books and its logo are trademarks of The Quick Brown Fox & Company LLC.

Library of Congress Catalog-in-Publication data available upon request.

ISBN (hardcover): 978-1-62953-774-0
ISBN (ePub): 978-1-62953-809-9
ISBN (Kindle): 978-1-62953-810-5
ISBN (ePDF): 978-1-62953-811-2

Cover design by Lori Palmer.
Book design by Jennifer Canzone.

Printed in the United States.

www.crookedlanebooks.com

Crooked Lane Books
34 West 27th St., 10th Floor
New York, NY 10001

First edition: November 2016

10 9 8 7 6 5 4 3 2 1

CHAPTER ONE

The man was staring.

Ara felt the weight of the stranger's gaze as surely as if he'd reached out to touch her. She pressed her arm against her clutch and felt the familiar outline of her handgun. The weight and solidness of it reassured her. It was, after all, the one thing she could count on.

The art gallery sparkled with sophistication and color. The paintings on the wall were oil abstracts done by a new and upcoming artist who was, according to the gallery owner, extraordinary.

Ara thought the paintings looked like something a two-year-old could do.

Her opinion, no doubt, was in the minority. So far this evening, she'd overheard nothing but praise for the artist. The rooms were filled with flashy people, mostly women, wearing expensive dresses and designer shoes. They mingled and laughed, holding flutes of bubbling champagne and eating tiny appetizers. Each time the door opened to allow a new person entrance, the music of New York City filtered in. Buses, shouting, the faint smell of sausage.

Still staring.

Ara licked her lips, her gaze carefully tracking the room. Nothing else seemed amiss. Nothing but the stranger who'd been watching them for the last fifteen minutes.

He bounced on the balls of his feet suddenly and began moving across the room, elegantly weaving through the throng. As he approached, she grew ever mindful, her entire body preparing. Her breathing slowed, her limbs relaxed, and she shifted her body protectively. Casually, she tucked her hand inside of her bag, her fingers wrapping around the cool metal of her weapon.

He bypassed her without a glance.

Ara watched as he greeted a woman who'd just come in from the brisk October night. They air-kissed each other's cheeks in an Upper East Side fashion before quickly moving toward the bar. She relaxed her tense grip on her gun, allowing the purse to slide to her elbow. He'd been watching the door, not them.

"Don't you just love the colors in this one, Holly?" Kat, the gallery owner, cut through Ara's thoughts. She was garishly dressed in a bright-orange jumpsuit—the color leaning closer to neon—and heavy turquoise jewelry. On anyone else, the outfit would have looked ridiculous. Kat made it work.

Next to her, Holly's understated elegance couldn't be more noticeable. Everything from the upsweep of her hair to the faint star detailing on her shoes was sheer perfection. She was a woman to whom dressing beautifully came easily and naturally.

Kat waved a hand toward the nearest painting. "The artist calls it *Moonshine*."

"It's amazing." Holly tilted her head delicately. "I think it would look stunning in Oliver's office."

She stepped a bit closer, her pale-blue eyes tracking over the frame. No doubt assessing its worth. "What do you think, Ara? Wouldn't this look wonderful? You know, in that space behind his desk."

Ara couldn't imagine having to look at the large painting, with its dark, black-and-blue streaks, every day. Depressing didn't even begin to describe it.

"It would look amazing," she said, smiling tightly.

Holly flashed her a bright smile and turned back to Kat. "I'll take it. And of course, I'd like to have it delivered tomorrow afternoon."

Ara half-listened to the conversation between the two women as she watched Sam, Holly's daughter, across the room. She'd been sulking for most of the evening, but now her peals of laughter could be heard even from where Ara was standing. She was talking to a young man, her heart-shaped face lit up with interest.

"Excuse me," Ara murmured to the other two women, then slipped into the crowd. Even as she crossed toward Sam, she discreetly scanned the room. Her gaze skipped over the waiter serving tuna tartare, the man in the corner who'd had two glasses of champagne, the old woman in a sequined dress arguing with another woman in fuchsia shoes and pearl earrings.

Ara had been to this art gallery many times before with Holly and Sam. She knew all the entrances and exits, the number of paces it took to cross the room in high heels, the positions of the security cameras. She might be outfitted in a tight red cocktail dress, her hair perfectly styled and a manicure gracing her fingertips, but it was all part of her job. Part of the ruse as Holly's "personal assistant."

No one would ever guess she was actually the bodyguard.

Ara took a glass of champagne off of a waiter's tray as he went past and held it in one hand as she sidled up to the painting closest to Sam and the young man.

"I agree—the colors here are extraordinary," Sam said, tossing her long blonde hair over one shoulder. "You have such a good taste, Nick."

They moved to the next painting. Ara floated along behind them, her attention fixed on them even though she was facing the gray-and-orange monstrosity on canvas in front of her.

Nick leaned close and whispered something in Sam's ear, and she laughed again, a musical sound, cultured and clean. The simple white dress she wore clung to her body in all the right places, and the pencil-thin heels exaggerated her already long legs. Sam looked nothing like her age. She could have easily passed for twenty-five.

Nick swiped his shaggy hair out of his eyes, a smile playing at the corners of his full lips. He was handsome, with chiseled features, broad shoulders, and a swoon-worthy smile. His hand was placed respectfully on the small of Sam's back. Yet something about him made Ara wary. His nose had been broken. His knuckles and fingernails were rough, as though he was used to hard labor. His suit was flattering, but it wasn't made from the best material, nor was it tailored to his body.

Обманщик.

The Russian word flitted through her mind, and she searched for the English version. *Imposter*—that was it. Her native tongue wasn't one she used much anymore, so sometimes it still took her a second to translate.

She looked over at Sam and took in the way her charge leaned into Nick—her face lit up with a smile, her cheeks flushed.

Nick was an impostor. *And sure*, she thought wryly, *it takes one to know one.* But while they both belonged among this group of wealthy elite about as much as a fish at a steakhouse, Ara knew how to fake it. Nick did not.

Nick whispered something else in Sam's ear, and when he pulled back, Ara could have sworn Sam's eyelashes actually fluttered.

Oh, this was not good.

Sam's lips brushed against Nick's cheek, and she tenderly trailed a hand down his arm. "I'll see you soon."

Sam turned and nearly ran right into Ara. She scowled at Ara before brushing past and crossing the room toward the big window near the front of the gallery. Ara fought back a sigh and followed.

It wasn't easy watching over a seventeen-year-old girl. Especially a stubborn, strong-willed, and rebellious one. For a moment, Ara felt a pang of loss.

Stop. That's all over.

And it was. She'd left her old life behind and moved up north for a fresh start. Finding a job she liked had proved more difficult—no police department would touch her anymore—so she'd wound up here, a private bodyguard for the spoiled, teen-age stepdaughter of an uber-elite billionaire.

At least the pay was amazing.

"Can't you hover from the corner of the room or something?" Sam waved her hand in a flicking motion. "How am I ever going to get a date with you on my heels?"

"Is that what you were doing?" Ara asked, ignoring Sam's tone. A waiter passed by, and Ara placed her untouched champagne glass on his tray. "Isn't he a bit old for you?"

"No." She opened her silver purse and removed a tube of lipstick. "He's twenty-one, if you must know. An appropriate age."

"I doubt your mother would agree." Ara passed a glance in Holly's direction. The woman had been fluttering around the room in a giant circle for the last few minutes.

"Oh, mind your own business." Sam applied the rouge color with expertise, using her reflection in the window to check for smears. "Besides, he works with the gallery as an art dealer. Perfectly respectable."

"You should still be careful."

Sam arched her eyebrows. "I already have one mother, Ara. I'm not looking for another."

"I suppose you're not. But I am hoping we can at least be friends." She rocked back on her heels, easing the pressure on the balls of her feet. These shoes were not her most comfortable ones. "Maybe one day you'll miss having me as your shadow."

"I wouldn't count on it." Sam snapped the purse closed just as Holly appeared at their side.

"There you are." She sounded a bit breathless. "I've been searching the room for you."

"We've been here for the last three minutes, Mom. You couldn't have been looking that hard."

Sam's tone was dismissive. Annoyance flashed across Holly's face, and she glanced at Ara as though looking for support.

Ara didn't say anything. She'd learned to keep quiet while mother and daughter dealt with each other.

"Well, listen—I've run into an old acquaintance of mine, Claire Hutchinson. She's a trustee for Princeton, and I want you to meet her."

"This woman that you want me to meet—did she refuse to give you the time of day before you married Oliver?"

Holly rolled her eyes. "Don't start again, Sam."

Sam's face flushed. "These people are fake. They didn't want anything to do with us a year ago."

Ara had to admit the teenager had a point. People had started taking a more serious interest in Holly, and subsequently Sam, once they found out about their connection to Oliver.

"This woman can help open the doors to Princeton," Holly hissed at her daughter. "Which you need, since your grades are absolutely atrocious."

"Yes, let's buy our way in."

Holly reached out and gripped Sam's forearm, her fingers turning white with the effort.

"Cut it out. You're lucky that Oliver is willing to pay for your college education at all." She leaned in closer to Sam. "You need to be pleasant and respectful for ten minutes while meeting this woman. Do you think you can accomplish that?"

It was a big request. Sam hadn't been pleasant and respectful to any adult since Ara had known her.

"Fine." Sam plastered on a fake smile. "I'll be nice. But only because college means I can move out."

Holly sucked in a breath and opened her mouth as though to say something but then seemed to change her mind. She swiped a hand over her tailored, mauve cocktail dress, smoothing out invisible wrinkles. "All right, let's go."

* * *

Ara was impressed. Not only had Sam been respectful—she'd been downright pleasant. The initial introduction had gone so well that Holly invited Claire to dinner. The restaurant was posh, with artistic chandeliers and more wine choices than food. The group was quickly ushered to an exclusive corner table.

The waiter fluttered around, making sure they had everything they needed before taking their order. Afterward, Holly and Claire kept up a steady stream of conversation, occasionally punctuated by a comment from Sam. Ara said very little. She knew her place: Blend in, don't talk unless spoken to, and then as little as possible. Basically, act like a piece of pretty furniture.

"I can't tell you, Holly," Claire said after the food arrived, "how delightful it is to see what a wonderful young woman you've raised."

Holly beamed. "Thank you, Claire."

"I'm horribly delayed in telling you how sorry I was to hear of the plane crash. It must have been an awful time for you."

Beside her, Sam drew in a sharp breath, and Ara reached under the table to gently tap her wrist. Sam grabbed Ara's hand and squeezed it so tightly, Ara felt her bones crunch together.

It was in these moments Ara remembered Sam was still a child. A little girl trapped in a young woman's body, without the tools or skills necessary to deal with the blows life had thrown at her. The loss of her father and her older brother in a plane crash two years ago was rarely discussed in the Boone house, even between Sam and her mother. It was as if, with her new marriage, Holly wanted to erase any painful reminders of the life she would never have again. Unfortunately, it left Sam floundering, alone and in pain.

Ara knew exactly what that felt like.

"It was very painful, as you can imagine." Holly's voice was low and trembled slightly. She pasted on a smile. "But of course, now we have many new, wonderful things to celebrate."

"Absolutely. Like your marriage." Claire gently cut into her fish and delicately lifted a piece to her mouth. "And to Oliver Boone, no less. Very impressive."

"Oliver works very hard at being *impressive*," Sam said.

Holly shot her a warning glance before turning her attention back to Claire. "Oliver is a very special man."

"Of course he is." Claire raised her eyebrows slightly. She had to be picking up on the tension at the table, but either good manners or simple decency kept her tone easy and polite. "How did the two of you meet?"

"I was working for ABC," Holly said, "and did a story on Oliver's investment into the New York Giants. He agreed to be interviewed. It was as simple as that, I'm afraid." She leaned in toward the other woman. "How is your son doing? Last I knew, he was at Princeton, aiming for law school next."

Claire smiled, but her face barely moved, not a wrinkle appearing. "He's wonderful. He's VP now. Charles, my husband, is so happy to have him working in the family business."

The conversation droned on. Next to Ara, Sam was scowling, pushing her food around on her plate and surreptitiously checking her phone for the time.

When dinner was finally over, Sam dumped her linen napkin on the table and said, "Excuse me. I'm going to run to the ladies' room. It was nice to meet you, Mrs. Hutchinson."

Claire gave her a polite nod. "You too, dear. Please contact me after your final examinations. I know Princeton would adore having you join the freshman class. I do hope you'll apply next year."

"I'll make sure she does," Holly assured her. Sam quickly slipped from the room, and Ara rose to follow her.

Before she could take a step, however, Holly said, "Ara, why don't you ask the valet to pull Claire's car around? And please text our driver and let him know we're ready to go. I'll just say good-bye to Claire, and then I'll come find you outside."

Ara debated arguing. She couldn't protect Sam and Holly from outside the restaurant. She shouldn't have even let Sam go to the bathroom alone, but explaining that fact wasn't possible right now. Not only would it reveal her as the family's bodyguard, but it would also embarrass Holly in front of Claire.

Smothering a frustrated sigh and making a note to have a conversation with her employer later, Ara gave a short nod. "Of course. I'll be right outside."

The quiet murmurs of the restaurant gave way to the bustle of city life as Ara stepped out. She handed Claire's valet ticket to the sharply dressed man at the station before texting David, the Boones' driver, asking him to bring the town car around.

Business done, she tightened the belt on her coat against the evening chill. One thing she loved about New York was the cooler weather. Long sleeves were a must for most of the year, and since that was all Ara wore, she fit in far better than she had in Texas, where the heat was blistering from March until October.

The door swung open, and Claire stepped outside, bundled in a fur coat, just as her car arrived at the curb.

"Ara, it was lovely to meet you," Claire said as she passed. "Have a nice evening."

"You too." Ara watched the older woman press a bill into the valet's hand before gracefully dropping behind the wheel of her Lexus.

Frowning, Ara turned toward the restaurant. Where were Holly and Sam? She'd expected they would come out with Claire. A quick scan of the interior through the windows didn't reveal them, and a sick feeling tightened in Ara's gut.

Silly. They're both probably in the restroom.

A black town car pulled up to the curb, and Ara held up one finger, gesturing to Gannon, the other bodyguard, and

David, the driver, that she would be a moment. She reached for the restaurant's door handle, swinging it open wide. Holly was going to have to understand that she couldn't just disappear from—

A blood-curdling scream broke through the quiet hum of the restaurant.

Ara's stomach dropped. It was coming from the back. From the restrooms.

She crossed the room in quick strides, simultaneously pulling the gun from her purse. Holly, eyes wide with panic, ran out into the main dining room. She caught sight of Ara and nearly collapsed.

"Sam! Oh my god . . . Sam!"

Ara gripped Holly's arm with one hand. "Where is she?"

"Th-th-they took her," she sputtered, the words unable to come. "A man . . . a van . . ."

Ara didn't wait for Holly to finish. She spun on her heel, running back toward the front door. The restaurant had a delivery entrance right next to the bathrooms. There was only one way in or out of it, and that was through the alley alongside the building.

She burst out of the restaurant, adrenaline coursing through her veins.

A white van. It peeled out of the alley. Tires screaming, it took a left-hand turn and raced through a red light, narrowly missing a Toyota before disappearing around the corner.

"Get inside to Holly," Ara ordered Gannon. He'd emerged from the town car and was waiting on the sidewalk. She flew past him.

Yanking open the door, she screamed, "Get out of the car! Get out of the car!"

She physically tugged David from the seat. The engine was running, and Ara took off from the curb, the force of her maneuver causing the vehicle's door to slam shut.

"Come on, come on," she muttered, taking a sharp turn and pressing the gas pedal as low as it would go. The town car shot forward, horns honking all around her.

Weave.

Swerve.

Her heart battered against her ribcage, and her palms were sweaty. It took all her concentration to keep control of the vehicle as she maneuvered through traffic, desperate to catch up to the blinking taillights she could just barely make out several blocks ahead of her.

She pushed the vehicle, leaning forward in the seat. *Two blocks left.*

God damn it, where was a New York City traffic jam when you needed it?

She flew through a red light, taking the town car onto the curb to avoid crashing into several cars in the intersection. *One block.*

Ara let up on the gas pedal, getting into the lane next to the white van. Unlike when it had pulled out of the alley, the driver was now going the speed limit, careful to not draw attention. The back and sides of the vehicle weren't marked. The only windows were in the front. It looked like nothing more than a regular delivery van.

The driver was midthirties. Dark hair and light skin. No passenger.

She pulled slightly ahead of the van and then, without warning, hurtled her vehicle directly into his path.

She kept her hands on the steering wheel but let her body go limp.

The van slammed into the front-passenger side of the town car, the sound of grating metal reverberating in Ara's head. The windshield and passenger-side glass shattered. Square shards flew across the interior. She'd instinctively closed her eyes but forced them open as the two cars skidded forward from the force of the impact and screeched to a halt.

She would only have seconds to gain the upper hand. She needed every one.

She leapt from the vehicle, gun in hand, and ran to the door of the van. Pulling it open, she pointed the gun at the man's head and said in a low, hard voice, "Put your hands up."

He was dazed. The sudden impact had caused his airbag to explode. Ara knew it wasn't something most people could easily recover from.

"W-W-What are you doing?" The driver shook his head in an obvious attempt to combat the effects of the airbag.

"Put your damn hands up," Ara ordered. "Now."

"Okay, okay." Wide-eyed, he raised his trembling hands. Ara couldn't see into the vehicle since the cab was completely closed off from the backside. "Get out. Slowly."

He dropped to the ground, and his legs nearly collapsed underneath him. Ara grabbed him by the back of the neck, pushing the gun into his head. "Now you are going to do exactly as I say, or I'm going to blow your damn brains out. Do you understand?"

He swallowed hard, hands still in the air, and nodded.

She shoved him—practically carried him—to the back of the van. "Open the doors."

Ara waited until he started to swing one door open before she took a step back and aimed her weapon. She blocked out the sound of the shouting on the street, the horns honking from the other drivers, the sound of her own heartbeat. Her entire focus was on the back of the van, on what she would find inside. Her trigger finger twitched, ready to fire.

She sucked in a breath as the last door swung open. The van was empty.

CHAPTER TWO

"**W**here is she?" Ara demanded.

The man, his hands still raised, shook his head in confusion. "Lady, I don't know what you're talking about. I'm just a driver."

"For who?" A whisper of doubt began to form in Ara's mind.

"Cheryl's Cakes over on sixth. I just did a delivery to the Four Seasons."

Her eyes narrowed. He sounded truthful, but anyone, with enough practice, could be a good liar. It was possible Sam had been transferred from the van to another vehicle. Doubtful, given the time frame, but still possible. And it was something she had to rule out.

"There's no lettering on this van." Honking horns punctuated her sentence. In a moment, the drivers of the other cars would be getting out to investigate. Someone would be calling the police and an ambulance, if they hadn't already. The cover of darkness and the positioning of Ara's body had shielded her weapon from almost everyone but the driver, but she couldn't keep a gun on him much longer. A decision had to be made. "You could be anyone."

"The invoice is in the cab of the truck."

"Show me."

With jerky steps, he moved to the front of the van and pulled out a clean, neatly written receipt, stamped with both the time and date.

Everything he said jived.

Cursing under her breath, she holstered her gun. "Sorry about this. Someone will be by to compensate you."

"But—"

She didn't wait to hear what he was going to say. Instead, Ara turned and rapidly took off down the street. *Damn it.* Following the wrong van was a mistake with potentially deadly consequences.

Pulling her cell phone from a secret pocket sewn into her dress, she speed-dialed a special number. When a gruff, deep voice answered, she said, "Code red. Daughter. I need a town car at Phillips immediately."

Mick, the owner of the deep voice, hesitated for just a second, and then there was a clatter as the phone hit a surface. Ara had covered one more block before he came back on the line.

"On its way. Police?"

His voice was even, but a touch of stress threaded its way through. Ara heard it but trusted him to keep a level head. As head of security, Mick's primary job was to be at the mansion, monitoring his staff and acting as a point of contact. He was military trained, big and bulky, with brains to boot. In all the time they'd been working together, he'd never let her down.

"Negative," she said, turning another corner. "But I'm not at the restaurant now, and someone might have called them."

She glanced behind her. No one was following. But the wreck would need cleanup, and there would probably be a police investigation. Money and a lot of red tape would be required to keep the mess from landing on the Boones' doorstep, which meant calling out the lawyers. "I also need Ricks to report to the corner of Third and Sixty-Fourth. I chased the bastards but didn't catch them. Wrecked the car."

"Holly?"

"Secured with Gannon."

"He'll control the situation." Mick's voice was full of confidence. "The car should arrive in two minutes."

"Good. I'll call you when we are en route."

She hung up and accelerated her pace, weaving through the pedestrians and running where she could. She'd crossed more ground than she'd thought, chasing the van.

The wrong damn van.

Ara's stomach twisted, and she felt bile rise in the back of her throat. Where was Sam? Who had her? And why? Oh God, what were they doing to her right now?

Don't think about it. She battled back the emotions threatening to overtake her. She couldn't afford them. Not yet. Right now, she needed her training, the skills and instincts honed during her years on the force.

She rounded a final corner, and the restaurant came into view. A momentary wave of relief crashed over her. No police cars. No panic in the street. Nothing to indicate anything had transpired only ten minutes ago.

Ara's steps slowed as she approached the main entrance. She couldn't walk in without knowing what the situation was. Through the front glass, she spotted waiters bustling around the tables. Patrons eating, talking, and drinking fine wines. It was a serene sight—quiet, low-key. Gannon had controlled the scene. Thank God.

She opened the door, and Robert, the manager, pounced on her. His thin frame was ramrod straight, his long face overwhelmed by a bulbous nose. "Mrs. Boone is in my office."

"Take me there."

She followed him through the restaurant, her gaze sweeping over the patrons. Checking to see if anyone was watching them, watching her. No one even gave her a passing glance. Robert led her through a silk-covered door into a large office. While it wasn't as posh as the restaurant itself, the space was decorated with a careful eye for detail. A gleaming wooden desk, high-backed visitors' chairs, and top-of-the-line electronic equipment.

Holly sat on a leather sofa, her eye makeup smeared across her face. She held a fistful of tissues in one hand, and the other gripped David's. Her blonde hair was mussed, strands drifting out of her French knot to wave around her reddened face.

David was whispering to her, murmuring words Ara couldn't hear. The Boones' driver was a strictly professional man in his midfifties, with unlined, ebony skin and black, short-cropped hair flecked with gray. He'd always been careful to keep professional boundaries, so the sight of Holly's delicate fingers tightly holding onto his massive, darker ones hit Ara square in the chest. It was a screaming, physical testament to the extreme situation they were in.

Gannon paced the room, a cell phone plastered to his ear. He was nodding silently along with whatever the person on the other end was saying.

"You may use this room as long as you need," Robert whispered, nervously wringing his hands. "The gentleman over there told us not to call the police."

He was talking about Gannon. The Boones were a high-profile family, despite Oliver's preference for privacy. Involving the NYPD would mean that within hours, everyone in the world would know about the kidnapping. Instead, they would gather evidence themselves, advise Oliver, and allow him to decide how to proceed. It was protocol, even if it went against everything Ara knew.

"Correct. Please don't breathe a word of this to anyone."

Relief flooded Robert's features. "Very good. If you need anything, please let me know."

He disappeared on whispered footsteps, the door clicking closed softly behind him. Ara stepped farther into the room, and Gannon looked up. Their eyes met, and he jerked his head in greeting. He didn't ask, and she didn't need to tell him. It was obvious she'd been unable to recover Sam.

"Excuse me, sir," Gannon said, talking into the phone. "Ara is back."

He held out the phone to her just as his words registered with Holly, who glanced toward the doorway. Spotting Ara, she flew from the couch.

"Did you find her?" Holly's nails dug into Ara's arm, even through the jacket she wore. "Did you catch them?"

Ara carefully held onto Holly, afraid that her words would cause the woman to collapse.

"No. I'm sorry."

Holly's face crumpled, hope fleeing from it, leaving wrinkles and cracks in its wake. It seemed she'd aged a decade in only a matter of moments.

"Oh my God, oh my God . . ." Her chanting turned to a desperate wail, and she sagged against Ara.

"David, please," Ara whispered. He rose from the couch, tears shimmering in his own eyes, and took hold of Holly.

"Come now, Mrs. Boone. Let's sit down."

Ara took the phone from Gannon's outstretched hand. This conversation needed to happen, but she would have preferred to do a sweep of the crime scene first. Oliver would have questions she wouldn't yet be able to answer.

Taking a deep breath, she turned her back to the room before placing the phone to her ear. "Yes, sir."

"You weren't able to find her." Her boss didn't sound haggard or stressed. He could have been talking about the weather, and yet Ara knew it was all just a cover. Oliver was pissed.

"No, sir."

"What happened?"

"I haven't had a chance to make a pass through the restaurant yet, sir." Her phone beeped in her pocket, signaling a text message. She ignored it. "I've only just returned. I wanted to ensure Mrs. Boone was secured and that the police had not been called."

"My wife has been taken care of and protected, thanks to Gannon's efforts." His words were biting, their meaning clear. Gannon, at the moment, was the savior. "He has also prevented the NYPD and the media from catching wind of this."

Ara bit her tongue so hard, she thought it might start bleeding. Now was not the time to defend herself or her actions, so she remained silent.

"Get Holly back to the house. Do not contact the police or FBI. Gather as much information as you can about how this went down. I'll meet you in two hours." His voice deepened, his tone turning to steel. "And Ara, I'm expecting answers."

"Yes, sir."

The echo of a dial tone answered her. She wasn't even sure he'd heard her reply. Tightening her jaw, she tossed the phone to Gannon before removing her own from her pocket. She glanced at the message and then turned her attention toward the bodyguard.

"A car is waiting outside. In fifteen minutes, I want you to take Mrs. Boone and load up."

Gannon arched his eyebrows. "Where are you going?"

"To take a look at the scene."

"I'll come with you."

"No. I need you here with Mrs. Boone."

His thick arms crossed over his chest. "I don't take orders from you."

"Then call Mick. If he gives you the okay to leave Mrs. Boone alone while you tag along behind me, then by all means." She opened the door, the scents of grilled beef and sweet butter wafting over her. Ara tossed a glance over her shoulder at the fuming Gannon. There was no way Mick would ever approve leaving Holly by herself, and he knew it just as well as she did.

"I'll meet you at the car in fifteen minutes."

* * *

The bathrooms were as poshly decorated as the rest of the place. Ornate faucets, spacious stalls, shimmery tiles, and individual cloth towels for hand drying. It was empty when Ara walked in, beads of water gathering in the silver sinks. She didn't know what she was looking for, exactly. She was just retracing Sam's steps, hoping to find something to help answer her questions.

Holly must have been talking to her newfound acquaintance for at least five minutes, and she had witnessed the man dragging Sam into the alley. It was a safe bet to consider the kidnapping occurred as Sam was coming out of the bathroom.

Directly outside the bathroom door was the hallway leading back to the restaurant. To her left was an emergency exit door. The red EXIT light glowed faintly overhead, a sign nearby providing clear instructions that opening the door would set off an alarm.

But there hadn't been any alarm.

Narrowing her eyes, Ara gave a shove on the bar, and the door flew open, depositing her into an alley behind the restaurant. Off to the side was the kitchen's delivery entrance, the door shut tightly against the cool night air.

She carefully examined the emergency exit door. No crowbar marks. No scratches near the lock. Nothing to indicate the kidnappers had forced the door open. Allowing it to close, Ara then opened it from the outside.

It swung freely.

"You shouldn't be out here."

The manager scurried down the hallway toward her. His previously pressed suit was looking a bit wrinkled, and worry lines crisscrossed his forehead.

"How long has this door been broken, Robert?"

His mouth thinned, lips nearly disappearing. "I don't think I should provide—"

"You know what I think?" Ara's tone took on a hard edge. "I think this is not the time for bullshit. A teenager was kidnapped from the back of your restaurant. Oliver Boone's stepdaughter, no less. Do you want to be responsible for what happens to her?"

Robert visibly blanched. "I'm not—"

"You are if you don't help me." She locked eyes with him. "Right now she's in the hands of God-knows-who and they are doing God-knows-what to her. Do you really want to be the person who kept her from being rescued for even a moment longer than necessary?"

She paused, giving him a moment to absorb the ramifications and possibilities. Robert's mouth gaped open before clamping shut again with a click. His gaze darted to the exit sign. "How can I help?"

"Just answer my questions." She jabbed a finger toward the door. "How long has the emergency exit been broken?"

"Uhh . . ." He swallowed hard and shifted uncomfortably. "Three months."

"How did it break?"

"We don't know. It may have been damaged long before that. We only discovered it by accident."

His answer confirmed her suspicions, but it also created more questions. The kidnappers had to have known the door was broken, but were they the ones who'd disabled the alarm in preparation? Or had they discovered it while casing the restaurant and used the knowledge to their advantage?

She glanced up at the camera lens peering out over the alley. "You have security cameras back here. How long do you hold onto the footage?"

Robert's cheeks turned pink, and he refused to meet her gaze. "They don't work."

"What?"

"They never worked," he said in a rush. "They were always just for show."

Ara closed her eyes and took a deep breath. In her head, she was screaming a string of obscenities. For such an expensive restaurant, it seemed overwhelmingly ridiculous that they'd never installed real cameras.

"Did anyone in the restaurant, other than Holly, see the attack?"

"No."

Robert held the door open as Ara released it and stepped farther into the alley. It was dark, the only light coming from the nearby building and a flickering street lamp. It smelled of urine, old food, and mold. Several dumpsters sat like hunched animals against the side wall.

"I've already asked all the kitchen staff." Robert waved toward the delivery entrance. "No one even saw the van."

"When was the last time someone took out the trash?"

"Eight o'clock."

She passed a glance at him over her shoulder. "How do you know that?"

"Because I asked our busboy to do it when I went back into the kitchen to check on things. I saw him go out the door myself."

Ara nodded. The kidnapping had happened at ten o'clock, and they'd arrived at the restaurant around eight thirty. Had they been followed? Or had the kidnappers known they were going to be there tonight because of their reservation?

No matter how she cut it, Ara kept circling around to the same answer. The kidnapping had been planned. Carefully. The kidnappers had known they would be at the restaurant, had known the emergency exit was broken, had probably known the cameras were fake.

She spotted a lump in the middle of the alley. As she drew closer, dread tightened her stomach.

Sam's purse.

Ara lifted the bag by the broken handle. Mud spattered the side, and the glittery fringe winked in the weak lamplight. A quick glance inside revealed everything was still there. Sam's wallet, her phone. The kidnappers had been thorough. By leaving the purse in the alley, there was no way Ara would be able to track Sam's movements via her cell phone's GPS.

Ara gripped the bag so tightly her knuckles ached with the effort. Spinning around, she faced the back of the restaurant, the concerned Robert hesitating in the doorway. Every detail had been planned. Every move calculated.

Except one.

How the hell had the kidnappers known Sam would use the bathroom?

CHAPTER THREE

The car ride back to the Boones' mansion felt like an eternity.

Holly, distraught and practically hysterical, had made for a very poor witness. Ara had briefly tried to question her during the trip back to Long Island, but it hadn't yielded any new information. Ara could do nothing more than try to comfort her in between planning and making the necessary phone calls. As a former reporter, Holly had covered all kinds of stories and understood well that the world was often not a kind place. She didn't need to be told about the dangerous situation her only living child was in.

The sound of her weeping had been almost more than Ara could take.

Things didn't get easier once they arrived home. Within ten minutes of walking through the front door, Ara stood in her office, facing Mick. His mouth thinned into a flat line, and perspiration dotted his hairline.

He wasn't her boss. As head of security, he oversaw every other bodyguard and security staff member, except her. She answered to no one other than Oliver and Holly. It was a requirement she'd given before accepting the position. Ara had done the bureaucracy bit, had clawed and fought her way up in the police department, ripping through red tape as she went. She wouldn't do it again. Working on her own, having the freedom to call her own shots, had become extremely important to her when she left the force.

Unfortunately, in this situation, it also meant all the responsibility fell on her shoulders.

And oh, did she feel the weight of that responsibility now. Like two lead balloons pressing down on either side of her. So heavy, the muscles in her shoulders ached and trembled. Still, Ara allowed no sign of her discomfort to show. She told Mick about the events leading up to and after the kidnapping using a cop's flat tone, giving the necessary details without embellishment or feeling.

Gannon paced the length of the room, the tap of his shoes against the tile floor repetitive and annoying. A distraction Ara could have lived without.

"What are the orders?" Mick's jaw was tight, his body coiled as though ready to spring into action.

"Gather as much evidence as we can, see if we can figure out who's behind this. Mr. Boone will be arriving within the hour. He'll make some decisions once he gets here." She turned her attention to Gannon. "Have you noticed anything unusual about Sam lately?"

He stopped his pacing abruptly. "Don't you think I would've said something before now?"

"I think these questions need to be asked. You're the one who picks her up from school and spends the afternoon with her." Her voice softened. She wouldn't get anywhere by antagonizing him, and she needed answers. "It's not personal, Gannon."

He studied her expression, and whatever he saw there made a difference. His posture relaxed. "I haven't noticed anything."

Ara didn't know whether she could trust that answer. Gannon had been with the Boones for many years, but Ara would've fired him long ago if she thought she could have convinced Oliver it was necessary. Gannon lacked the observation skills and training necessary for a bodyguard.

"Where have you been taking her after school?" she asked.

"To see her friends. The mall." He gave a half shrug. "The usual places."

"Have you noticed anyone following her?"

"No. Like I said, there hasn't been anything out of the ordinary."

A furrow appeared in Mick's brow. "She's been happier lately. Although things here in the house haven't improved that much, Sam seems calmer."

"Happier?" Gannon laughed. "Just last week, she yelled at me for following her and her friends through the park."

"Happier is a relative term. She hasn't been as snappy lately."

Ara nodded. "I agree. It's a subtle difference, but there has been one."

"You said you recovered her phone from the back of the restaurant. She's always on the damn thing. Maybe she met someone or has been talking to someone we don't know about."

Ara rubbed the back of her neck, where the mixture of tension and adrenaline was giving her a raging headache. "She changed the passcode. I've tried different combinations, but I haven't been able to figure it out."

"Do you really think Sam is stupid enough to meet with someone she met online?" Gannon scoffed. "She's a pain in the ass, but she isn't an idiot."

"You don't have to be an idiot," Ara said. "You have to be vulnerable, which Sam is."

"These predators are master manipulators. He would work on saying all the right things." Mick tightened his meaty fists. "If she trusted him, Sam would've—could've—told an outsider all kinds of things about the Boone household. Including where she was tonight."

His words twisted Ara's stomach. The thought had already occurred to her, but to hear him say it aloud made it seem more real, more of a possibility. She feared for a moment she would throw up.

She could not fall apart. Sam needed her. There was a job to do, and damn it, she would not make another mistake. She'd already made too many.

"The perimeter of the house needs to be monitored physically," she said.

Stress lines appeared on Mick's forehead. "You think they'll use her to gain entrance?"

"I think it's a mistake to assume they won't. Sam knows the gate codes and the alarm codes."

"We should change them immediately."

Ara held up a hand. "Let's ask Mr. Boone what he wants to do. I don't want to change the codes and have the kidnappers hurt Sam because of it."

"That's a risk."

"Any move we make at the moment is a risk, which is exactly why we need to be on high alert. Right now, we don't know who the kidnappers are or what their end game is." Ara squared her shoulders. "There are other people—and another child—in this house. They need to be protected."

Mick gave a firm nod. "You're right. They need to be our top priority. Gannon, come with me."

The men stepped from her office with a renewed sense of purpose, exactly as Ara had hoped for. Once the door was shut and she was alone, she collapsed into her chair.

Despair and guilt threatened to overtake her as images flashed in her mind. She could easily visualize all the things being done to Sam right now. The endless possible ways the kidnappers could be hurting her.

And it was all her fault.

She slammed a fist down on the desk. She never should have left them inside the restaurant. She *knew* better. She'd allowed the fear of losing her job to prevent her from actually doing it, and now Sam was paying the price.

Kidnapped.

By whom? And for what purpose? Ara could think of only two possibilities.

One was exactly as she told the security team—the kidnappers hoped to use Sam to gain entrance to the house. Once inside, they could threaten Oliver's biological child, Charlie. Oliver would give any amount demanded to keep Charlie safe.

The second possibility—and the most likely scenario—was that the kidnappers were amateurs. Any kidnapper who'd done his research on the family would know Sam wasn't the best target. She and Oliver had a barely tolerant relationship, and that fact wasn't a secret. But they probably figured Sam was worth some kind of ransom. If that were the case, Oliver would be receiving the demand soon.

Oliver would pay to get his stepdaughter back. For Holly's sake, especially. But not nearly the same amount he would for his own child.

As much as Ara hated to say it, she was hoping for the second scenario. One, it would mean the kidnappers would most likely keep Sam alive. She was no good to them dead, and Ara had a real chance to find her and get her back. Two, it would mean the other members of the household were safe. All their energy and resources could be dedicated to Sam's safe return.

As her mind twisted with different scenarios, her stomach churned. She, of all people, understood the terror Sam would be feeling right now. The helplessness. Ara's heart battered against her chest as the memories washed over her. The smell of the leather seats. The feeling of a heavy hand on her inner thigh. The cool, metal clasp of handcuffs.

The laughter—the cold, mean laughter.

Stop it.

She couldn't help Sam if she was embroiled in her own past. She swallowed hard and forced herself to box all those thoughts up, to hide them away. There would be time later for grief and self-flagellation, but right now, she needed the anger.

Ara stood up from the chair, the sudden force of her movement causing it to roll and slam against the back wall. All her energy and focus needed to be on getting Sam back. That was her job.

She glanced at her watch. Mr. Boone would be here in thirty minutes, and she needed to have options. Answers. Recommendations.

There was work to do.

* * *

"You think these men are amateurs?" Oliver's voice held the perfect amount of disdain and incredulousness. "They snatch Sam from right underneath your nose and escape into the night, and you think they're amateurs?"

Ara fought the urge to shift in her shoes. Oliver's stare was cold. Deceptively so. She knew that underneath the indifferent exterior was a man bubbling with rage. But Oliver Boone hadn't made a fortune by running with his emotions. No, he gathered all the facts first, and then he sliced you where it hurt the most.

"Not the kidnapping itself," she said. "I only meant that the kidnappers went after Sam instead of Charlie, your son."

Oliver's spine straightened a fraction. "You think their ultimate target might be my son?"

"I think it's a possibility we can't ignore."

His gaze narrowed as he considered her answer. His hands were locked together on the top of his broad desk. Oliver cut an imposing figure, even sitting. His athletic frame was once the picture of male perfection, but now, in his sixties, his age was starting to show in the sag of his skin, the curve of a small belly.

What he hadn't lost with time was his immense power. If anything, it had grown. He carried himself like a man who was assured of his place in the world.

"How would taking Sam help them get to Charlie?" he asked.

"Well, for one, she's an easier target."

At ten, Charlie was well insulated and far more protected. It would've been more difficult for the kidnappers to take him. But Sam was a teenager with an independent and rebellious streak. She had often attempted to lose her security detail.

"Once the kidnappers have her," Ara continued, "Sam would be able to provide them with any information they need about the household. Including how to get in. Which is why, for safety reasons, I'd like to recommend the codes be changed for the house and the gate."

He rose from the chair and went to look out of the window. His office faced the front of the house and the driveway leading to the gates. "What happens to Sam if they try to gain access to the house and can't?"

"I don't know."

He waited for a long moment, and Ara studied his profile. A muscle in his jaw worked as he thought through the options.

"Change the codes." Oliver turned to her. "It won't prevent me from opening the doors if they show up with Sam, but it'll make it impossible for them to sneak onto the grounds."

"Understood."

"In addition, Charlie is not to leave this house. Not for school, not for activities. Not for any reason whatsoever until Sam is returned. I don't even want him outside on the grounds. And I want Alex to be with him at all times. Eating, sleeping, playing video games. He isn't to let Charlie out of his sight for a moment."

Alex was Charlie's primary bodyguard.

"I'll make sure of it." She paused. "Sir, we don't know for sure that the kidnappers have taken Sam for the purpose of gaining entrance into the house. She could've been their primary target."

"For ransom."

Ara nodded. "It's the most logical conclusion. I want Charlie protected, the household kept safe, but I don't think it's likely the kidnappers will show up here."

"How in the hell did this happen? How in the hell did they know what restaurant you would be at?"

Ara eyebrows creased. "The reservation was made two weeks ago. That's one of Mrs. Boone's favorite restaurants, particularly after attending an event at the gallery. It wouldn't be hard to find out where we were going to be. The truth is, sir, they only had to wait for the right opportunity. If Sam hadn't been snatched tonight, it would've been next week. Or next month." She licked her lips. "The other possibility is that Sam herself told the kidnappers."

"How?"

"We watch over her, but we don't keep track of her online activities. It's entirely possible someone has been communicating with her, has gained her trust. She may have, unwittingly, helped them take her."

Oliver's face paled as he considered the possibilities. "Would they . . . are they . . ."

He couldn't say the words, but Ara knew what he was asking all the same. It cut her like a thousand knives, ripping open painful scars from wounds that had never healed.

"If their purpose is to hold her for ransom, they probably won't hurt her." She couldn't bring herself to tell him the entire truth. That every fear he was imagining in his head was only the beginning.

He heard it anyway. "Probably?"

It came out a whisper, a touch of heartache underlying the single question.

Ara briefly closed her eyes before focusing back on him. "She's no good to them dead, and it's not smart for them to hurt her."

Oliver's posture was tight, and he was quiet for a long moment. She could feel the tension in the room growing with every tick of the grandfather clock behind her.

"As we've discussed, kidnapping for ransom is the most likely scenario." Oliver's tone became hard, more definitive. "It's one of the reasons I have you watching over Sam and Holly. It's the specific reason I hired you, especially."

"Yes, sir." She swallowed. "And under normal circumstances, I would've never left Sam alone, but Mrs. Boone asked me to order the car around front. She requested a few moments alone with her dinner guest. I complied with her wishes."

"Are you blaming Holly?"

"I—"

"Shut up," Oliver snapped. His eyes blazed as he jabbed a finger in her direction. "Don't ever, ever say that again. Not to me and especially not to Holly. This falls on you. This entire mess is your fault."

His words echoed her own emotions, but that didn't make them any easier to hear.

"Do you understand me?" he continued. "If there's someone to blame, it's you."

Belatedly, she realized what he was doing. "Absolutely, sir. It's not Mrs. Boone's fault."

The anger left him as quickly as it came. His shoulders turned inward, and for a brief second, tears shimmered in his eyes. "She blames herself. She's falling apart, and I can't even tell her that Sam will be okay."

"We'll find her." Ara stepped forward but resisted the urge to place a reassuring hand on Oliver's arm. "I'll find her. I promise."

He shook his head. "Don't, Ara. Don't make promises you can't keep."

She opened her mouth to respond, but a knock at the door interrupted her.

"Come in," Oliver barked.

The door swung open and Mick walked in. He was wearing a set of gloves, a letter in his hands. "This was just delivered to the front gate. No return address. I have the courier waiting down at the gate with Gannon. He claims a man paid extra to have this envelope delivered within the hour. The transaction was made in cash. He doesn't believe they have security cameras inside the courier office."

Oliver reached for the envelope with an impatient hand.

"No, sir," Ara said. "You aren't wearing gloves, and we need to touch the envelope as little as possible. There probably aren't any fingerprints, but we can't be sure."

He gave a sharp nod of understanding. "Open it."

Ara handed Mick a silver letter opener from the desk. He deftly swept through the paper, the slicing sound carrying across the office, before he dumped the contents onto the black glass covering Oliver's desk.

When Ara saw the familiar locket, her heart stopped. Sam wore that piece of jewelry every day of her life. Inside, Ara knew, was a photograph of her late father. It had been his gift to her on her fifteenth birthday.

"Good God," Oliver whispered. This was the demand they had been waiting for.

"Open the letter," Ara ordered Mick.

The notebook paper was plain, folded in thirds. And the letter was written in Sam's own hand. Another personal touch, and proof that she was alive. At least, she had been.

$15 million dollars. You have 72 hours to gather the money. If you call the police or fail to deliver the money, we will kill her.

We will contact you again soon.

"That's it?" Oliver asked incredulously. He came around from behind the desk to reread the note. "This barely tells us anything."

"It tells us that Sam is still alive." Ara gestured to the locket on the desk. "It tells us that she's valuable to them."

"But it doesn't give us any clues on how to find her." Oliver spun away to pace the room. "And it doesn't ensure they will *keep* her alive. It's just enough to keep us hopeful that if we follow their instructions, we have a chance to get her back."

"Most kidnappers get the money and then the victim is found alive," Mick offered. "If she remains compliant—"

"Does Sam strike you as the compliant type?" Oliver threw his hands up.

"You need to start gathering the money together," Ara said. "This amount won't be easy to get within seventy-two hours, especially with today being a Sunday."

"I'm not paying a damn dime."

"What?" Ara blinked, certain she'd heard him incorrectly. She never once considered he wouldn't pay the ransom.

"We aren't playing the game by their rules." Oliver reached for his phone, picking up the receiver with rapid, jerky movements.

"Who are you calling?"

"The director of the FBI."

CHAPTER FOUR

Luke drove his car down the tree-lined street. Fall was making her presence known. Deep red, tawny yellow, and brilliant orange leaves decorated the branches of the trees and fell, with October's swift breezes, across the road. The early-morning light made the whole scene appear ethereal. Only an hour outside of Manhattan, but he might as well have been a world away.

Huntington, Long Island, was an oasis of calm. Giant mansions sat on wide green yards, protected from prying eyes by massive oak trees and security gates. Living in Huntington meant having all the comforts of being close to Manhattan without actually having to live among the crowds and the noise. The catch was affording it. Luke knew from his quick research on the Boone family that they could buy a whole block and still have a fortune left over.

He swung his car into the driveway and faced an intricate iron gate. He rang the buzzer and raised his eyebrows at the camera.

"Can I help you?" The man's voice was gruff, meaty; Luke pictured someone with huge muscles to match.

"Luke Patrick, FBI."

"Come to the front door." The gate swung open soundlessly, and as Luke drove up the driveway, he shook his head. Gaining access had been easier than he could have imagined.

Big mistake.

A mermaid fountain sat spraying water in the center of the mansion's circular drive. Luke parked his car on the left side and climbed out. His gaze swept over the perfectly manicured lawn, the stone detailing on the estate's walls, the statues gracing either side of the walkway. The obvious lack of security.

The heavy, wooden main door of the house swung open, and a man charged out.

Oliver Boone.

Luke didn't need an introduction. He recognized the man from the photograph he'd pulled up when he'd been assigned the case. Although, with his hair flying and his clothes rumpled, Oliver looked slightly different from the polished, put-together CEO in the picture.

Oliver stalked toward Luke on long strides, shoulders back and head high. Even exhausted, this man was formidable.

"Where the hell have you been?" Oliver demanded as he grew closer, followed closely by a petite woman. "We've been waiting for you."

"Mr. Boone." Luke kept his tone calm but authoritative. "I can assure you I've been working hard on Sam's case from the moment I received the call this morning. I'm sorry to have kept you waiting, but I wanted to gather as much information as I could before coming here."

Kidnappings were tricky business. Sam had been missing for nine hours, no witness had been interviewed, and the crime scene had been severely compromised. Luke would've choked Oliver Boone just for that if he could. He'd put Sam's life in extreme danger by delaying the call to authorities. Every moment counted in these situations, especially now that a ransom had been demanded, and Luke was stepping in with one hand already tied behind his back.

Before driving out to Huntington, Luke had gone to Phillips, the restaurant where the kidnapping had taken place. He'd woken the owner from a dead sleep and forced him to open the space. It was imperative he see the scene of the crime, get a feel for the layout and the chain of events. He didn't know much—only that the daughter had been taken out the back of the restaurant by a masked intruder and had been driven off in a white van—but he felt more knowledgeable walking in the actual space. It gave him an edge reports and photographs couldn't replace.

Oliver drew up sharply in front of him. "What information have you been able to gather? Is there progress on the case?"

"I have a forensic team going through every inch of the restaurant for evidence as we speak." Luke drew in a breath and silently reminded himself to be patient. "I'm also doing my best to locate all the patrons who were in the restaurant last night. It would've been easier had the authorities been called immediately."

Oliver's jaw tightened. "This is a sensitive case. I don't want the media—"

Luke held up a hand to ward him off. "The agents doing the questioning will be discreet. No one will be told of Sam's kidnapping."

Luke studied the woman standing just behind Oliver and slightly to his side. Not the wife, he knew that. Friend? Family member? Her short hair was cut flatteringly around her angular face, complementing her meadow-green eyes. She was dressed in simple jeans and a long-sleeved shirt. Tennis shoes on her feet.

"And you are?" he asked.

"Ara Zuyev. I'm a member of the Boones' security team."

She wasn't American. At least, not American-born. Russian, if her name was any indication. Luke knew some of the security detail had been present at the restaurant. Had Ara been one of them? He would have to do a background check on her, along with the entire security team and possibly the household staff. He made a mental note to tell Thomas, his second in command, to do just that once he arrived.

Luke turned his attention back to Mr. Boone. "Forgive me, sir, but your security team is lackadaisical at best."

"That's—" Ara started to say, but Luke cut her off.

"I was able to enter the gates of your home without anyone verifying my ID at the gate. If I had been a kidnapper posing as an FBI agent, you, sir, would be in serious trouble." His gaze flickered to the woman. "Even with your bodyguard."

Ara glared at him.

"I'm putting an FBI officer at the gate," Luke continued. "He'll check everyone going in or out. I assume you have security cameras around the perimeter of the property?"

"Of course," Ara answered.

"Good. I'll want copies of all the video from the last month."

"That's intrusive." Oliver's face reddened. "I don't think it's necessary to have you going through an entire month of security footage for a kidnapping that didn't even take place here."

Privacy. It seemed to be important to Oliver, very important. He was famous because of his wealth, yet the man avoided interviews and the public eye as much as possible. For someone like him, having strangers go through his home would be difficult.

Well, tough. To a certain extent, Luke could understand Oliver's hesitation and protective instincts, but he couldn't allow them to interfere with his job. Sure, Oliver was probably used to having people jump to give him what he wanted. But that wasn't going to happen with Luke. It would be better if everyone realized right up front who was running the show from this moment on.

"Look, Mr. Boone, I will do everything I can to protect your family's privacy, but any further delays could mean the difference between getting Sam back alive or dead. You need to listen to me and follow my advice." He locked his gaze onto Oliver. "You do want her back alive, don't you?"

"Of course. I—"

"Good. Then that's settled."

A flower delivery van curved around the driveway and came to a stop next to Luke's car. "My team is here."

"Your team?" Oliver repeated, staring as various people piled out of the van. Cameras, forensic equipment, and other objects were meticulously organized inside. "I was assured by the director it would only be you. Again, I must insist— I don't want the media catching wind of this."

"Well, I can't very well find your stepdaughter all by myself." Luke tucked his hands in his pockets. "I assure you, we have everything under control. As you can see, anyone watching the house would think you'd simply had flowers delivered for an event."

He waved a few key personnel over and doled out orders: tap the phone in case the kidnappers call, search the missing girl's room, get a man on the gate, gather the security video from the house. Once his team had dispersed, he turned his attention back to a gaping Oliver and a furious bodyguard.

"Are we going to go inside, or should I start the questioning out here on the driveway?" he asked, walking toward the house. "I want to see the ransom note. Then I need to speak with Mrs. Boone."

Oliver ran to catch up with him. "You can't talk to my wife. She's a wreck. Questioning her—"

"Is exactly what needs to happen." Luke stepped over the threshold of the open front door. It was warmer inside the house, the marble entryway and soft-peach walls both elegant and inviting. "Mrs. Boone saw the event take place."

Oliver swung a hand in his bodyguard's direction. "Ara was also there. She can answer your questions."

Ara remained silent, but Luke could feel her gaze heavy on him. Watching, assessing how he would handle the situation.

"I'll speak to her, too." He moved further into the foyer. "Where is the ransom note?"

* * *

He'd dismissed her.

Ara watched him pull on a set of disposable gloves with ease and fumed. Luke Patrick represented everything Ara had hated in the cops she'd previously worked with. He might be the best the FBI had to offer, but in her opinion, that didn't matter if he didn't give a damn.

And Luke Patrick didn't care about Sam.

It was obvious in his flat expression. In the control he exerted from the moment he opened his mouth. And in the arrogance that colored his every word.

This was a job to him. Nothing more.

It didn't help that the security team had screwed up. Again. She was going to kill Gannon for allowing someone through the gate without first verifying their ID. It didn't matter that they'd been expecting Luke, and it also didn't matter that they'd known his name beforehand. Gannon should have double- and tripled-checked.

Luke examined the ransom note as though it held the secret to life. The sunlight from the large corner window caressed his face. Ara studied his straight nose, closely shaven jaw, shortly cropped dark hair, and sharp blue eyes. His expression remained placid, as cool and still as an iced-over lake.

"How did it arrive?" Luke asked.

It wasn't clear who he was addressing. Habit had Ara looking toward Oliver, who was sitting in his office chair. When he remained still and quiet, she was forced to respond. "By courier."

"Did anyone touch the paper?"

"No."

Luke carefully folded the page and placed it back into the envelope before turning his attention to the locket. His gaze tracked over the simple piece of jewelry before he opened it to study the photograph inside.

"It's Sam's father," Ara offered.

"He died in a plane crash. Last year." Luke glanced from the locket to her. "Along with an older brother, Jacob."

He'd done some research at least. That fact mollified Ara slightly, and she nodded. This wasn't about her or her feelings. This was about finding Sam and getting her home alive. To make it happen, like it or not, Ara was going to have to work with Luke.

"Yes," she said. "That necklace was a gift to Sam for her birthday. The last birthday she had with him before he died." Ara swallowed hard, past the lump of guilt and anguish that lodged itself in her throat. "She wore the necklace every day. She was never without it."

Luke snapped the locket closed and placed it back into the envelope. He pulled off his gloves and removed a small notepad and pen from his jacket pocket.

"Explain to me what happened at the restaurant."

She gave him a rundown of the facts and what she knew. He listened carefully, never interrupting. Ara wasn't sure if that was his style or if it was because she instinctively provided him with the necessary information before he could ask.

"How long have you been working for the Boone family?" He leaned against the desk and crossed his feet at the ankles. It was a deceptively casual stance. One Ara recognized as a simple investigator's trick. Luke was about to dig in and go for the jugular.

"For the last six months."

His mouth thinned, and he didn't have to say what he was thinking. She already knew.

"I didn't have anything to do with Sam's disappearance, if that's your next question."

He let her words linger, absently running a hand down his tie. The tick of the grandfather clock seemed extraordinarily loud in the silence, and Ara fought the urge to speak. It was what he wanted. For her to continue to explain and deny.

Finally, he met her gaze. "Aren't you quick to clear yourself?"

"It's the most logical next step, isn't it?" She lifted her chin. "I used to be a cop. I know how this works."

If he was surprised by her answer, he didn't show it.

"Do you often separate yourself from the people you're protecting?"

"What do you mean?"

"Exactly what I asked." His voice was smooth and easy. "Do you often go outside or to a different room, separating yourself from the individuals you are supposed to protect?"

"Generally, no." Ara's cheeks flushed. She understood exactly what he was getting at. She'd left Sam and Holly alone. Conveniently during the time of the kidnapping. Either that made her part of the scheme or it made her completely incompetent.

"I didn't have anything to do with the kidnapping," she said. "I wouldn't have left them alone in the first place, except Mrs. Boone requested it. She's my boss. I can't argue with her in the middle of a restaurant in front of her guest. Not if I want to keep working here."

He studied her, disbelief evident in the arch of his brow, and Ara felt a fresh wave of anger rush her. Damn him. What would he have done in her position? It wasn't like Luke Patrick would ever go against an order from the FBI director. Not if he wanted to keep his job.

Luke rose from desk in a fluid, graceful movement. "I'm ready to interview Mrs. Boone now." He turned to Oliver. "Where is she?"

CHAPTER FIVE

Oliver escorted them to Holly's sitting room. It was decorated in soft-purple pastels offset by cream highlights. Delicate feminine touches were everywhere, from the silk-covered couches to the vases of fresh flowers.

Oliver ordered them to wait before disappearing through the doors leading to the bedroom. The silence left in his wake was awkward and uncomfortable. Ara wanted to ask Luke if he believed her about her lack of involvement in the kidnapping, but she held back. She would not appear weak in front of this man. If she did, he would never respect her.

Luke wandered around the room in a large circle. Ara had no idea what he was thinking about. Or looking for. He paused at a family photograph hanging on the far side of the wall, a large portrait of Oliver and Holly on their wedding day. Next to it was one taken the same day, this time with the children. Charlie, all dark-eyed mischief, radiated happiness. Sam, on the other hand, was barely smiling.

The bedroom door opened, and Oliver brought Holly into the sitting room, his arms around her. Ara nearly gasped at the sight of Holly. She was deathly pale, her long blonde hair stringy and uncombed, her eyes bloodshot. Once settled on the sofa, she appeared tiny and fragile, like a delicate doll about to break.

Oliver sat next to her, held her hands in his, and Holly leaned into him. Ara understood—had always known—the clear attraction between the couple. For Oliver, Holly helped provide a softening around the edges of his life, which was mostly spent in the cutthroat world of business. She was cultured and proper enough to throw the best dinner parties and manage a household, but also intelligent enough to hold her own in conversations with him about his companies.

For Holly, Oliver provided her with comfort and kindness. A sweetness and thoughtfulness she responded to. He also represented protection, a shelter against the harsh realities of life. With him, there was nothing that couldn't be fixed or attended to.

Sam's kidnapping had blown all her illusions to smithereens.

Oliver glared up at Luke, his tone a clear warning. "As you can see, my wife is having a very hard time. Please ask your questions carefully."

Luke sat down in the armchair angled toward the sofa. "Mrs. Boone, my name is Luke Patrick. I'm the FBI agent assigned to investigate this case."

His face grew soft, gentle. Ara instinctively understood that Luke was being kind not because Oliver ordered it but because he knew it was the best way to get what he needed.

"I'm sorry, but I must ask you a few questions," he said. "As I understand it, you were having dinner with a friend last night, correct?"

"Yes. Claire Hutchinson. She's a trustee at Princeton, and I wanted Sam . . ." Holly's eyes flooded with sudden tears. Ara grabbed some tissues from a nearby table and handed them to her. They looked at each other for a moment, and Ara saw the depth of her pain, the regret mixed with the agony of the unknown.

"I asked Ara to pull Claire's car around. I wanted to impress her. I never should have . . ." Her shoulders shook violently. "It's all my fault."

"No," Ara said firmly. "It's my fault. It was my job to keep Sam safe."

Oliver flashed her a grateful glance, even as he hugged Holly tighter. "Shush, shush, darling."

"You need to leave," Luke quietly ordered, his gaze locked on Ara. He was upset with her. His fingers flexed against the arms of the chair. "You can't be in here."

"No," Oliver said, his mouth tight. "Ara stays."

"You have no need for a bodyguard—"

"This is my home and my wife. I will decide what we need and don't need." Oliver countered coolly. "Ara was there when the attack on my stepdaughter occurred, and she may remember important information. She stays."

Ara thought for a moment that Luke would insist, but when Holly's crying subsided, he turned his attention back to her, obviously abandoning the argument.

"I know this is difficult, Mrs. Boone," he said, "but I need to speak with you about what happened. It's the best way for us to find your daughter. Every bit of information helps."

"Of course. Of course it does." Holly pulled away from Oliver slightly, straightening her shoulders. A glint of resolve hardened her features, and she tucked a few loose strands of hair neatly behind her ears. Inwardly, Ara smiled. This was Holly Harper, strong news reporter. She was buried, sometimes long forgotten, but she existed.

"Claire left, and then you went to the back to check on Sam. Is that right?"

"Yes." Holly swiped at her red face with the tissues. "As I stepped toward the back of the restaurant, where the bathrooms are, I caught sight of a man wearing a black ski mask pushing Sam out of the exit door."

"What did the man look like?"

"I told you, he was wearing a mask."

Luke smiled slightly. "Was he taller than Sam? The same height?"

"Oh, I see what you mean." Holly's eyebrows creased in thought. "He was the same height as her, but Sam had on heels, so he must be an inch or two taller. I would say around five nine or so."

"Good." Luke nodded. "That's very good. What was he wearing, other than the ski mask?"

"Blue jeans. A black jacket. Sneakers."

"Any logos anywhere? Any identifying markers?"

"Not that I noticed. I'm sorry, it all happened so fast."

Luke gave her a reassuring smile. "It's all right. When you saw Sam fighting with the man, what did you do?"

"I ran after them. I was just a few seconds behind, but when I got the door open . . ." Her voice trailed off as fresh tears welled in her eyes. "It was too late."

Ara's stomach twisted at the pain vibrating in Holly's voice.

"The white van—did you catch a glimpse of the license plate?" Luke asked.

"No. It was dark in the alley." Holly turned in toward Oliver, obviously drained from both the stress and the questions.

"She didn't see anything," Oliver snapped. "I think it's time you left her alone."

"Almost done." Luke remained calm in the face of Oliver's annoyance. "Mrs. Boone, how is your relationship with Sam lately?"

The simple question caused Holly to crumple. A sob rose from her chest. She pressed a hand to her mouth, as though desperate to keep a scream inside. Ara's own protective instincts flared and her fists clenched at her side.

"You're finished," Oliver said. "No more."

"Do you want Sam brought home again?" Luke looked back and forth between Holly and Oliver. "Then let me do my job."

"Your job is to find her, not torture my wife with personal questions about her relationship with her daughter." Oliver rose, pulling Holly along with him. A sudden, sharp knock at the door caused Holly to jump.

"Come in," Oliver barked.

The door swung open, and an FBI agent entered. Behind him, lingering in the hallway, was Charlie, Oliver's son. He was dressed in his pajamas, his hair tousled, his eyes swollen and red.

"Charlie." Holly crouched down and extended her arms, and the boy rushed to her side, burying his face in her neck. Fresh tears stained both of their faces.

"Is it true?" Charlie asked, his voice muffled. "Did someone take Sam?"

Holly's only answer was to clutch him tighter. A mother who'd lost her own child but was still willing to offer comfort to another. Ara felt a lump form in her throat, and she swallowed hard against it.

"I'm sorry to intrude, but sir," the FBI agent said, "I have some information you need to hear."

Luke rose, leaning toward the man expectantly. "Go ahead, Thomas."

"The boy remembered a teenager who came to the house last month, along with some of Sam's regular friends. He'd seen the guy a few times before, but the last time . . ." Thomas's dark eyes darted in Oliver and Holly's direction. The message was clear. He wasn't sure how much to say.

Ara's heart skipped a beat.

"Just spit it out," Oliver ordered. "We're going to find out eventually anyway."

Thomas's gaze shifted to Luke, who gave a small nod of permission. His mouth pursed, the lips tightening just a bit. The room was deadly quiet, and Thomas's words carried across it, unmistakably clear.

"He tried to sell the boy drugs."

CHAPTER SIX

It was like a bomb had gone off.

Luke carefully watched every expression, every emotion that flitted across the faces in the room. Ara closed her eyes.

Holly gasped, her mouth dropping open in shock.

Oliver's jaw clenched so tight that Luke was afraid he would crack his molars.

"Charlie, is that true?" Holly pulled back so she could look him in the eyes.

"I didn't tell you because I didn't want to get Sam into trouble."

"You are going to tell me exactly what happened." Oliver's face flushed with anger. "And you are going to tell me right now, or so help me—"

Charlie scooted a little closer to Holly. Luke read the situation and stepped in quickly.

"Mr. Boone, I know this is upsetting, but yelling won't make this any easier."

Oliver broke away to pace the room like a caged animal.

"I'm sorry," Charlie whispered. "I'm so sorry. Maybe if I'd told, Sam wouldn't—"

"You're telling now," Luke cut in. "And everything you remember can help us find Sam."

"We went through the house security footage and found an image." Thomas opened the folder he was carrying and pulled out a photograph. He handed it to Luke, who studied it carefully. The suspect had the clean-cut good looks of a movie star, with jet-black hair and a strong jaw.

"Do we have a name?"

"Only a first one. Grant."

"He goes to Sam's school," Charlie offered. "I know that because he came with one of Sam's friends, Kelly."

Luke nodded. "Okay. And you told Thomas that he offered you drugs."

Charlie nodded, passing a nervous glance at his father. "I didn't take them."

"Of course you didn't," Luke agreed smoothly. "What kind of drugs did he offer you?"

"Pot. Some strange pills."

"Were you alone with him?"

Charlie shook his head, brown hair waving with the movement. "No, Kelly was there. She told him to cut it out. To leave me alone and save the stuff for Sam."

Holly collapsed on the sofa with a soft wail. Oliver cursed.

Luke stepped forward and put a hand on the boy's bony shoulder. So small and delicate—like a bird's. He must have been terrified to confess what he knew. Yet he'd done it anyway.

"You're a brave boy, Charlie. Thank you for telling us."

His chin trembled. "Will you find her? Will she be all right?"

"I'm going to do everything I can to bring her home." Luke met the boy's gaze. "You have my word on that."

"Charlie." Oliver pointed at the door. "Go to your room. I'll come find you later." He waited until the door clicked shut behind him before turning on Luke. "Do you think this druggie had something to do with Sam's disappearance?"

"It's a lead we have to consider. He was here in your house, presumably had a certain amount of information about your family from Sam." Luke glanced down at the picture. "She could owe him money. Or he could be looking to get rich quick."

When you mixed drugs and rich teenagers, all kinds of bad things could happen. Kidnapping wasn't the worst he'd seen.

"I knew she was getting into to trouble." Oliver ran a hand through his hair. "But I didn't think things had gotten this bad."

Holly was shaking on the couch, her hands trembling so badly, she appeared to be in an earthquake of her own making.

"I just can't believe it," she said. Oliver moved to place a reassuring hand on her shoulder.

"None of you had any idea Sam was involved in drugs?" Luke ignored the parents, directing the question toward Ara. He didn't need Holly and Oliver's answer. It was clear they weren't clued in to what had been happening right under their roof.

Ara's back was ramrod straight, her face smooth. In the short time Luke had been observing her, he'd never seen her so expressionless.

She was hiding something.

She'd known.

He thrust the photograph in her direction. "Do you know what this kid's last name is?"

Her gaze flickered down, but no recognition crossed her face. "No. I've never seen him before."

"Who is Kelly?"

"Sam's best friend. Kelly O'Neill. She lives a few streets over."

Adrenaline coursed through him as he quickly made a plan.

"Thomas, I want an address on this girl now." Luke spun on his heel, had almost left the room before he remembered the parents. He looked over his shoulder at Oliver. "I'll contact you when I have some more information."

Oliver reached out to touch Holly's shoulder and gave Luke a nod.

Luke tore out of the room into the hallway, Thomas right next to him. "I want this kid found. Wake up the principal, go through the yearbook if you have to. I want to know where he lives and whether he has any priors. I also want every agent on the case to have his image. Let's find this guy."

* * *

Ara raced out of the room, hot on the heels of the two FBI agents. Thomas broke off at the base of the stairs, heading toward the dining room and the control center the FBI had created there.

Luke, the picture of Grant clutched in his fingers, went straight for the front door. She followed close behind. So close that when he stopped abruptly, she rammed right into him.

"What do you think you're doing?"

She lifted her chin. "I'm coming with you."

"No, you're not."

He turned his back on her and walked away. She hurried through the door after him, this time keeping pace with his frantic steps.

"You need me." The bright sunlight blinded her, and Ara blinked several times, trying to clear her vision. "I know all of Sam's friends and they know me. They'll tell me things they'd never tell you." She grabbed his arm, forcing him to a stop. "Let me help."

"You've helped enough."

"What does that mean?"

He didn't answer but kept on to his car. It beeped as he hit the fob, and he reached for the door handle.

Ara shoved his shoulder slightly. "I'm talking to you."

"And I answered you," he said smoothly. That professional mask was back, and she found it infuriating. "No."

She crossed her arms over her chest. "Because you think I'm responsible for her kidnapping. You think this is my fault."

"Do I think it was smart of you to leave her alone? No. Are you a potential suspect?" He raised his brows slightly. "I think you're intelligent enough to figure out the answer to that. However, even if those two things weren't true, you still can't tag along with me while I interview witnesses.

"This is an FBI investigation," he continued, placing a slight stress on FBI. "You are neither an agent nor a police officer. You are a bodyguard, and as such, have no place in my investigation."

Luke opened the car door. "Now, if you'll excuse me, I have a missing teenager to find."

He drove away, his taillights barely winking as he sped around a curve in the driveway. Ara clenched her jaw. Spinning on her heel, she headed for the parking garage on the far side of the property. If Luke Patrick thought she would be so easily dismissed, he was mistaken.

She was going to find Sam. And she was bringing her home.

CHAPTER SEVEN

Fear churned Sam's stomach. She'd nearly thrown up twice, and her heart felt like it was about to leap right out of her chest. There were no windows in the back of the van, and the obscurity only fed her anxiety. Alone, in the dark and the cold, a million questions fluttered through her head.

Along with the echo of her mother's scream.

Metal scraped against metal, and the van lurched forward. Sam bounced against the floor and winced. The engine went silent. She swallowed hard and tried to slow her racing heart.

The back doors of the van swung open, and Sam blinked against the sudden flood of bright light assaulting her eyes. A shadowy form, male, stood motionless at the doors.

"Sam?" he asked, surprise and confusion heavy in that one word.

The squint of her gaze lessened as her eyes adjusted. Nick's gorgeous face slowly came into focus, bewilderment creating lines in his forehead.

"What are you doing here?" he asked.

She scooted toward the edge and held out a hand to him. He took it, his warm palm stark against her own freezing fingers. She climbed down from the van, her legs trembling slightly. She was missing one shoe. She kicked the other off, sending it clattering, and stood barefoot on the icy, concrete floor of the warehouse.

She scanned the space around them, the paintings and workbench in the corner, the overflowing garbage can, the wide expanse of gray walls. Sam strained, listening for any noise coming from the other side of the metal warehouse door.

Nothing.

No sirens.

No one chasing them.

The passenger door to the van opened, and a well-built man with short dark hair and a crooked nose climbed down. When he caught sight of Sam, he grinned broadly, his jet-black eyes twinkling with excitement.

"We did it."

His words swept over her, and Sam broke out in a wide smile. They did it.

A sudden high, a rush of excitement, flooded her veins, and she let out a whoop. "Oh my God, I was so scared we were going to get caught when my mom saw us wrestling. I thought for sure we were done for."

"Nah." Eddie threw a hand in the air dismissively. "That part was the best. Now they'll know right away you're in trouble. So much better than if you'd just disappeared."

"Hold up," Nick stepped in between them. "What is going on?"

"I've been kidnapped." She wrapped her arms around his waist, leaned into his warmth. But it was like hugging granite, hard and rigid.

"What in the hell are you talking about?" Nick pulled her back and turned toward his cousin. They looked nothing alike. Nick, with his shaggy blond hair and baby-blue eyes, towered over his dark-eyed, dark-haired relative. "Eddie, what in the hell is going on?"

"Exactly what Sam told you." Eddie gave Sam a wink. "We kidnapped her."

"It was fun, too." Gina, Eddie's girlfriend, came around the side of the van, her gum snapping like punctuation marks. "If I'd known kidnapping was going to be so much fun, I woulda done it a lot earlier." She tossed her dyed blonde hair over her shoulder. "I told ya, Eddie, I make a good getaway driver."

"Ah baby, you were fuckin' awesome." Eddie grabbed Gina's wrist and pulled her over to him. He planted a sloppy kiss on her mouth.

"Eddie, cut it out." Nick punched his cousin lightly on the arm, drawing his attention back to him. "Will someone explain to me what in hell is going on?"

Eddie punched Nick back harder, as a warning. "I already told ya, dipshit, we kidnapped Sam. Right out of the back of the restaurant. Her mom saw us and started screaming. It couldn't have gone any better."

"What time is it?" Sam asked. She'd dropped her purse when Eddie had shoved her into the back of the van. It had all been part of the plan. She didn't want the police to track her using her cell phone. "We shouldn't wait too long before we send the ransom note."

"Ransom note?" Nick's face flushed, and his gaze darted from Sam, to Eddie, and back again. "You guys are kidding, right?"

"No, we aren't kidding. How in the hell are we going to get the money if we don't send a ransom note?" Eddie asked.

Sam could see the moment Nick realized they weren't playing some sort of weird joke on him. When he understood exactly what had transpired.

"You planned this," he whispered, his eyes growing wide. "Oh my God, you planned this."

"Of course we planned it. God, you are fuckin' slow sometimes, dude. You can't kidnap people without a plan."

"You can't kidnap people at all!" Nick shouted. "What in the hell is wrong with you?"

"What is wrong with *me*?" Eddie took a threatening step closer, and Sam knew this wasn't going in a good direction. Both of the men had fiery tempers—a family trait they did have in common.

"Eddie, shut up," Sam snapped, stepping between the two of them. She turned to Nick, held up a hand as he backed away from her. "Don't worry. I knew all about it. I'm in on it."

He stared at her as though she'd suddenly sprouted another head. "What in the hell—*why*?"

"To get back at Oliver. I want to hurt him where it counts. He doesn't give a crap about me, but he does care about his money." She caught his gaze, disappointment and anger leaking into her voice. "I thought you'd be thrilled."

"Thrilled? Why in the fuck would I be thrilled?" Nick ran a hand through his hair. "This is some crazy shit. Crazy, illegal shit!"

"I hate to break it to you, Nick." Gina snapped her gum. "But you already do crazy, illegal shit." She gestured toward the back of the van where three paintings leaned against the wall of the vehicle. "Stealing artwork and replacing it with forgeries isn't exactly the work of Mother Teresa."

Eddie snorted, his arm swinging over Gina's slim shoulders. "Mother Teresa. Good one, babe."

Sam crossed her arms over her chest. Gina was right. What right did Nick have to act all goody two-shoes now? The rush of her success was being eaten away by his reaction. She'd pulled it off, gotten herself kidnapped. They should be partying, enjoying the high—not fighting over it.

"My forgeries aren't the same thing as kidnapping." Nick's voice rose, echoing off of the empty warehouse walls. "It's not even close. Eddie, what the fuck? They are going to be sending FBI agents and all kinds of shit after us."

He stepped closer to Eddie, his fists clenched. "I didn't agree to this."

A thunderous look came over Eddie's face. He unwrapped his arm from around Gina, and pushing Sam aside roughly, stepped up to Nick. They were toe-to-toe, nose-to-nose. Sam sucked in a breath.

"You didn't agree to this?" Eddie gave Nick a slight push, forcing him to take a step backward. "Who the fuck do you think you are? Without me, you'd still be doodling in your notebook with nothing but empty dreams and a job at McDonalds."

"This is serious shit."

"Don't you think I know this is serious shit?" Eddie's face turned bright red. "But I've got some problems of my own going on, Nick."

Something passed between the two men, something Sam couldn't read. Nick's temper deflated.

"What did you do, Eddie?" he whispered.

"Nothing." Eddie's gaze darted toward Sam before turning back to Nick. "I just owe some money. Sam's kidnapping is the answer to my problems. And to hers."

Nick shook his head. "You're a damn fool. This isn't the answer to any of our problems. Not by a long shot." He looked past his cousin and locked eyes with Sam. "This needs to end right now. You need to go home, Sam."

"She can't." Eddie adjusted his stance so that he was between them. "Didn't you hear her? Her mom saw us wrestling. It's too late, Nick. It can't be undone." He pushed a finger into Nick's chest. "I'm your blood, and I'm telling you, I need this money."

"We'll get it another way."

"There is no other way!" Eddie shouted. "Don't you think I would've done something else if it was possible? And the way I see it, you owe me. So stop being a damn pussy about things!"

Nick's mouth opened as though he was going to say something, but the look in Eddie's eyes must have stopped him, because he shut it again. Spinning on his heel, he stomped over to a corner of the warehouse. The clatter of the easel hitting the floor as he kicked it sounded like a gunshot across the space.

Sam blew out a breath, the tension almost more than she could take. "I'll go talk to him."

"Leave him." Eddie swung his arm around Gina again. "He's just being a baby, as usual. He'll come around. He always does."

Sam bit her lip indecisively. No one knew Nick better than Eddie. They were as tight as brothers, and despite their arguments, the loyalty between them ran deep. But a twinge of guilt had Sam crossing the room anyway.

Nick was leaning against a workbench, fists clenched. Sam reached out, stroking his long, muscled back, his T-shirt soft against her fingertips.

"Everything is going to be okay."

"This isn't going to work, Sam." He spun around to face her. "You're playing with things you can't understand."

"What things?"

His gaze darted across the room to Eddie before focusing back on her. "I can't tell you."

"Can't or won't?"

He ignored her question. "Damn it, Sam, why didn't you tell me you were planning this?"

"Eddie told me not to. He said you would try to talk me out of it."

"He was right. I would have." Nick let out a sigh and drew her into his arms. She breathed in the scent of him. "This was a mistake, Sam."

His tone was so ominous, so stressed, a tinge of fear pricked her. She fought against it.

"Stop worrying." Sam pulled back and tilted her head up so she could look into his face. "No one is going to get in trouble."

He shook his head. "I never should've introduced you to Eddie. I should've known he would talk you into something stupid. Hell," Nick gestured to the paintings, "he's already got me doing something stupid. You didn't stand a chance against him."

Nick didn't like doing the paintings. He was always worried about getting caught, but it was also something he couldn't stop. The money he got for them went straight into art school, something he couldn't afford otherwise.

"Look, no one is going to get in trouble," she reassured him. "I'm a very smart girl. This has been planned and planned. Absolutely nothing is going to go wrong."

She could tell from his expression; Nick didn't believe her.

CHAPTER EIGHT

Ara knew from her time with Sam that Kelly wouldn't be at her house. She would be at Sharon Dade's. The FBI agents would be spinning their wheels and wasting time. Ara figured she had maybe an hour's head start. The sooner she got Grant's location from Kelly, the sooner Sam could be rescued. Luke Patrick might not want her help, but damn it, he was going to get it anyway.

The clock in the car's dash read ten thirty. Kelly and Sharon wouldn't even be awake yet. They would've been out, in the city, partying until the early morning hours. If Holly hadn't insisted on dragging Sam to the gallery opening, she would have been with her friends. It had been one of the last things they'd fought about.

Ara passed through the massive iron gate and parked her car in front of the Dades' stone mansion. It was gorgeous, with stunning rose beds and ivy climbing the walls in intricate patterns.

"Good morning, Ms. Zuyev." Richard, the butler, could barely cover the surprise in his voice as he opened the front door and stepped out onto the small porch. "There must be some mix-up. Ms. Sam is not here."

"I know." Her stride toward him was purposeful. "I need to speak to Kelly."

"Ms. Kelly is still sleeping. The ladies were out quite late last night." He took a step back, allowing her enter the foyer. "If you would like, I can arrange for some refreshments and—"

"No, Richard." Ara cut him off. She wasn't going to wait until the girls woke up. "I need to speak with her now. It's an urgent matter."

She began climbing the wide staircase as she spoke. Richard, flustered and thrown off guard by her rude behavior, followed her up the steps.

"Ms. Zuyev, surely this can wait until this afternoon. Ms. Sharon will be very upset to have you . . ."

His voice trailed off as Ara swung open Sharon's bedroom door, flipping on the lights and charging in as if she owned the room.

There was a moan from the king-size bed. Sharon, her hair a wild mess and mascara ringing her eyes, jolted upright. She blinked in the sudden light and, seeing Ara and Richard standing in her room, drew the covers up over her chest.

"What do you think you're doing in my room?" Her face flushed. "Get the hell out."

The bed covers shifted, and another moan came from a lump in the center. "Oh God, don't yell. My head."

"Get up," Ara snapped. She marched around the side of the bed and yanked on the blankets, throwing them to the floor. "Get up right now."

"Ms. Zuyev, please." Richard stood in the doorway uncertainly, his eyes wide.

"What are you doing?" Sharon screeched. "Get out of my room, both of you!"

Richard fled as though the devil were coming after him.

Kelly pried open one eye and spotted Ara standing over her. "Rise and shine. I need to talk to you."

Kelly tried to bury herself in the pillows until Ara removed them. "Get up now, or the next move is to dump cold water on you."

It was either the threat or Sharon's continuous stream of curse words—or perhaps a combination of the two—that finally got Kelly sitting up. She yawned broadly and swiped dirty-blonde hair out of her puffy face.

"What is going on?"

"Sharon, shut up," Ara ordered.

"Screw you," the teenager spat back in a final insult before hurling a pillow in Ara's direction.

Ara let the room grow quiet, making sure she had both girls' attention before focusing in on Kelly.

"I need to know where Grant is."

Kelly's forehead creased in confusion. "You busted in here to find out where Grant is?" She gave another yawn before throwing herself back down on the bed. "How should I know? I'm not his mother."

"Sam's missing." She carefully watched every emotion as it crossed Kelly's face. "And I think Grant might have had something to do with it. Where can I find him?"

"What are you talking about?"

"She was taken last night from a restaurant by a man in a mask. She's been missing for almost twelve hours, and I'm trying to find her."

Sharon shook her head. "You're screwing with us."

"No," Ara said flatly. "I'm not."

Kelly's face paled more and more as the realization of what Ara said sank in. "Sam's . . . missing?"

"Yes." Ara sat down on the bed. "I need to know about Grant. I need to know where I can find him."

"But why would you think Grant has anything to do with this?"

"Because," Ara said, "he's been selling drugs to Sam."

Kelly glanced at Sharon, and some silent message passed between them. Ara took a guess.

"He's been selling to all of you, hasn't he?"

The girls joined hands, and Kelly bit her lip. "He sells to everyone at school—not just to us."

"What is he selling?"

"Anything you want."

"What was he selling to Sam?" The question lingered in the air. Neither of the teenagers seemed eager to answer it. "Look," Ara continued. "I need your help. I need you to tell me the truth."

Sharon sighed. "He started off selling her pot. We used to smoke it at parties, you know. But lately, Sam's been into pills more. Uppers and downers. She likes to mix them with booze."

Ara had always had her suspicions about the drinking and the pot, but she'd never been able to confirm it. Sam had always been careful to do it in places where her security detail wouldn't see, like at friends' houses or sleepovers.

"She owes him money." Kelly's voice was low, near a whisper. "She owes him a lot of money."

"How much?"

"A few thousand," Kelly said weakly. "She kept telling him she was good for it, but her stepdad cut her allowance off after she failed her last three classes. She could only get money from her mom and it wasn't enough to party on."

Sharon's mouth dropped open. "Oh, God, Kelly . . . the fight."

"What fight?" Ara's gaze darted back and forth between the girls. "What fight?"

"They got into it bad a few nights ago." Sudden tears flooded Kelly's eyes. "Grant threatened her. Said that if she didn't pay, he would make her sorry."

The words churned Ara's stomach, and her heart beat faster. "Where is he, Kelly? How do I find him?"

* * *

Huntington Country Club was elite, sophisticated, and exclusive. Ara breezed through the entrance, giving a nod to the doorman. The staff recognized her on sight, thanks to Holly's frequent visits, and no one stopped her as she crossed toward the banquet room.

The gathering was in full swing. The photograph of a chubby-cheeked baby in a snow-white dress was propped up on an easel. The room was decorated in pink and silver. Ara passed by a table loaded down with gifts in glittery paper.

A baptism after party, perhaps? Or a delayed baby shower? Whatever the occasion, the infant was obviously the guest of honor.

Guests mingled, drinking mimosas out of fluted champagne glasses in front of large windows overlooking the golf course. Ara wandered around the room, looking for Grant. The crowd made it difficult, and her patience had started to wane when she finally spotted him. He was speaking to an older man, nodding politely. Grant had handsome, natural good looks. His dark hair gently waved away from his face, making the most of his square jaw and almond-shaped eyes.

Before she could move, Grant placed his champagne glass on a waiter's tray and casually walked out of the ballroom.

Damn it.

She hurried across, muttering apologies as she bumped people. She caught a glimpse of his back as he turned the corner. The direction he headed was for club personnel—the kitchen, maintenance, and other offices were that way. Where was he going?

By the time she made it to the corner, there wasn't any sign of him. She stood for a moment, uncertain, but the click of a door handle sent her moving forward.

The maintenance closet.

Her eyes narrowed. Grant was obviously doing something he didn't want anyone else to know about. Good. That much better for her.

With a last look over her shoulder, Ara turned the handle and slipped into the room.

CHAPTER NINE

"**W**hat are you doing in here?" Grant quickly fumbled with the dollar bill he was rolling. He shifted his body in a desperate attempt to block the white powder sitting on the shelf in front of him.

"This isn't the ladies' room?" Ara creased her eyebrows in confusion. Her gaze quickly darted over the shelves. Gloves. Napkins. Toilet paper and scrub brushes. A broom, along with a mop and a bucket, sat in the corner. He could use one of those for a weapon. Bash her over the head with the stick, jab it in her ribs. "What are you doing in here?"

"Nothing. I just needed a minute of peace." He glared at her, his statement pointed. A fine sheen of sweat coated his forehead. "Away from everyone."

"I understand that feeling." Ara leaned against the door, managing to both block the entrance and appear casual. "My boss is a real bitch, but the pay's good, so I put up with it. Still, there are times I have to escape."

Grant's wary expression didn't waver, but he took a second look at her. No gleam of recognition flashed in his eyes, and he continued to be silent. She sighed wearily and peered out at him from underneath her lashes. "I'm Ara."

"So?" He didn't lose his guarded expression. If anything, his body seemed to tense more.

"And you are . . ."

He smirked. "None of your business."

"You look familiar. Don't I know you?"

"I doubt it." He passed a glance down her wrinkled slacks. "It's not like you and I run in the same circles."

She snapped her fingers, and Grant jumped slightly. "No, I do know you. You're Grant Turner."

"Listen, I'm not sure what you want, but I'm not interested in having this little chat. Get out of here and leave me alone."

Ara shook her head. "Sam told me you'd be a pain in the ass. She warned me."

Grant's whole body grew rigid. "Sam?"

"Sam Harper. You know her, right? You're her supplier. You've been giving her drugs for a while."

He stood stock-still, barely breathing, his gaze fixed on the floor.

"I know she owes you money. I can get it for you. Whatever you want." She stepped closer. "I work for the family. This can all be taken care of, it can all go away, if you just work with me. I can help you, Grant."

He jerked his head up. "I'm not sure what game you're playing, but you need to go." He threw out an arm, nearly hitting Ara in the face. "Get out of here. Now."

"No can do." Ara grabbed his shirt, pivoting her body suddenly, and smashed Grant up against a wall.

"Hey, let me go!"

"Where is she, you little piece of shit?"

"Who?" He struggled in her grasp, but she had him pinned, and he wasn't strong enough to break the hold. "What the hell are you talking about?"

Ara leaned in, right next to his face. "Sam. Where. Is. She."

"I don't know." Panic made his voice crack. His eyes darted around, desperately seeking help and finding nothing but cleaning supplies and paper towels. All out of reach.

"You're lying. You supplied her with drugs, and when she couldn't pay, you threatened her."

His face flushed. "Fuck you." He kicked out with his legs, nailing Ara in both shins. Pain rushed through her, and her grip on his shirt loosened. He wriggled free.

Furious, she shoved him back against the wall again hard, his head slamming against the brick with a thunk.

His right hand flew up, fist rocketing into her stomach, knocking the wind from her. She doubled over, gasping for breath, and he skirted around her.

No.

She could not lose him. She could not let Sam down.

Ara grabbed his foot at the last moment, and Grant went flying toward the cement floor. A crack echoed as his face smashed into a shelf on the way down. He flailed, kicking out with his other foot. She struggled to hold onto to him, but his shoe slipped off in her hand.

Grant, his face bloody, swung open the door of the maintenance closet and started screaming.

* * *

Sam watched in awe as Nick worked. The brush looked tiny in his large hand, and she was struck by the gentleness of his strokes. He'd already created the bulk of the painting—flowers, a lily pond, the forest. Now, he was filling in the detail work.

The original painting stood next to the replication Nick was making, and he referred to it often. Checking and double-checking the brush strokes, the angle of the sunlight streaming through the branches of the trees.

"You should eat some pizza." Sam picked up her own slice, bit off a piece. "Especially while it's still hot."

"I can't. They're coming to collect the originals tomorrow. I need to finish before that." He carefully placed his brush against the canvas and stroked upward. As if by magic, a bird materialized.

"Almost done." He stepped back and judged his work, dipping his brush into a can of paint thinner to remove the excess color. "What do you think?"

She set down her pizza and wiped her hands quickly on a napkin before approaching the side-by-side paintings. Carefully, she scrutinized them.

"It's very good. I almost wouldn't know it's a forgery."

He arched his eyebrows at her. "Except . . ."

She waved her hand in the upper-right corner. "The sunlight in the original is a bit stronger here. And a slightly different shade. Perhaps add in more primary yellow."

He cocked his head, his gaze intense. "You're right. Damn, you have a good eye."

A rush of pleasure flooded over her. "The owners will never know it's not real."

"I hope not." He loaded up his small brush and squinted at the canvas. "At some point, our luck is going to run out. I've been talking to Eddie about getting out now, while we have the chance. Before we get caught, you know."

"What does he say?"

"Not much." Nick passed a glance behind him to where Eddie and Gina were sharing a laugh. "I'm trying to only steal from people who won't know the difference. Rich assholes with loads of money who wouldn't know real art if it bit them." He shrugged and turned his attention back the paintings. "But there's always the chance someone will surprise me."

"Like I did."

He glanced at her and gave a heart-stopping smile. "Like you did."

The sharp scrape of metal echoed across the space. The large warehouse door opened, and bright sunlight streamed in. A black Mercedes pulled up and stopped next to the van. Before the engine shut off, the warehouse door shut, casting the entire place back into dim shadows and poor fluorescent lighting.

"What the hell?" Nick dropped the paintbrush on the table and bypassed Sam, heading straight for Eddie. She quickly followed but only caught the end of his sentence.

". . . can't know Sam's here."

"It's fine," Eddie hissed. "They already know."

Two men in dark suits and shiny shoes climbed out of the Mercedes. Their looks were so similar, Sam's initial impression was that they were brothers. They were both young, muscles bunching under their jackets, with thick dark hair and pale skin. The driver sported a goatee and mustache combination. The passenger was clean shaven, but his tie was a bit more adventurous, a wild combination of multicolored stripes.

Sam tugged on Nick's sleeve. "What's going on?"

He didn't answer her but gently pushed her slightly behind him. The protective gesture caused Sam's stomach to clench with nerves. She gripped the back of his shirt.

"Sasha, Maksim," Eddie greeted each man in turn, shaking their hands and clapping Maksim on the back. "Good to see you."

Maksim smiled, flashing neat, white teeth. "It's only good when your luck takes a turn."

The men laughed, although Sam didn't understand why.

Sasha looked beyond Eddie to Gina, who was standing back, quietly waiting. "Are you going to greet me, Kotik, or are you going to leave me waiting?"

Nick was stiff, tension streaming off of him in waves. Something wasn't right, and Sam's heart pounded in her chest. She had the instinctive urge to run.

Gina stepped forward, brushing her mouth gently across Sasha's. If Eddie was shocked by the tender gesture, he didn't show it. His cheeks were practically bursting from his broad grin.

Maksim said, "Let's get down to business."

"Of course." Eddie bounced on the balls of his feet. "I told Ivan I wouldn't let the boss man down."

He started walking toward Nick and Sam, and the men followed. Sasha kept a tight grip on Gina's waist.

"Nick, you both know." Eddie waved at his cousin dismissively. "And this is Sam."

Maksim's dark eyes locked onto her. His face was stunningly beautiful, like a piece of marble carved to perfection. But something about him sent a shiver of fear trickling down her spine. It didn't help that he was coolly appraising her as though she were an object he was buying.

"What's going on?" Nick asked. His gaze darted to his cousin before locking back on the men.

"Eddie, you didn't tell him?" Maksim tsked. His voice was accented heavily, and Sam could barely make out what he'd said over the rush of blood in her ears.

"Tell me what?" Nick growled. "Damn it, Eddie . . ."

"I didn't have a choice." Eddie answered, his tone cold. He turned back to Maksim. "I've kept my end of the deal, as promised. I've delivered the girl, and my debt is paid."

What in the hell was Eddie talking about? What deal?

Nick's face flushed. "No, that's not what's going to happen." He stepped toward Maksim and tempered his voice. "Listen, we can get you the money, but you can't have Sam."

Sam's knees went weak. Faster than she could blink, Sasha rotated Gina in front of him, holding her by the neck. Gina yelped in pain and shock.

"What are you doing?" Eddie froze as Sasha placed his gun to Gina's head.

"Nobody move, or I'll shoot her brains out."

Eddie licked his lips, his eyes wide with horror. "What are you doing? This wasn't part of the deal."

Maksim smirked. "The deal is off."

CHAPTER TEN

Luke paced the small interrogation room at the police station. It smelled like a combination of sweaty feet and burned coffee, but it was quiet and empty—two things he required at the moment. He'd spent the last few hours dealing with angry parents, one high-priced attorney, and a smart-mouthed druggie.

Precious time wasted. And he was no closer to finding Sam.

What he had now was a list of questions he couldn't answer. Most of them about Ara. Not only had she left Sam alone during the time of the kidnapping, but now she'd inserted herself into the investigation. Why? Because she was trying to help? Or because she was trying to hide something?

Luke sat in the uncomfortable metal chair and opened the file folder on the table. He scanned Ara's record faxed over from the Austin Police Department. There was a phone number scrawled at the top. He pulled out his cell phone and dialed.

"Maxwell," a voice barked.

"Captain Maxwell, this is FBI Special Agent Luke Patrick. It's my understanding you wished to speak to me directly about Ara Zuyev."

"Yes. I gathered from your colleague Thomas that Ara is in some kind of trouble."

"I can't talk about the particulars of the case, but I would like to know your honest impressions of Ara."

"You've seen her service record?" Maxwell asked.

"I have. It's a bit of a mess."

The captain barked out a laugh. "She was a bit of a mess. Smart, determined, passionate about the job. Several times she went above and beyond, which is why she was promoted and kept around despite her failings."

"What kind of failings?"

There was silence, and then Maxwell sighed. "Listen, Ara had a lot going for her and could've been a hell of a cop. But she had a way of circumventing the rules when it suited her. Before she moved to my squad, she'd been cited twice for insubordination. I thought I could work with her . . . I thought with a little more discipline, she would pull through. I was wrong."

"What happened?"

"During an op, she disobeyed a direct order. Our entire case imploded as a result. Even worse, a necessary suspect died."

Luke sat up straighter. "She killed someone?"

"He died as a direct result of her disobedience. Ara didn't pull the trigger, but she might as well have."

"Is that why she left the force?"

"Yes. Truth be told, we didn't give her much choice. It was either resign or take a desk job. There was no way I could allow her back into the field again. She chose to resign, and honestly, I wasn't sorry to see her go. Neither were a lot of other members of the team."

"She didn't get along with them," Luke said.

"That's putting it mildly. She's something of a hothead."

"I've noticed." Luke switched the phone to his other ear. "Captain, is she dangerous? Do you think she'd become involved in something criminal?"

There was a very long pause. He could practically hear the captain wrestling with himself, and he understood that battle. "Sir, whatever you say on this phone call will remain between us. I wouldn't ask if I didn't need to know."

"I understand." Maxwell cleared his throat. "Ara operates under her own set of rules. Do I think she could be involved in something criminal if it suited her purposes? Yes, I do."

"And she has the brains to pull it off."

"She does," he confirmed. "If there's anything you take away from this phone call, Agent Patrick, it's that Ara can't be trusted. She'll turn on you in a heartbeat if it serves her own agenda."

The warning replayed over and over in his head even after Luke ended the call. He thought researching Ara's background would help answer his questions, but all it seemed to do was confound them. Clearly from the attack on Grant, Ara was working her own agenda. But what was it? Was she behind Sam's kidnapping?

He rose from the chair and gathered the folder from the table. He might not have all the answers he needed, but it wouldn't be the first interrogation he'd done half-blind. It was damn well time to figure out what in the hell Ara was doing.

* * *

Luke bypassed the officers dressed in blue, following the signs directing him to the jail. He'd ordered Ara be placed in a holding cell by herself, and the NYPD had complied. The cell was nothing more than monotonous gray walls, metal bars, and a battered toilet/sink combination. No windows. No sound. Nothing to keep her company or distract her, except for the frigid temperatures.

He found her pacing the length of the cell, her face tight and haggard. Her short hair was mussed, her pants dusty, any makeup she'd been wearing now long gone. At the sound of his footsteps echoing off of the concrete and metal cage, she spun in his direction.

"Did you find her?" Ara's hands gripped the metal bars. "Is she okay?"

Her question had fresh frustration twisting in his stomach. It was quickly followed by a lingering feeling of failure. He tamped the emotions down, years of practice keeping his voice cool and controlled. "No. We haven't found her."

"But Grant has to know where she is," she insisted. "Did you ask Kelly about the threats he made against Sam? About the money Sam owed him?"

"Grant Turner has been questioned thoroughly. He knew nothing about Sam's kidnapping, nor was he involved in any way. You went after the wrong person."

She stepped back, her lips trembling slightly. "That's not possible. He threatened her."

Luke shook his head. He kept his gaze locked on Ara's face, watching every twitch of her body language. "Sam owed him three grand. Grant shits and that kind of money comes out. He doesn't need Sam's money, not really. He's dealing for the fun of it."

"But . . . but . . . he threatened her."

"He probably did. But threatening and kidnapping are two very different ball games. The money isn't enough of a motivation for him to kidnap and possibly kill over. You should've stayed out of it."

Her jaw clenched. "If I had, you'd still be chasing your tail looking for Grant. I found him long before you did. We're wasting time. Get me out of here so we can find Sam."

"No."

Her eyes widened. "You need me."

He raised his eyebrows. "You assaulted a teenager and interfered with a federal investigation."

She sucked in a breath and blew it out again slowly. "All right, I shouldn't have attacked Grant. But you can't deny that my connection to Sam gives me an inside track to her life and her friends. You shouldn't have locked me out of the investigation."

She played the game well, changing tactics with an ease that must have made her a good interrogator.

He was better.

"I refused to allow you to tag along during a federal investigation," he said. "I had my reasons."

"Because you think I had something to do with the kidnapping." She swallowed hard, her face turning slightly pale. "You're making a mistake."

"Am I?" His voice was cold and harsh, as stark as the gray-cement walls. "I had my team research you. Thoroughly. It seems you've had an interesting career path."

"What are you talking about? I quit the police force."

"After a suspect died." Luke studied her expression. She knew exactly where this was going. "Seems you have quite the temper. What happened, Ara? Did Sam piss you off? Were you tired of listening to her complain?"

She backed away from the bars. He thought he saw her hands tremble before she clenched them into fists.

"You conveniently left Sam alone right before she was kidnapped," he continued. "You claimed to not know she was doing drugs, and yet you've been her primary bodyguard. You ran to question her friends before we could get to them. Something to hide?"

Ara glared at him. Her lips were so tightly pressed together, they were nothing more than white slashes.

"You won't get the money, you know." Luke rocked on his heels. "Oliver has already said he won't pay it."

"I told you, I didn't have anything to do with Sam's disappearance." Her whole body was shaking, and she spoke through gritted teeth. "God damn it, I'm trying to find her."

"Are you?" He cocked his head. "Or are you trying to muddy the waters?"

"If I had kidnapped Sam, do you think I'd be stupid enough to end up behind bars?"

"Frankly, I don't know. According to the Austin PD, you were stupid enough to disobey orders and leave a suspect to die."

All the color drained from her face. "I never meant for that. I tried—" She stopped suddenly as their gazes met.

"You tried?"

"It doesn't matter. You've already made up your mind about me." She jutted out her chin. Defiant. Proud. "What I did, the choices I made . . . if I had to do it all over again, I would."

Luke studied her expression, and Maxwell's warning echoed in his mind.

She can't be trusted. She'll turn on you if she thinks it serves her own agenda.

"Where is she, Ara? Where's Sam?"

"I don't know."

He stared at her, the silence stretching out between them. Ara's shoulders relaxed, her hands unclenching. Other people might rush to fill the quiet; she seemed to grow more comfortable with it.

She wasn't going to tell him what he needed to know.

Frustrated, Luke moved away from the cell toward the door.

"Wait," she said.

He glanced over his shoulder. She was pressed against the metal bars, a hand outstretched toward him. "Please, let me help you. I want to find Sam. Ask yourself this, if I was behind the kidnapping, then why in the hell did I chase the van afterward?"

"You followed the wrong one. Was it by chance or by design?"

For the briefest moment, their eyes locked, and before Ara's gaze dropped, Luke could've sworn he saw the shimmer of tears.

She took a deep breath. "What can I do to prove to you I didn't have anything to do with Sam's kidnapping?"

"You can't." A sudden twinge of sympathy for her tugged at him. The shock of it caused him to pause. "Right now, you're in the perfect place. If you had something to do with Sam's kidnapping, I have time to find it. And believe me, I will find it."

"There isn't anything to find."

"Maybe." He hardened himself, remembering the trouble she'd caused him, the holdup in the investigation that might have cost Sam her life. "But, if nothing else, you're out of my way. And out of my investigation."

CHAPTER ELEVEN

Luke stared down the table at his team. The dining room table at the Boone house had been transformed into a temporary headquarters. Laptops, cell phones, papers, and photographs were scattered in organized chaos. His hands tightened on the leather chair he was standing behind as he asked, "What have we been able to glean from her other friends?"

"Nothing we didn't already know," Thomas answered.

"What about Sam's phone?"

"We've torn it apart, looked at everything from text messages to the websites she was visiting. We've got nothing."

"I want you to pull her records from the phone company. If she had something to hide, she probably would've deleted it before anyone could see it."

Thomas pointed to one of their analysts. "Get on that."

"No one noticed her being followed?" Luke shoved off the chair and paced around the room. "This doesn't make any sense to me. She's around people all day long: her family, her friends, drivers, bodyguards. Not one of them noticed someone following her, watching her."

Thomas shook his head. "We've interviewed everyone on the list. No one has noticed anything strange in the last few months."

"What about the patrons at the restaurant? The staff? Where are we on those interviews?"

Vicki, a petite fireball of an agent, tilted her chair in his direction. "We've done two-thirds of the patrons and all the staff. Most of them remember seeing her that night, but no one saw the actual kidnapping. It's a dead end."

She tapped her pen on the pad of paper in front of her. "We were able to use the traffic-light cameras and get a visual of the van. Stolen plates, traced back to an SUV in LaGuardia's long-term parking."

No help.

"The driver of the van appears to be a woman," Vicki continued. "I've sent the image off to our labs to have it magnified and cleaned up. We should have it in a few hours."

"Call them and tell them I need it in thirty minutes. No excuses." Luke blew out a breath. "If they give you any grief, tell them to take it to the director."

"What about the ransom note?" He turned his attention to a nearby agent, Jacob, who was eyeing him with a weary expression. The two of them had worked together for almost Luke's entire career, and Jacob knew Luke didn't take failure well.

"No fingerprints on the note or on the necklace," said Jacob, "other than Sam's. Our handwriting expert confirmed the note was written by Sam."

"So we are able to confirm she was alive at the time the note was written." Luke bounced on his feet. "The courier—"

His thought was cut off by another young agent bursting into the room, her ponytail swinging. "Sir, you need to come with me right now. The kidnappers have called his cell phone. He's talking with them right now."

Luke slipped into Oliver's office soundlessly. The man was standing behind his desk, rigid, his face haggard and pale. To his right, another agent, the sound/audio master, was recording the conversation. His gaze met Luke's briefly, serious concern and concentration etched across his features.

The cell phone lay on the desk. It was on speaker, and from the first word, Luke immediately recognized that the kidnapper was using a voice-distortion device.

". . . didn't follow our instructions." Anger came through loud and clear, even though it sounded as if the man was underwater. "We know the FBI is with you."

Damn it. Luke ran a hand through his hair. They'd been careful. Extremely careful. How the hell did they know the FBI was involved?

Was this an inside job? A family member? A member of the security team?

Ara?

"As punishment for disobeying our orders, the ransom amount is now thirty million dollars." Oliver blinked, and his Adam's apple bobbed as he swallowed hard.

Leaning over the desk, he bent closer to the phone. "I need more time to gather the money."

The kidnapper laughed. "No. You have forty-eight hours to get us the money, or the girl will die." Luke's jaw tightened as his temper rose. "I'll call you again in forty-eight hours to arrange the exchange."

"Wait," Oliver demanded. "Before I give you this money, I want assurances that Sam is alive and unharmed."

"She's alive and unharmed," the kidnapper repeated back to him, mockingly.

"No." Oliver's voice hardened. "I want to speak to her myself. I want proof that she's alive, or you won't get a dime from me."

"Are you threatening me?"

"I'm telling you that nothing will happen until I know Sam is still alive."

"You're trying my patience."

"Maybe." Oliver narrowed his eyes. "But you're the one who kidnapped my stepdaughter. The least you can do is give me some sign of good faith that Sam will be returned to her family unharmed."

The kidnapper was silent for a moment. "Stay next to your phone. I'll contact you in a few minutes."

Then there was nothing but a dial tone.

* * *

Sam was freezing. Goose bumps trailed along her skin, and her teeth were chattering. They had taken her clothes, leaving her in nothing but her bra and underwear. Every time she moved, the zip ties around her hands cut into her skin, and the knot at the back of her blindfold dug into her skull. She didn't know how long she'd been left alone, but by the growl of her stomach, it'd been a long time.

The cold and the hunger were made worse by the silence. She couldn't hear anything, no talking or footsteps. But she knew they were out there. Maksim, the one in charge, had promised to hurt her should she move one inch.

After what they'd done a few hours ago, she believed him.

How had she ended up here? Where had everything gone so wrong?

He'll pay it. He'll pay the ransom.

The mantra playing in her head was the only thing giving her any sense of hope, even as the tiny voice in the back of her mind whispered she wasn't really Oliver's child. There was a chance he wouldn't pay, especially if he found out this was all her fault.

The echo of her mother's scream, the image of her frightened face flying down the hallway of the restaurant, brought a round of fresh tears to Sam's eyes. She would give anything to feel the warmth of her mother's arms, the brush of her lips across her forehead.

A door creaked open, and Sam's heart jackrabbited in her chest. Oh God, what was happening now? Instinct had her shrinking against the wall, desperate for a place to hide. Were they coming to finish off the job? Were they going to shoot her?

Footsteps echoed and halted in front of her. The jangle of keys and the strong scent of aftershave. Someone grabbed her upper arms and pulled her into a standing position.

She fought against him, trying to pull her arm out of his hand. She screamed against the duct tape stretched over her mouth.

He smacked her across the face. The force of it knocked Sam's head back against the wall. Stars played behind her blindfold, and her knees gave out.

"I'm not going to kill you, so fucking stop it." It was Sasha. She trembled, and his grip on her upper arm tightened. He pulled her forward. "Move it."

Her feet weren't coordinated after so many hours sitting, and she stumbled. She struck her knee against the edge of something, and pain shot up her leg. Sasha was not sympathetic. He kept yanking until she was shoved into a chair.

Cracked vinyl. It was slippery under her fingertips, and the seat of the chair listed to one side. The scent of cigarette smoke was strong. She gingerly reached out, and her fingers met something wooden. Probably a table.

"Remove her blindfold," Maskim ordered. When it was off, Sam blinked against the sudden assault of bright light. As the world came into focus, so did the man sitting across from her.

Maskim's black hair was combed back from his face. Up close, she could see that the small scar at the corner of his nose was the only imperfection in his skin. He'd removed his jacket and tie. Now in all black, he was dressed like death, the button-down shirt open at the collar, revealing the curve of his throat and a touch of his collarbone.

Maksim calmly took a drag on his cigarette. The smell of the smoke was making Sam nauseous, and bile burned the back of her throat.

"I'll remove the tape over your mouth, but you have to promise not to scream." Maksim picked up a pair of pliers resting on the table. "If you so much as make a whimper, I will be forced to pull out one of your teeth."

He took another drag on his cigarette. "Nod once if you understand my terms."

She gave a quick shake of her head in agreement. Maksim waved the pliers toward Sasha, who ripped the tape off with such force, it felt like half of Sam's face went with it. She swallowed down the sharp cry bubbling in her throat, her eyes locked on the pliers still in Maksim's hand.

"Now." He crushed the cigarette into an ashtray and leaned back in his chair. "You are going to do something for me. And you are going to do this because you don't want me to kill you, right?"

She met his questioning gaze and gave a silent nod.

"Good. We're going to make a phone call to your stepfather."

Sam's heart raced.

"You are going to tell him that you are unhurt." Maksim waved the pliers. "If you do this, then he will pay us, and you will get to go home. Understand?"

She nodded again. They were going to put her on the phone. This might be her only chance to get a message across, to help her family understand what was going on.

What could she say?

She closed her eyes and breathed in deep. She cleared her mind of everything. The pain and terror. The feeling of the hard chair underneath her. The smell of the cigarettes. She focused solely on finding a message.

The idea flittered through her mind, and Sam's hands shook. It might work. She opened her eyes as Maksim finished dialing the cell phone.

"I have her." With that brief introduction, he shoved the phone under her mouth.

"Hello? Sam?" Oliver's voice came through the loudspeaker, and sudden, unexplainable tears flooded her vision.

"I'm not hurt," she managed to choke out. Before Maksim could jerk the phone away she said quickly, "Ara, I miss you."

Sasha pulled on a chunk of her hair, twisting it painfully, and tears streamed down her cheeks.

"You have your proof," Maksim said into the phone. "The clock is ticking. I'll call again in forty-eight hours."

He hung up and glared at Sam. "What the hell was that?"

"She's my friend." Her voice trembled. "If I never get to see her again, I wanted her to know I miss her."

His eyes narrowed. Whatever he saw in her face must have convinced him because he said, "Take her back to the room."

Sasha replaced her blindfold and the duct tape before manhandling her back into the other room. Without another word, he dumped her on the floor and left her in the dark.

The sound of the door shutting was all the trigger Sam needed. She let loose, her body racked with sobs, the tears wetting the blindfold. The duct tape across her mouth muffled the sounds, but also made it more difficult to breathe. She forced herself to stop crying, but she couldn't stop the fear from staying lodged in her throat.

That phone call was probably the only chance she had to get a message to her family about how to save her. She had no illusions that she was going to get out of this alive, even if Oliver paid the money. Maksim and Sasha were going to kill her. She'd seen it in their eyes, as clearly as if it had already happened.

With her message, she'd placed all her hope in one woman. *Please, please, Ara. Figure it out.*

CHAPTER TWELVE

Giving a presentation after so many years in the FBI should've been a piece of cake, but Luke felt the weight of this case coming down on him. The tension in his neck and shoulders was giving him a massive headache.

He had very little information, almost no leads. He was failing, and judging from the frown stretched across FBI Director Robert Johnson's face, his boss was thinking exactly the same thing.

He said nothing for a long moment but then finally waved at the chair across from him. "Sit down, Patrick."

"I prefer to stand."

"Sit. Down. I'm getting a crick in my neck looking up at you."

Luke hesitated but then sat, his back ramrod straight.

Johnson leaned back in his chair. "I've listened to the phone call between Oliver and Sam. What do you make of the last thing Sam said? The part about missing Ara."

"I don't know. Is it a message of some kind? Or is it a real sentiment? Ara was her bodyguard. And I have a feeling she knows more about Sam's life than she lets on. It could be nothing."

"Or it could be something."

Luke nodded. "Or it could be something. I've been thinking about what it could mean, if it is a message, but I'm coming up empty."

"Have you played it for Ara?" Johnson asked.

The thought had occurred to him almost immediately, but Luke had rejected it. "No. I don't think it's a good idea. The message could be a way for the kidnappers to communicate with Ara, to send her instructions of some kind."

"Have you come up with any direct evidence to show she's a part of the kidnapping plan?"

"No. We've been able to clear Grant from the suspect list, so her attacking him, while troublesome, didn't put the case in jeopardy."

"What do you make of the fact that she left Sam alone at the restaurant?"

"Negligent. But she has a reasonable explanation that's backed by Sam's mother. Plus she tried to follow the van in an attempt to get Sam back." Luke could hear the words as they left his mouth, and he knew where the director was going.

"I understand how it sounds," Luke acknowledged. "But Ara has a questionable history that makes me wonder about her real intentions. And sir, I believe she knows more than what she's saying."

"She probably does. Which is what you're going to find out when you interrogate her." Johnson's deeply lined face wobbled with every word, the folds of his chin disappearing into his tightly buttoned shirt. "There's no other way to decipher the message. Let Ara hear it, see if it means anything to her."

"So you don't believe she's a viable suspect?"

"I think the risk is low and worth taking," Johnson answered. "Find out what you need to know to appease your conscience and ensure she isn't in league with the kidnappers, but then use her."

"It will take time. Time that I won't have to work on other leads."

"That's why you have a team," Johnson replied. "Assign them to do other things while you're figuring out what in the hell Sam is trying to say. This message she gave us might be the lead we need to crack the case."

"I know." Luke ran a hand through his hair. "It's part of what makes it so damn frustrating. I just wish there was some other way to figure it out without using Ara."

Johnson's beady eyes locked on Luke. "You're a damn fine FBI agent. Nearly as good as your father."

Luke's jaw tightened at the supposed compliment. It felt more like a backhanded slap.

"Nearly as good" seemed to be his legacy. At first, he'd been proud to follow in his father's footsteps. Dan Patrick had been a career FBI agent, solving more cases than anyone else, his quick mind and fast trigger finger the stuff of legend. Many of the old timers, like Johnson, had served for decades with him. Now, so many years into his own career, it felt like Luke would never get out from behind his father's shadow.

"You Patricks tend to be stubborn and independent," Johnson continued. "It normally serves you well, but it can get in the way. It's my job to tell you when that happens."

"And you think I'm being unnecessarily cautious?"

"I think time is running out and you can't be as thorough as you'd like. Our backs are against the wall here." He sighed. "I agree that Ara's actions with Grant were reckless, and you're right to be cautious, given what we've learned about her past. But I don't see any way around it. And at this point, we need to use any lead we've got. Including Ara."

Luke blew out a breath. "I don't like it, but I agree it's our best course of action. I'll play Ara the message."

Johnson gave him a nod. "Find Sam. Bring her home. And then catch the bastards. You do that and you'll have written your own legacy."

* * *

Ara paced the tiny interrogation room. Her bruised knuckles ached, and her stomach was still sore from Grant punching her. Yet none of her physical pains compared to the emotional and mental agony she was trapped in.

Had they found Sam? Had Oliver agreed to pay the ransom?

She wanted to bang on the door, punch the walls, do something to expel the frustration boiling inside. It wouldn't help. Only finding Sam would ease the heavy weight of guilt she carried.

Damn Luke Patrick. Damn him to hell. If Sam died because he'd refused her help, it would be on him.

As if called by her thoughts, the door opened and Luke himself strolled through. His gaze flicked over her, taking in her wrinkled clothes and messy hair.

Rather than be embarrassed, she gave him the same appraisal. Ara's lips tightened. Why the hell did he look so good? Black suit and white, crisp shirt, freshly shaven face.

He'd obviously taken time to shower and change his clothes. All while Sam was at the mercy of men doing God-knows-what to her.

Bastard.

Heat rose in her cheeks, and her fists clenched. He caught the movement and arched his eyebrows.

"Are you going to hit me, too? Or do you only use teenage boys for boxing practice?"

She didn't answer him. He moved into the room, closing the door behind him, and set a bag down on the table. He pulled out a sandwich, Coke, and some chips.

"You should eat something." He gestured to the chair closest to her.

"Is there a point to this meeting?" She crossed her arms over her chest. "If so, you should just get on with it."

"Sit down."

Ara didn't move. She wouldn't give him an inch, wouldn't allow him to bully her. She'd had just about enough of this whole thing. She'd been alone for hours with nothing but regret and horrible memories to ponder. Now she had a person in front of her she could pour all those emotions on.

A flicker of something crossed his face. "Can I trust you, Ara?"

The question came out so low, she almost thought she'd imagined it. But then he pinned her with those sharp blue eyes of his, searching for the truth.

"What game are you playing now?"

"No game," he said, his steady gaze never leaving hers. "There have been some developments in the case."

Like a switch, her anger melted, and fear mingled with horror took its place. She almost couldn't choke out the words. "Did you find her?"

"No. Not yet."

Relief rushed over her, so heady she swayed. Her hand grabbed the back of the chair to steady herself. "What's going on?"

"Before I can tell you more, I need to know if I can trust you."

"You can." She straightened up. "For the last time, I didn't have anything to do with Sam's kidnapping."

He didn't miss a beat. "Prove it."

"How?"

"Answer my questions." Luke sat up, folding his hands together on the table. "All of them."

She narrowed her eyes. He'd had plenty of time to ask questions. Why now? What had he learned?

What if he's done more research? What if he asks about . . .

No. Her past was long buried and done, and there was no way for Luke to dig it back up again. Moving to the United States had wiped the slate clean. And besides, she couldn't find Sam from behind bars. If Luke was offering her a way out of jail, she had to take it.

"You have questions for me about Sam." She took a deep breath and tugged at her long sleeves, making sure her scars were covered. "Let's do this. Ask them."

He gestured again to the chair across from him.

"I'd rather not, if it's all the same to you."

"Fine." He rose from his own chair and stepped away from the table. She recognized the move for what it was—an interrogation tactic. He wouldn't allow her to tower over him or be in any kind of position of power.

It rankled her, but she admired it as well. She would have done exactly the same thing in his shoes.

"Do you know of anyone who would want to hurt Sam? Or get back at her in some way?"

"No. She's your typical teenager. She gets into trouble sometimes, but it's nothing extreme."

"What do you consider extreme?"

She let go of the back of the chair and started pacing. "Lately, she's been acting out more. Skipping school, not doing her homework, more of the club scene. Hanging out with kids that probably aren't a good influence on her. At the same time, she's seemed happier. Less snarky. It's hard to explain."

"Did you know that Sam was involved with drugs?"

She let out a breath. "I suspected, but I didn't know for sure. I . . ."

He arched his brows. "Now is not the time to stay silent. If you know something, you need to say it."

He was right, but she hated this all the same. "You said Grant didn't have anything to do with Sam's disappearance?"

"He didn't. But you knew she might be involved with drugs and never said a word. That leaves me questioning your motives."

"I didn't say anything because I didn't know for sure she was." She sighed. "The truth is, I suspected she was doing them while Gannon was guarding her, and it caused a lot of fights between us."

Luke's brow creased. "I thought you were Sam's primary bodyguard?"

"I am. Well, I was up until school started. Oliver decided it would be better for me to stick with Holly during the day. Sam spent her afternoons guarded by Gannon." She frowned. "When you talked to Grant, did he confirm that Sam owed him money?"

"He did. Why?"

"Because I don't understand why Sam wouldn't pay him. She doesn't get much cash from Oliver, but she has a credit card she uses most of the time. What was she doing with her cash if she wasn't paying Grant?"

Luke titled his head in thought. "We've interviewed Gannon. He hadn't noticed anything out of the ordinary."

Ara stilled. "Did you do a background check on him?"

"We did." She could tell by his facial expression that nothing had come of it, but questions were starting to play in his mind. "What are you doing, Ara?"

"I'm trying to help you. I'm trying to figure out what is going on."

"Are you? Or are you trying to point fingers at other potential suspects?"

She spun to face him. "Do you think I like doing this? Do you think I want to believe Gannon might've had something to do with Sam's disappearance? I don't. But she's missing. I didn't help the kidnappers, but I can't ignore the fact that someone else in the household might have, and Gannon is the one person who was with Sam the most, outside of me."

She took a deep breath. "What can I do to make you believe me?"

He paused. "Tell me about the raid in Austin."

Ara stiffened. "You already know about it."

"I want to hear your version."

Panic set her heart pounding, and she spun away from him, taking a few shaky steps toward the far wall. Why couldn't he let this go? "This has nothing to do with Sam."

"You're right. But I won't work with someone I can't trust. I've been warned away from you by Captain Maxwell, and I need to know is if his assessment is correct."

"Then pull the reports."

"I already have. They're contradictory at best. And I can't let you on this case, give you potentially sensitive material, without knowing if I can trust you." His voice turned soft, as comforting as a caress. "Tell me what happened that day, Ara. Let me judge for myself."

Oh, God, she couldn't do this. She didn't want to say the words aloud. She'd survived worse than the fallout from the raid—far worse—yet the loss of her career as a police officer was like an open sore she couldn't bear to poke.

But what choice did she have?

Ara closed her eyes, gave herself a heartbeat to shore up her resolve.

"I was part of a task force investigating a new network of human traffickers and drug dealers," she said, still facing away from Luke. "These guys were new to the business but were working in conjunction with established cartels and had ties to the Russian mafia. They were particularly nasty. They'd cut out the tongues of anyone suspected of talking to the cops, and it seemed every time we managed to get a foothold into their organization, our contact would end up dead."

"Undercover officers?"

She spun around but refused to look him in the eye. "We sent in two. Their bodies were found a month later. That's when Captain Maxwell formed the task force. Our mission was to breach the network and take out a few of their operatives. The plan was to offer them a trade. Little to no jail time if they flipped on their superiors and named the men who'd killed our undercover detectives."

She started pacing the length of the room again. Luke tracked her movements, his expression grave.

"It took more than six months to get a lead. No one would talk to us. Finally we got a tip about a house the traffickers might be using as a temporary holding place."

She remembered standing at the edge of the woods, the oppressive Texas heat crushing down on her. In her mind's eye, she could see the house down below in the clearing. The warped front steps, the reflection of the morning light off the tin roof.

"We were just about to begin the raid when a van full of new girls arrived. I wanted to move out, to capture the suppliers along with the men in the house. Captain Maxwell overruled me."

"You didn't agree with his decision?"

"He felt we didn't have the manpower necessary to take down all five men. I believed we did."

"What happened next?"

"We waited until the delivery was complete." The words were sterile, so mild compared to what had actually happened. How could she explain that she'd stood by helplessly while a line of little girls piled out of the back of an industrial van? How could she explain the terror on their faces? The way her heart wept at the sight of their malnourished bodies?

She'd watched the leader, a man known only to her by his street name, Viktor, as he assessed each girl in turn. She'd shared every touch with those poor children—every strike, every insult, every swipe of Viktor's hand as clearly as if he'd been doing it to her.

Even now, the memory made her want to puke.

When her eyes met Luke's, she froze. Gone was the mask of indifference he normally wore. Now he stared at her with a mixture of horror and grief, and a strange kind of understanding.

Ara swallowed past the lump in her throat and dropped her gaze from his. "After the suppliers left, we commenced with the raid. The first suspect, Whip, was an easy capture."

"And the second? The leader, Viktor?"

"He disappeared into the basement. I led the way down. It was terrifying because we hadn't been able to do much recon

before the raid. We had no idea what we were walking into."
She bit her lip. The basement had been pitch black, the stairs
creaky. She'd been afraid they wouldn't hold her weight, let
alone her teammates following behind her. "Viktor panicked.
He was spraying gasoline all over the basement."

She shook her head. "I have no idea what the hell he was
trying to do, except maybe burn the evidence." This time, she
met Luke's eyes and held them. "He had all the girls down
there with him, handcuffed to the beds. He made a move for
his weapon. I tackled him, handcuffed him, and held him
down while the other members of my team pulled those girls
out one by one."

"What went wrong?"

"They left one behind."

The echo of that child's cry still played in Ara's night-
mares sometimes.

Por favor. Por favor.

"I couldn't leave her there. She was frightened and alone, in
the dark, and the basement's soundproofing wouldn't allow me
to make contact with my team." She squared her shoulders. "It
was her or Viktor. So I made the decision to take her up and
leave Viktor down in the basement. I handcuffed him to one of
the beds. I figured I would take the girl upstairs, pass her over
to one of my team members, and then go back for Viktor."

She didn't tell Luke about the deep well of satisfaction
she'd felt when Viktor's handcuffs had clanked closed around
the metal bed frame.

"When I took her up the stairs, I realized all hell had
broken loose. The team tracking the suppliers had lost them.

They were interrogating Whip, trying to get him to give them some information to help. He wasn't being cooperative."

"Is that when the explosion happened?"

She nodded. "We found out later it was a spark from the water heater that set the basement on fire. It ignited all the gasoline Viktor had spread on the flooring." She leaned against the wall, suddenly extremely tired. "He died."

"One of the reports said you went back into the house. That you tried to save him."

Ara closed her eyes. She could still smell the scent of burning wood. The smoke seemed impenetrable. The heat coming from the kitchen was intense, singeing her arm hair.

Fear clawed up her spine, and time seemed to slow. Sheer force of will had her ignoring every instinct for retreat. Instead, Ara shut her eyes against the sting of the smoke. Placing a hand on the wall, she used it as a guide, moving further into the house.

Go. Go. Go.

Her fingers skipped over the opening to the bathroom. She saw the hallway in her mind, the kitchen, and the doorway to the basement. *Only ten more steps ahead. Nine. Eight.*

It was like moving toward hell, the heat pouring over her in waves. The building hissed and groaned. It wouldn't be standing for much longer. She couldn't breathe. Dropping to her knees, she crawled forward, desperate to get to the basement.

Opening her eyes, Ara snapped back into the present. "I did. But it was too late. There was nothing to be done. Captain Maxwell was furious with me. He felt I should have left the girl downstairs and taken up Viktor first, since Viktor was our best bet at breaking open the ring and catching the men who'd killed our fellow police officers."

Luke looked at her for a long moment. "What do you think?"

"I think our undercover officers were dead, and they were going to stay dead whether we caught their killers or not. But that little girl had her whole life ahead of her. She hadn't done anything wrong, and she didn't deserve to spend one more minute down in that hellhole." Tears welled in her eyes, and she swiped them away, embarrassed.

Luke didn't say anything. The only sound in the room was the whir of the heater and the dim chatter seeping in from the station outside the closed interrogation room door.

Finally, he met her gaze.

"I agree with you."

CHAPTER THIRTEEN

The words hung in the air between them, the tension so thick Ara could feel it prickling her skin.

"We don't have much time," Luke continued. "There have been some new developments in Sam's case, and I need your help."

"My help?"

"We both want the same thing here, Ara. To find Sam."

She hesitated for a moment, judging whether his offer was sincere. "I want full access to Sam's case. I can't help you if you don't give me all the information."

"You're not a federal agent."

"I just spilled my guts to you. I think I've earned the right to hear everything."

Luke blinked, and his mouth twitched. He didn't seem to like the idea, and she waited while he thought about it. Finally, he nodded. "On one condition."

"Okay."

"You don't go rogue." He leveled a cold, hard stare at her. "I don't want you running off chasing leads without me. Either you work this as part of the team, or you're off."

Ara met his stare with one of her own. "Fine."

A truce, then, if an uneasy one. Pulling out the chair, Ara sat down and looked up at him expectantly. Luke pushed the sandwich closer to her.

"Eat. You'll need your strength."

She unwrapped the sandwich, and her stomach gave an anticipatory growl. She took a bite. "You talk while I eat. I can multitask."

"We've heard from the kidnappers."

Fifteen minutes later, Ara had been fully informed about the case, and she'd inhaled all the food and the Coke. Obviously, he was right about one thing. She'd been starving.

"Do you have a recording of the phone call?"

Luke pulled out his cell phone and accessed a file on it. A man's voice came through the speaker.

"I have her."

Luke stopped the recording. "Do you recognize him?"

She frowned. "No, but that's not surprising, considering he's using a voice distorter. I could be this guy's sister and I wouldn't recognize his voice. Have you sent the recording off to be cleaned up?"

Luke nodded. "I have the best audio guys working on it, but it takes time." He hit play again. This time it was Sam's voice that came through the speaker, undistorted and frighteningly clear.

"I'm not hurt."

Ara's lunch turned to stones in her stomach. Only three words, but she could clearly hear the terror in Sam's voice. She didn't believe for a moment Sam wasn't hurt.

But at least she was alive.

"I miss you, Ara."

Shock froze Ara in place. She barely registered the kidnapper's distorted voice coming back on to remind them of the ticking clock and the need for money.

Luke shut off the recording. "Why did Sam mention you?"

"I don't know." She frowned. "Play it again."

She focused more carefully on the second run-through. Sam's words were rushed, and Ara's name sounded fainter than the rest of the sentence. Like they'd been taking the phone away from her as she said it.

Ara got out of the chair and started pacing the room. "It must be a message of some kind, but I have no idea what it means."

"How can you be sure?" Luke leaned back in his chair, watching her movements. He was playing devil's advocate, she realized. Helping her to work through what her gut was telling her. Forcing her to use logic.

"Sam tolerates me, nothing more. She resents having to be followed around and protected." She paused in her stride. "We're not close, not enough for her to call out to me, and not her mother. That doesn't make any sense at all."

She resumed her pacing. "However, she would assume that if something happened to her, I would be in the room when the kidnappers talked to her stepfather. I'm the one who follows her around, and I was there on the day of the

117

kidnapping. One thing Sam can count on is that I'll come looking for her."

"You know Sam better than you think. Walk me through it. What is she doing?"

Ara frowned, trying to place herself in Sam's position. "I've been kidnapped. I have one chance to get a message through, one shot at giving a clue." She spun and faced Luke. "She can't say anything that would make them suspicious."

"So she says something that can be interpreted in many different ways." Appreciation dawned in Luke's expression. "Smart."

"Sam's a smart girl." Ara gestured to the paused audio recording. "Maybe too smart for me, because I can't figure out what the hell she wants me to get from this."

"If you were a cop on the case, what would you do?"

Luke's question cut through Ara's racing mind. It provided her with focus and sudden clarity.

"Take me back to the restaurant."

* * *

The afternoon shadows were deepening as Ara and Luke entered Phillips. It was too late for the lunch crowd and too early for dinner, so most of the tables were empty. Soft lighting played perfectly off the wooden floor and linen tablecloths.

Luke flashed his badge to the maître d'. A short conversation later, Ara was finally able to walk to the back of the restaurant where they'd been seated for dinner on the night of the kidnapping.

"What happened during dinner?" Luke asked.

"Nothing out of the ordinary." Ara shrugged, touching the back of a chair. "Holly had met with an old friend who was a trustee at Princeton. She was trying to woo her in the hopes of giving Sam an edge next year when she starts applying for colleges."

"Did you notice anyone watching you? Acting strange?"

Ara bit her lip, thinking back to that night. Nothing had felt out of place or tickled her intuition.

She shook her head. "It was a regular dinner. Up until it was time to leave, anyway." She caught Luke's questioning gaze. "Holly asked me to step outside so she could have a moment with her friend. Despite what you may think of me, I don't make a habit of leaving my employer unprotected. But I did as she asked."

"What about Sam?"

"She was upset." Ara's voice picked up in pace. "She didn't want to be at the dinner in the first place. Then Holly's friend brought up the plane crash, and Sam became extremely withdrawn after that. When dinner was over, she ran off to the restroom. I think she wanted to have a moment to herself."

Ara followed the path Sam took that night, and Luke followed her.

"Do you know if Sam ever made it to the bathroom?" Ara asked.

"No, but my suspicion based on the timeline is that she did. Otherwise Holly would have missed the assault altogether." Luke stepped in front of Ara, blocking the exit door with his body. He seemed to sense she needed to walk through the event, to understand it from every angle.

Ara nodded, opening the bathroom door and standing in the threshold. "Okay, so Sam comes out of the bathroom, and he grabs her."

"Holly reported she caught them wrestling as they went out the door."

Luke grabbed Ara around the waist, twisting her so that her back was against his front. She could feel the firm muscles of his chest, the heat of his body pressed against her. He lifted her slightly so her feet were off the ground, then backed out the emergency exit into the alley.

"Sam drops her purse during the struggle, or the kidnapper forces her to release it," Ara said.

"Then he shoves her into the back of the van."

Luke set her down gently, and she spun to face him. This close, she could smell the warm spice of his aftershave.

She jerked her arm out of his grasp and backed away from him.

Luke put his hands in his pockets and began walking toward the entrance of the alley. "They went this way in the van."

"Right." Ara shook her head to clear her mind, to refocus herself, and followed him. "They took a left out of the alley." She pointed down the road. "And then went that way, toward the highway."

She eyed the street up and down, but nothing seemed to stick out. She bounced on the balls of her feet. "One thing I never understood about the whole operation was how the kidnappers knew Sam would use the bathroom. Were they here, waiting, hoping that at some point she would pass by?"

She blew out a breath. "I mean, I suppose it's possible they did, but it seems risky to me. And why didn't I ever spot them following us? We were so careful—I was so careful. I can't believe I never noticed them, even if they were professionals."

"I had the same questions."

Luke's low tone caught Ara's attention. "What? What do you know?"

He pulled out his cell phone from his suit pocket and scrolled to something before handing it over to her. "I pulled Sam's phone records from the company. Thomas sent the results to me as we were driving over here."

Ara scrolled through the messages on the phone, and her heart started pounding with a mixture of dread and confusion. Blinking twice, she reread the final words.

"Wrapping up dinner now," she said aloud. "I'll go to the bathroom within the next five minutes."

Luke nodded, answering her unasked question. "She had something to do with this."

Ara shook her head. *No way. Not Sam.* "That's not possible. Why would she do that?"

"You tell me. Why would she?" Luke expression was filled with both understanding and sympathy. He already knew why. He was just waiting for her to figure it out.

Ara's mind twisted. It only took a few moments before she caught up to his thinking. "Oh, God, she wanted to get back at Oliver." She nearly spiked Luke's phone to the ground before she caught herself. "What the hell was she thinking?"

"She's a seventeen-year-old. They don't always have the best foresight." Luke slid his phone out of her hands and tucked it back in his pocket. "She's been through a lot of changes in the last two years. The loss of her father and brother, the remarriage of her mother, the new design of her family."

"The changes in her mother," Ara added. "Holly's distant with her, more and more every day." She closed her eyes as she absolved the full impact of the evidence. "Sam's rebellious and difficult and a smart-mouthed pain in the ass, but I never thought she would do something like this."

"She's hurting. The kidnapping would give her a double strike. She could gain her mother's attention and get back at Oliver by taking something he values dearly—his money."

"I've been torturing myself," she whispered. "Thinking I let her down, that she was suffering because of my mistakes. And all this time, she's been playing me for a fool."

Luke reached out and touched her arm. His palm was warm, the grip firm, and she could sense the strength behind it. "It wasn't just you she played for a fool."

She looked up. Luke's eyes were darker now. Had they always been that dark?

Luke released her arm and stepped back, and Ara let out a breath she hadn't realized she'd been holding. She wasn't attracted to Luke. It was simply a side effect of the situation.

Focusing on the exit of the alley, Ara forced herself back to the case. She replayed everything she knew, including the phone call Luke had played for her just an hour before.

"Wait a minute." She spun back toward Luke to find him watching her, that expressionless mask he wore firmly back in place. "The way Sam sounded on the phone . . . it didn't seem fake to me. She's smart, but she's not much of an actress."

She bit her lip. "She's in danger."

Luke nodded. "I believe she is, too. The ransom increase, the change in communication with the kidnappers. Something went wrong. Whatever Sam got herself into, whatever she had planned, didn't go the way she thought it would. It may be why she's trying to get a message across to you. Because she's in real danger, and she didn't know any other way to tell us."

"Whose number was she texting? Have you been able to trace it?"

"It's a burner phone. Already been shut off," Luke said. "The only solid lead we have at the moment is the message she sent to you."

"Which means I have to figure out what the hell she's trying to tell me." Ara ran a hand through her hair. "This isn't right. I don't think the message has anything to do with the restaurant. It's something else."

"What?"

Ara sighed. "I don't know."

CHAPTER FOURTEEN

Gannon looked nervous.

The massive man was sitting on the overstuffed couch, attempting to appear nonchalant, but his foot was jumping and his fingers kept flexing. Luke took the chair across from him and offered a disarming smile.

"Sorry to keep you waiting. Seems I'm burning the candle at both ends."

"No problem." Gannon cleared his throat. "Although I already told the other agent . . ." He waved his hand around.

"Thomas."

"Yeah, Thomas—everything I know. I haven't thought of anything new."

"I just have some follow-up questions. Nothing too major, but every detail helps."

"Sure."

"It's come to my attention you were guarding Sam in the afternoons. Is that true?"

His eyes darted around the library before settling back on Luke. "Yeah, but only since school started. Before that she was mostly with Ara."

Luke nodded. "Right. Just to be clear, where was Sam going after school?"

"The regular places. Her friends' houses. The mall. Usual stuff."

"Did you accompany Sam to those places?"

He swallowed hard. "Well, it depends. If Sam went to Sharon's house, for example, I would hang out outside or downstairs while I waited for her. If she went somewhere public, like the mall, I would follow her from store to store. Keep an eye on her, you know?"

"And you were watching Sam every afternoon?"

Gannon straightened in his seat. "What are you implying?"

"I'm not implying anything. I'm asking if you were with Sam every afternoon after school."

"Of course. It's my job."

Luke pulled out a photograph from the file folder resting on the table between them and turned it toward Gannon. "Then explain to me how you were at the horse track, placing bets, during the time you were supposed to be watching Sam?"

He paused, his body still. "I took off one afternoon."

"Don't." Luke voice came out cold. "Don't lie to me anymore. I have records, Gannon. You were placing bets several afternoons a week."

It'd taken his team time to find it, but once they went back in Gannon's financials more than several months, they'd uncovered his gambling problem. Gannon had suddenly come into an influx of cash and was using that money to place his bets.

"It's time to come clean with me," Luke said. "Now."

Gannon's mouth opened and then shut. Color rose high on his cheeks. Luke waited him out, and finally the big man across from him let out a long, slow breath. "Sam was paying me to give her the afternoons off."

"She was paying you in cash."

Gannon nodded. "Yeah."

It confirmed what Luke had suspected. Sam couldn't pay Grant because she was paying Gannon instead. Having the afternoons off, without any bodyguards, gave Sam the freedom to connect with someone and plan her own kidnapping without anyone knowing.

"Listen," Gannon sat closer to the edge of the couch. "It's not what you think."

"What do I think?"

"It was innocent. Sam couldn't stand being followed around all the time. She wasn't used to it. Before her mom married Oliver, she could go where she pleased without a babysitter and she missed it. She begged me to help her. To let her have some time to be normal." His voice lowered, and his gaze dropped to his hands. "And the truth is, I needed the extra cash."

"If this was all so innocent, then why didn't you tell us when she was taken?"

His head shot up. "Are you kidding me? If I'd told you the truth, I would've been fired."

"By not telling me the truth, you may have cost Sam her life," Luke retorted. "Didn't that occur to you?"

Gannon's foot started jumping again.

"Where was Sam going during her afternoons off?" Luke asked.

"I don't know. I would drop her off at the mall and then pick her up."

"From what time to what time?"

"Right after school until seven or so. She would meet me in the west parking lot, the one near the food court."

"Was she meeting with someone?"

Gannon shrugged. "Maybe. Sometimes she had gone shopping because she would come back with bags of stuff. But other times she was empty-handed."

"You never asked her?"

"Once. She laughed and told me to mind my own business."

Which meant yes. All this time, he and his team were spinning their wheels trying to figure out how the kidnapping had gone down, and with whom, and Gannon had been sitting on important information that could've helped them. The idiot wasn't only going to lose his job. If they didn't find Sam in time, Luke was going to charge him.

But now was not the time to say that.

"Did you ever see her with anyone?" he asked, careful to keep his tone professional.

Gannon shook his head. "No, I promise. I would tell you if I had."

Luke leaned back in the chair. "Okay. Let's go again. From the beginning."

* * *

Ara climbed out of the shower stall and wrapped the towel around her. The bathroom was foggy with steam, the mat soft under her bare feet. She'd convinced herself a long, hot shower would make her feel better. She was wrong.

Sam's face felt etched in her mind, a continuous movie she couldn't stop. What was happening to her right now? She had to be terrified. More than terrified. It was an indescribable feeling, the helplessness that came with being at another person's mercy. Ara knew. She'd experienced it firsthand.

She gripped the countertop and cursed. This wasn't helping. Sucking in a deep breath, she opened the door and padded into her bedroom. She rummaged around for clothes, pulling out a pair of jeans from the bottom drawer of her dresser. Opening the one with her shirts, she swore again.

No long sleeves.

Her gaze dropped over her shoulder to the back of her arms and the long, ragged scars there. They were thicker at the top and tapered down toward her elbows. Those scars were a physical reminder of her own personal nightmare. She never discussed the incident, kept it locked down behind a wall of armor. The scars were hidden away too. The clothes she wore protection against unwanted questions and unsolicited comments.

And, if she was honest, she covered them for own benefit as well. Every time she looked at them, all she could hear was the echoing sound of gunshots. And the screams.

Ara closed her eyes, but it only made things worse. Her stomach churned, and she feared for a moment she would be sick. She focused her gaze on a spot on the carpeting and forced herself to take a deep breath. Then another one.

Sam's kidnapping had rubbed all her old wounds raw. The ghosts of her past felt too close. How would she survive if Sam died? Her shoulders already carried the burden of other deaths, the guilt of being a survivor. She didn't think she could add Sam to the load.

Forget it. She would be wearing a jacket anyway. No one would know. And Sam wasn't going to die.

She dressed quickly and combed her hair, leaving it to curl loose and damp around her face. She considered going to the dining room but couldn't bare it. Having Luke hovering over her with quiet expectation was too much. Yet neither did she want to be in her own room, the memories threatening to overtake her. She needed to clear her head. She needed to focus on Sam.

Ara climbed the staircase to Sam's room. She hesitated before touching the handle, suddenly feeling nervous about stepping into the private space. Sam was always so protective of her area.

Not that it mattered now.

Ara swung the door open and came face-to-face with the familiar surroundings. The large canopy bed, the silk walls, the expensive clothes littering the floor. Two days ago, Sam had been whirling through this room, a bundle of bad attitude and cockiness. It was never quiet when she was around. There were always friends, music, television.

Now, the silence of the room was deafening.

Ara walked across the plush carpeting, carefully stepping over items on the floor. Clothes, books, discarded food wrappers. Sam's room was always a mess, but it had grown substantially worse since Holly had forbidden the housekeepers from cleaning it last month, after a huge blowout between Sam and her mother.

I miss you, Ara.

Sam's words played over and over again in her head in a continuous loop. What did they mean? What had the girl been trying to tell her?

Ara spun in a circle around the room, eyeing the objects, hoping for some sort of inspiration.

Nothing.

Frustrated, she sat down on the unmade bed. The sheets and comforter were in a tangled heap, the scent of Sam's shampoo wafting up from them. It brought tears to Ara's eyes. She wiped them away with a trembling hand.

She should be furious with Sam, and a part of her was. But overriding all of that was an overwhelming fear. It was clear, from the desperate tone of Sam's voice, she was in way over her head. There was no question in Ara's mind. Sam was in serious danger.

Ara had been racking her brain throughout her shower, trying to figure out who Sam could have planned this with. Most of her friends were flighty teenagers, rich kids with God complexes. They wouldn't have had the skills necessary to effectively plan and execute a kidnapping.

No, it had to be someone else.

Ara's shoulders slumped, and she sighed, long and slow. She'd come into Sam's room looking for inspiration. It seemed all she'd found was sadness and more questions.

Her gaze caught sight of the painting above Sam's desk. It was an oil abstract in bright, cheerful colors that matched the room's overall decor. Another one of Holly's art purchases, no doubt. Probably from the same gallery as the depressing painting she'd bought for Oliver the night of the kidnapping.

Ara blinked. Her heart thudded in her chest.

The gallery.

Her own words flitted through her mind.

Maybe one day you'll miss having me as your shadow.

She gasped and rose from the bed. Is that what Sam was referring to? The conversation they'd had at the gallery?

Her lips tightened together. Her gut was screaming, and adrenaline coursed through her. She was onto something. She could feel it.

But what? What was the message?

She struggled to replay the conversation in her head. Ara had been telling her to be careful because Sam . . .

Because Sam had been flirting with the man at the gallery. *Nick.*

The name popped into her head along with a fresh wave of excitement. Was Nick the clue to this whole thing? Was he the person Sam was trying to tell Ara about?

She ran from the bedroom and downstairs, nearly trampling over Luke as he came out of the library.

"Whoa, where are you going in such a hurry?" He grabbed her arm, steadying her. His grip was firm, and Ara swore she could feel the heat of his palm through her leather jacket.

"I was coming to find you." She peered through the open doorway and caught sight of Gannon on the couch, his head in his hands. "What's going on?"

Luke passed a glance over his shoulder and shut the door. "Gannon says that in the last few months Sam's been paying him for time off."

Ara's heart leapt. "Time off? What does that mean?" She blinked. "He was leaving her alone?"

"Seems so. For hours at a time."

"So it's possible she was meeting with someone."

"More than possible given what we know about Sam's involvement in her kidnapping." Luke's mouth tightened at the corners. "Unfortunately, Gannon doesn't have a clue about who this mystery person might be."

"I do."

CHAPTER FIFTEEN

There was a flurry of activity happening inside the gallery. Waiters bustled around, a janitor was sweeping the floor, and several people were hanging tags next to paintings. Obviously another event was taking place that night.

Ara led Luke past the first room toward the back, following the sound of the gallery owner's voice. Kat was in deep conversation with another woman, her hands gesturing expressively. Her long hair was elegantly styled, accentuating strong cheekbones and a cleft chin.

Before Ara could open her mouth, Luke stepped in front of her, taking the lead.

"Excuse me, ladies," Luke interrupted smoothly. "I was told one of you was the gallery owner."

Kat glanced over her shoulder and then did a double take. Her gaze lingered on Luke's broad chest before moving upward to his close-cropped hair and chiseled jawline.

"I'm the owner." She licked her lips and then stuck out a hand for Luke to shake. "Katherine Carmichael, but you can call me Kat."

Luke took it, and Kat held onto to his hand longer than necessary. Ara clenched her fists at her side. "Pleased to meet you." Luke's expression held a hint of amusement as he released her hand.

The other woman nudged Kat with her elbow. Kat laughed and stepped back from Luke, gesturing to her friend. "Oh, I'm sorry. This is Megan O'Conner."

"Ma'am." Luke gave her a simple nod but never took his gaze off of Kat. "I need to speak with you about an important matter, and I'd like to do so in private. Is there somewhere we could talk?"

"I'm sorry, Mr. . . ."

"Patrick. Luke Patrick."

She plastered on a polite smile of regret. "I can't possibly get away . . ."

Her voice trailed off as Ara stepped around Luke, directly into Kat's vision. Kat's eyes widened in surprise before she caught herself and leaned in, brushing both of Ara's cheeks with her soft lips. "Ara? Goodness, I didn't even see you there. How are you?"

"Just fine."

"There hasn't been some kind of mistake with the painting, has there? I have it scheduled for delivery tomorrow."

Ara shook her head. "No, no. Everything's fine. I'm here with Luke, actually."

Kat's eyebrows arched only a touch—not from a skilled practice at hiding her emotions, but because Botox wouldn't allow them to move more than that.

"I think Holly would really appreciate it if you would take a few moments to talk with us," Ara said. "In private."

Megan's curious gaze drifted back and forth among the three of them. She was eating up every word of this, to be distributed later at luncheons and brunches.

"Of course." Kat smoothed back a strand of her hair and gave them a winning smile. "But only for a few moments. I have a huge opening tonight, as you can see."

"I assure you it won't take but a few minutes of your time," Luke said.

I assure you. Ara nearly snorted before she caught herself. Luke really was a chameleon. A touch of admiration for him blossomed as Kat made her apologies to Megan and then led them to her office.

The expensive touches in the gallery extended into the office. Everything was high end, from the modern desk to the striped visitors' chairs. It was also immaculately clean, not a paper out of place or a pen in sight. The effect was like stepping into a decor magazine.

"Please, have a seat," Kat said, waving toward the visitors' chairs as she stepped behind the desk. "Can I get you something to drink? A glass of champagne, perhaps?"

"No, thank you. And allow me to properly introduce myself. Luke Patrick, FBI." He flashed his badge. Kat's eyes widened, and a hand fluttered to her throat.

"FBI?" Her glance darted to Ara. "What is this about?"

"Nick," Luke answered, drawing Kat's attention back to him.

"Nick? What in heaven's name could you want with my delivery boy?"

Luke withdrew a notepad and a pen. "Let's start with his last name."

Kat's eyes narrowed. "Not until you tell me exactly what is going on here."

"A federal investigation. What is Nick's last name?" When Kat didn't answer him, Luke clicked his pen closed. "Fine. We'll do this the hard way. I want all your documents regarding Nick, and I want them right now. Employment records, addresses, pay stubs. Everything you have."

A fine sheen of sweat appeared across Kat's forehead, and her hands trembled ever so slightly before she flattened them against her desk. "Whatever you think Nick has done, I can assure you, he is completely innocent."

"Right now, I'm more concerned with your obstruction of a federal investigation." Luke cocked his head at her. "Would you like to spend a night or two in jail?"

Her face paled and then flushed a deep red. She rose from her chair, all semblance of politeness erased from both her demeanor and her expression. "Don't you dare threaten me. I know my rights. If you want my records or information about Nick, you come back here with a warrant. Anything less and you won't get a lick of information from me."

They didn't have enough for a warrant. There was no solid evidence linking Nick to Sam's kidnapping. If they couldn't gain Kat's cooperation, they would be walking out of this gallery empty-handed.

"Please." Ara stepped forward, her voice low. "We need your help. We don't want to get Nick into any trouble—we just need to speak with him."

"I fail to understand exactly what is going on here, but I'm absolutely appalled you would trick me into a confrontation with the FBI. Does Holly know you are here? Does she know about this horrible meeting?"

"Yes," Ara lied. Holly wasn't in any position to discuss the incident, and given the opportunity, would probably have consented to beating Kat to get the information out of her, if need be. "And she requires your cooperation. Mr. Boone will be very unhappy to learn you've delayed an investigation essential to his family."

"How is it essential?" Kat demanded. "Just what do you think Nick has done?"

"I can't tell you that. I can only say that we wish to speak with him. Nothing more." Kat hesitated, and Ara's heart quickened in her chest.

Please, please.

"I'm sorry, Ara." Kat tilted her chin up, the decision made. "But I cannot provide information regarding my employees. Not even for the Boones. Come back with a valid warrant, and I'll comply."

* * *

"Damn it," Ara swore as she left the gallery. "Is there any way you can get a warrant?"

"Not likely, although for the Boones, we might be able to find a judge who will stretch the rules a bit." Luke ran a hand through his hair. "How sure are you that this Nick might be involved?"

She shrugged. "I can't be sure at all, but you saw Kat's reaction in there. The whole thing seems hinky."

Luke nodded and pulled out his cell, speed-dialing a number. "Thomas, what do you have?" A pause. "Text it to me."

He hung up and started for the car, calling over his shoulder. "Come on."

"Where are we going?" She hurried to keep up with his long strides.

"Thomas looked through Sam's phone records and figured out Nick's number. He was able to get the address associated with the account."

Twenty minutes later, Ara climbed out of the vehicle and double-checked her surroundings. "Are you sure this is the right street?"

"Yep." Luke slammed the car door. "It should be down this way."

She kept close to him even as she scanned the street. It was dimly lit and ghostly quiet. The buildings were crumbling down around themselves, huge chunks of concrete missing from the sides. Many of the lower windows had old-fashioned bars across the front, a weak attempt to discourage theft. Crumpled newspapers fluttered down the road. In the distance, the wail of a police siren became louder and then faded.

Ara hunched down in her jacket as a cold wind whipped past her. She tucked her hand in her pocket, feeling the familiar weight of her gun. It reassured her.

Across the street, a man lingered like a ghost in the doorway of a building. When he saw Ara and Luke coming toward him, he scurried away. She glanced at the peeling number at the top of the building's doorway. Fifty-two.

Next door was a single-story. Frowning, Luke pulled out his phone and the text Thomas sent him. "Number fifty-four. This is it."

"What the hell is going on?" Ara asked. This couldn't be where Nick lived. It was a hair salon. And not a very nice one, judging from the dirt caked on the window. The sign on the door listed the opening hours. It was way past closing time, and the inside was pitch black. Ara cupped one hand around her face, trying to peer through the glass. "There's a back room. It's possible Sam's inside."

"Only one way to make sure." He unholstered his weapon. Ara pulled hers from underneath her jacket. Luke paused, but only for half a beat. "Is that registered?"

She nodded. "I'm legal."

Luke leaned back to survey the building and the street. "There isn't an alley, which means the only doorway is right in front of us." He put a hand to his ear and winked at her. "You heard that scream, too, right?"

There was no scream, but without a reasonable belief that Sam was inside, Luke couldn't break in.

"Absolutely. It sounded like Sam's voice."

Pushing her aside, he raised the butt of his gun before tossing her a glance over his shoulder. "Cover me. Go low."

The familiar words kicked Ara into motion. She changed her stance into a lower crouch, held her weapon with practiced precision.

She gave him a nod and whispered, "Go."

Luke smashed the glass of the door with the butt of his gun and it shattered into a million pieces that danced across the dirty tile floor inside. Ara braced herself for the wail of an alarm, but none came. Slipping a hand inside, Luke flicked the lock open and pulled the door outward.

Ara's heart was pounding out of her chest. She carefully stepped across the broken glass, the pieces crunching underneath her feet.

The main room wasn't large, just big enough for a single barber's chair and a tiny receptionist desk. It smelled like fruity soap and sweet aftershave.

Luke moved quickly toward the one door in the back of the room. She followed right behind him. Efficient, smooth, like a well-oiled machine. If the situation wasn't so serious, Ara might have been able to admit she liked it. That she'd missed it. But all her energy was focused on what was behind that door.

On Sam.

Silently, she took up position on the opposite side of the frame, crouching lower. Luke glanced down at her, questions in his eyes.

She nodded. She was ready.

He reached out, his hand steady, and grasped the knob. With a twist, he flung open the door, and they both entered, guns raised.

The room was empty.

Ara rose from her crouch, despair and a strong sense of failure washing over her. "She's not here."

The room was nothing more than a storage closet. A broken mirror, a dirty mop and bucket, shelves lined with shampoo and hair dye.

"Who does this place belong to?" she asked.

"An eighty-year-old barber with no criminal history."

"So the kidnapper gave a fake address when he bought the phone." Ara tucked her gun back in its holster. A sharp wind whistled down the street, and a touch of it flew in through the smashed window. She shivered inside her coat. "What a surprise. Can we tie the owner to Nick in any way?"

Luke didn't answer her but instead whipped out his phone and dialed quickly. "Thomas, I need a team." A pause. He glanced around the room. "She's not here. But I need to know if this place has anything to do with Nick." Another pause. "No, I doubt it. It seems to me he gave a fake address. If I go with my gut, the team won't find anything linking this place to him, but we have to be sure. Yeah . . . yeah . . . ten minutes. Good."

He hung up. "Don't get your hopes up. Chances are this place has no connection to the kidnappers. The smartest thing for them to do was pick a place at random."

Luke sighed. "You could be wrong about the message Sam was trying to send you. Nick may have nothing to do with this. And Kat's questionable behavior could be nothing more than a coincidence."

Ara glanced at the barber's chair, at the mirror hanging crooked on the wall, at the messy papers littering the receptionist area. "I don't believe in coincidences. We're on the right path. I can feel it."

CHAPTER SIXTEEN

Thwack.

The sound of the glove hitting the punching bag echoed across the exercise room. Luke watched as Ara paused, wiping sweat from her brow with the sleeve of her shirt before attacking the bag again with a furious intensity.

She was graceful and far more powerful than her small frame indicated. In hand-to-hand combat, Ara would make a formidable opponent.

He rubbed his forehead, trying to erase the ache that seemed to have permanently entrenched itself there. He couldn't remember the last time he'd eaten or slept. This case demanded all his attention, and still it felt like he was going nowhere fast.

No new leads.

And still so many unanswered questions. How had the kidnappers discovered the FBI was involved? Who tipped them off? And what about Sam's message to Ara? Were they interpreting it correctly, or had they missed something?

No. He shook his head. Nick and the gallery were tied into this somehow. He would bet his entire paycheck on it. The way the gallery owner, Kat, had reacted to the flash of his badge confirmed something wasn't right.

But what? He had no evidence or proof to tie anything together. His team was frantically gathering as much info as they could on the gallery, but so far, they weren't coming up with anything useful.

And time was running out.

"How long have you been standing there?" Ara's voice cut through his thoughts. She swiped a damp strand of hair out of her eyes, her chest heaving with the effort from her blows.

He swallowed hard, his mouth inexplicably dry. Luke forced himself to follow the line of her neck up to her face. Her expression was guarded, like an uncertain doe attempting to decipher if he was a predator or not.

"Has there been any news?" she asked, yanking off the boxing gloves and tossing them onto a nearby bench.

"No. I have my team researching the gallery for leverage, and there's another group tearing through Sam's room and computer. So far, no other mention of Nick." He rocked back on his heels. "I've sent the composite you created with the sketch artist out, but we don't have any new hits."

Ara blew out a frustrated breath. "Damn it!" She spun around again and punched the bag, this time with her bare hands.

"Don't do that." Luke stepped forward and grabbed her arm, preventing her from taking another swing. "You'll tear up your knuckles."

Tears shimmered in her eyes, and for a moment, he thought it was from the pain in her hand, but then she whispered, "I can't stand it."

Luke didn't have to ask her what she meant. The waiting, the tedious running down of lead after lead, the feeling of failure. He got it. He was feeling exactly the same way.

He wanted to tug her closer, to comfort her and forget for half a heartbeat about this damn case he was losing.

But he didn't. Luke had learned long ago to listen to his head, and not his heart.

She broke his hold and sagged against the wall, sliding down it until her hands rested on her knees. "What are they doing to her?"

"Thinking about it will only tear you apart."

She laughed, mocking and hard. "You really are a cold bastard, aren't you?"

Her words knifed through him, but he only shrugged.

Ara met his gaze and sucked in a sharp breath. "I'm sorry. I'm . . ."

"I know."

There was an uncomfortable pause. Ara bit her lip and said, "Truth is, sometimes I wish I could be more like you."

"Cold-hearted?" He smiled a bit to take the sting out of it.

"Contained."

"Ah." Luke crossed and sat down next to her on the floor. "Well, that's a family trait. A requirement of all Patrick men."

She glanced at him out of the corner of her eye. "Why?"

"Because you need it to become an FBI agent." The corners of his mouth twitched. "Just like your father before you."

"Is that why you did?"

"Yep." He paused. "At least, it started out that way. Now, it's about more than that."

Ara leaned her head against the wall. "What's your father like?"

"Hard. Rigid." He pictured his dad. The dark suit, the stern face with the faint scar along the left cheek. "But he was a hell of an agent."

"Was?"

"He retired. Now he lives on a farm in Tennessee, and every time I call, he never fails to remind me of the Patrick legacy." Luke realized he'd said more than he meant to. He glanced at her. "Do you miss it? Being a cop?"

"Sometimes." Ara straightened her legs out in front of her. "I used to all the time. But Sam . . . what's happening now . . . it reminds me of why I didn't always make a good cop."

"You feel it."

"Too much." She touched her chest. "The responsibility crushing down on you. So heavy you almost can't breathe."

They sat in silence, and for the first time, it was easy between them.

"I've been thinking about Nick," she said, breaking the stillness. "Trying to remember everything Sam told me about him."

"And?" When she didn't answer, Luke waved a hand in front of him slightly. "It might make it easier if you talk it through."

"Yeah, okay." Ara licked her lips, her gaze focused on a point on the floor. "Sam told me he was twenty-one. She was flirting with him. It was obvious, and I disapproved since he seemed so much older than her. He also had a look about him. Like he wanted to fit in with the wealthy but couldn't quite pull it off. He wasn't born with money."

"Working class."

Ara nodded. "Definitely." Her eyebrow creased in concentration. "Sam told me he was an art dealer, but Kat knew him as the delivery driver." Ara was staring off again, a strange look on her face.

"What?"

"Their interaction . . ." She frowned. "Sam told me she was trying to get a date with him, but something about their body language indicated they knew each other."

Luke straightened up. "What do you mean?"

Ara gasped. "Of course." She scrambled to her feet and grabbed Luke's hand. "Come on. I think we might have video of this guy."

* * *

Ara watched the images flicker across the screen in rapid succession. The Boones' security system was top of the line, with cameras in nearly every room of the house. The bedrooms and bathrooms remained private. It'd always made sense to Ara, but now she wished her employer hadn't been so particular.

She was chilly in her damp exercise clothes, and goose bumps prickled her arms. Finally, she spotted what she was looking for and gave a cry of excitement.

"There." She pointed to a nondescript van that parked in the driveway. A young man dropped out of the driver's seat. Blond hair, a long-legged walk, broad shoulders.

Nick.

"When was this?" Luke's voice had an edge to it.

"August twelfth. Two months before the kidnapping."

They watched in silence as Nick removed a large, painting-sized package from the back of the van and approached the house.

"Can you change the camera angle?"

"Of course." Ara moved to the foyer. Nick was greeted by the main housekeeper, Rose, and directed upstairs.

Right to Sam's bedroom door.

She came to the door, barefoot, wearing jeans and a simple T-shirt. Her hair was loose and flowing over her shoulders. Ara had to swallow hard at the image. So damn young.

She focused her attention on the interaction between Sam and Nick. There was a brief conversation. Sam smiled broadly, flashing perfect teeth, before she opened the door wide and they disappeared.

"Can you change it to inside the bedroom?"

"No." Frustration had Ara's lips tightening. On screen, Rose reappeared, her quick stride taking her down the hall. They waited several minutes, but when no one else came by, Ara began fast-forwarding the video.

Nearly thirty minutes later, the door to Sam's bedroom opened. She was laughing. Her hand brushed against Nick's arm.

Beside her, Luke sucked in a breath.

The two of them continued down the hall and stairs. Out the front door. Obviously flirting, based on body language.

Nick's face flushed a few times, and Sam elbowed him in jest. He gave a final wave before climbing into the van and driving off. Sam waited until she couldn't see him anymore, and then she turned back toward the house.

There was a skip in her step.

Ara stopped the video, her stomach tight, her mind whirling.

He'd known Sam.

He'd been inside the house.

The importance of that did not escape Ara. Since Sam and Nick had known each other, it was entirely possible they'd met at other times. Secretly.

"He gained her trust," Luke said aloud, completing Ara's own line of thought. "Slowly. They dated, kept their relationship a secret."

"And the whole time, he was planning."

He spun toward her. "When was it confirmed Sam and Holly were going to the gallery opening?"

"One week before. At least, as far as Sam was concerned. Holly had confirmed several weeks earlier, and dinner reservations were made, but she didn't tell Sam about it until the Sunday right before the exhibit." She bit her lip. "They had a huge fight about it because Sam didn't want to go. She had made plans to go to some club with her friends."

"Was it the type of argument a young teenage girl might tell her boyfriend about?"

Ara nodded. "Exactly the type. Which means that the text you found on Sam's phone the night of the kidnapping could've been to Nick."

"And she would've been deleting all of Nick's texts because she didn't want her mother to learn about the relationship." Luke continued pacing, his steps coming as fast as his words. "Let's play this out. Sam and Nick meet, and when they start dating, he convinces her to keep it a secret from everyone, claiming her parents wouldn't approve of him. She starts paying Gannon to give her time and space so they can meet without being detected."

"This kind of relationship would have appealed to Sam," Ara said. "She was rebellious. And she knew Holly would never approve of her dating someone so much older, especially someone who worked as a delivery boy. He would have fed right into Sam's notion that her world was fake, that the people in it didn't care about anything real. She was already feeling some of that anyway and—"

"He would've played on it," Luke finished her thought. He jabbed a finger at the frozen image of Nick. "He's the mastermind. I'll bet you anything. Nick came up with the brilliant plan to kidnap her, convincing her it was the perfect way to get back at her stepfather and her mother."

Luke charged out of the room. Ara chased after him, catching up in the dining room. Several members of the FBI team were hunched over laptops, but they glanced up, their concentration broken, when Luke burst in.

"I need to know who Nick is, people. I need a last name. I need an address. And I need it right now."

"I might be able to help with that." Thomas spoke from a corner of the room, hanging up his cell phone and tucking it into his pocket. A broad smile cracked his face. "I have some leverage for you to use at the gallery. The owner will hand over everything she has, and she'll be grateful to do it."

CHAPTER SEVENTEEN

Shaking with fury, Luke marched into the art gallery, Ara hot on his heels. Two different employees tried to stop him, but he bypassed them without a word, bulldozing his way right into Kat's office.

Kat jumped in her chair, her startled gaze drawn to the pair of them in the doorway. She placed a hand to her throat. As Luke drew closer, he could see the rapid pulsing in the curve of the woman's neck.

"You scared me." Kat's tone was accusatory. "What exactly do you think you're doing?"

"I want all the information you have on Nick." Luke's tone left no room for argument. Kat caught the dark look on his face, and her own paled, made starker by the bright dusting of blush on her cheeks.

"I told you, Agent, you need a warrant. Do you have one?"

"No."

"Then I suggest—"

150

"I suggest," Luke said, leaning closer to her, crowding her, forcing Kat to move backward in her chair, "that if you don't want to go to jail, you comply with my request."

"Threats again," Kat's words were meant to be tough, but her voice shook slightly. "Those don't work with me."

"I have evidence that you are forging artwork and substituting the fakes for the originals when the paintings are delivered to the buyer."

Kat's face paled even more, and her whole body began to tremble. "That's . . . that's ridiculous."

"That's the truth," Luke spit out. "Did Nick know what you were doing? Was he in on it? Is that why you're so protective of him?"

Ara stepped forward. "You've sold several pieces to the Boones. It would be a simple matter to have an art appraiser out to the house to assess whether or not the paintings are the real deal." She gave her a mean smile. "It could be done within the hour."

"Once that happens," Luke added, "the FBI will have enough evidence to launch an official investigation. Immediately. Is that what you want?"

The desperate look on Kat's face answered for her.

"Give me the records." Luke lowered his voice, making it smooth and comforting. "Now that your secret is out, there's no need to keep us from questioning him."

"You want to talk to him about what I'm doing?"

"No." Luke backed up, and Kat visibly exhaled. "I want to discuss a completely different matter with him. But if I have to arrest you in order to be able to comb this place over for his information, then I will." He cocked his head at her. "Do I need to do that?"

"No." With a shaking hand, she opened the drawer next to her. "I don't have much on him. Just a telephone number and an address."

She handed a manila folder over to him. When he flipped it open, his heart sank at how little paperwork was inside.

"What about paystubs? 1099s?"

She flushed, and her hand gripped the handle of the drawer tighter. "I always paid him in cash. It was per delivery."

He pinned her with a dark stare. "If you're lying to me . . ." The threat hung in the air between them, unspoken.

"I'm not." She swallowed hard. "I promise. That's all I have."

* * *

"It seems our Nick is something of an enigma." Luke took a turn into Mike's Mechanics. It was the address listed for him in Kat's records. The area around the shop was a mix of old and new, ancient brownstones mingling with their modern, glass-fronted counterparts. Mike's stood out, the storefront twice the size of others in the area. His garage doors were wide open, cars spilling out in organized chaos.

"At least we have his last name now," Ara replied. "Your team will work their magic to find Nick Flores."

"In the meantime, we follow the trail of breadcrumbs." Luke climbed out of the car. The scents of gasoline and oil hung heavy in the air. The doors to the shop were open, and an older man with graying hair and a potbelly was crouched over a car. He looked up when they approached, his bright-blue eyes startling against his dark skin.

"What can I do for you folks?"

"We're looking for Nick Flores?"

"Nick?" The old man's eyebrows drew together. "Haven't seen him around lately." He reached for a rag and wiped his greasy hands. "Has something happened?"

"Why would you think that?"

"Because when two cops show up on your doorstep, it's usually not a good thing." He caught the look of surprise on Ara's face and chuckled. "It's the way you move, sweetheart. A cop all the way. I should know. In my youth, it paid to know what makes a cop a cop, even when they aren't wearing the uniform."

"And you are . . ."

"Mike Travis." He swung a dirty hand in the direction of the sign over his shop. "Owner."

"When's the last time you saw Nick?" Luke asked.

"I'd like to know why you're looking for Nick before I start giving out information about him. Is he in some kind of trouble?"

"I can't give out the particulars," Luke said, "but what I can say is that if I don't find Nick soon, things might get a hell of a lot worse."

Mike was quiet for a moment, his gaze drifting between Luke and Ara. Sizing them up, perhaps trying to determine their intentions. Ara met his stare, and he sniffed. "Is that your assessment as well?"

"We need to find him. It's . . ."

"It's important," Luke finished for her, stepping toward the man. "And we don't have a lot of time to waste. So I'm going to ask again, when was the last time you saw Nick?"

Mike let out a breath. "It would be last Friday. He was doing some work for me in exchange for storage of his van."

"His van?"

"Yup." Mike threw the dirty rag onto his workbench before leaning against it. "He has a delivery job of some sort. Drives an old Ford for it. He doesn't get paid much and needed a place to store it. We made up a nice bartering system. He does some work for me around the shop in exchange for a parking space."

"Where's the van now?"

Mike shrugged. "Dunno. He must've come and picked it up on Saturday morning. It wasn't here when I came in. Haven't seen the van or him since."

"Is that unusual?"

"Kinda. On Friday, we discussed him doing some work for me today, but he hasn't shown up. That's not like him . . ." Mike's voice trailed off as his eyes widened. He stood up, squaring his shoulders. "Has something happened to the boy? Is he hurt?"

"We don't know. We're trying to locate him." Luke's tone was even, but it did nothing to ease Mike's sudden worry. The lines in his forehead deepened, and his mouth formed a frown.

"So you're lookin' at him for some kind of crime then."

"Would you be surprised if we did?"

"Hell yes." Mike's face flushed. "Nick's a real good kid. He's no innocent flower, mind you, but for the most part he keeps his nose real clean. A hell of a lot cleaner than I did at his age."

"Do you know where he lives? Do you have an address for him?" Luke asked.

Mike hesitated.

Ara caught his gaze. "I get it. You care about him."

"Whatever you think he's done, he hasn't."

"Which is exactly what Nick will tell us when we find him," she said. "But we need to find him first. It could mean the difference between life and death. If you care about him, you'll help us."

She paused, letting her words sink in. Beside her, Luke was stiff.

"Okay," Mike said. "Come with me."

Luke let out the breath he'd been holding and glanced at her. The corners of his mouth tipped up just slightly, just enough to tell her she'd done a good job.

Together, they followed behind Mike as he hurried to the back of his shop and into a messy office. Piles of grease-stained paper formed mountains around an old telephone and beat-up computer. Mike went straight to the metal filing cabinet and opened the first drawer. It gave a squeal of protest.

"His dad isn't alive anymore, died two years ago, but his mama's a real nice lady. She used to work down at the convenience store over on the next block."

He pulled out a folder and opened it. His stained finger trailed down a page until he found what he was looking for.

"Damn, I think this is his old address. They moved right after his daddy died."

"It's all right. Write that one down for us anyway."

Mike scribbled it on a scrap piece of paper he unearthed. He handed it to Luke, chewing on the inside of his cheek. "There is another place you might try though."

"Where?"

"Nick has a warehouse he paints at."

Luke's heart jumped in his throat. Beside him, Ara stiffened as the words registered with her.

"He's an aspiring artist," Mike continued, "and creates these amazing—"

Luke cut him off. "Where is it? Where's the warehouse?"

CHAPTER EIGHTEEN

The warehouse was only fifteen minutes away from Mike's garage. It was nestled in an industrial area, the buildings showing their wear with chipped concrete facings and faded roofs. Nick's was easy to spot, the last on the row, the smallest of them all. When they drove past, Ara scanned it carefully. Not a whisper of movement.

But her instincts were screaming.

"Don't even think about it," Luke hissed as he picked up speed and drove them around the corner.

Ara realized her hand had crept toward the door handle. She forced herself to pull it back. "Sam's in there."

"Maybe." He found a position for the vehicle that was out of the way of traffic but allowed them to still see the front of the building. "Maybe not."

Despite his words, a muscle had tightened at his jaw, and his movements were high energy, as though he'd also had a rush of adrenaline flood over him.

This was the break they'd been waiting for. And Luke knew it as much as she did.

The FBI agents descended and were organized within forty minutes of Luke's phone call. Ara waited outside with a bulky babysitter named Mark, who was ordered not to allow her anywhere near the warehouse during the raid. Tension coiled in her stomach. It felt like she was crawling out of her skin.

She wanted to be in on the action. Desperately wanted to break down the doors, rush inside, and help in the search. Standing outside, doing nothing, made her feel helpless and useless.

Out of control.

Hold on, Sam. Just hold on.

A flash of metal from the top of a building caught Ara's eye. The snipers were almost in position. The raid was about to begin. Her body felt tight, muscles rigid. She couldn't tell one agent from another, couldn't see where Luke was as they approached the warehouse. The team moved together, a coordinated mass of helmets and vests.

The sound of the battering ram hitting the door echoed across the space separating Ara from the agents. She sucked in a sharp breath as the door gave way. The scent of tear gas, the flurry of pounding boots and men shouting were all carried on the breeze.

The moments stretched out. Seconds. A minute or two at most. But it felt like an eternity. Ara strained to see through the cloud of dust, to catch a glimpse of the first agents as they exited the building. Her heart pounded so hard against her ribcage, it hurt.

There. A shadow formed into a man dressed in dark green. Followed by another. Slowly, the agents filed out of the building, their rifles angled safely away. No mad rush, no shouts. Just the dragging steps of men who were unhappy with the outcome.

"What happened?" Ara asked. She started toward the building, but her arm was grabbed by her babysitter, halting her movements.

"Let me go," she demanded.

"I've been ordered to keep you here," he insisted, his jaw set in a stubborn line. "Don't make me arrest you."

"That's my job."

The familiar voice was weary, and Ara spun to find Luke approaching them. He'd removed the gas mask and helmet. His face was red with exertion, his eyes shadowed.

Her lips trembled. Luke didn't have to open his mouth. For once, she could read everything he was about to say all over his face.

"No." She backed away from him, holding out a hand. "No."

"Ara—"

She pounded a fist into her thigh and swallowed a scream. Sam couldn't be dead. God damn it, she couldn't be.

It was all her fault. She'd failed her. She'd killed her. As surely as if she'd pulled the trigger herself.

Luke grabbed her arms and shook her so hard her teeth clattered together. "Listen to me." Ara blinked, forcing herself to focus on him, to clamp down on the emotions that had tears springing to her eyes.

"There is a woman's body inside. She's blonde and the same size as Sam." He paused.

"Just spit it out."

"They shot her in the head. We can't ID her yet."

Ara closed her eyes as if it would block out his words. But they replayed in her mind.

We can't ID her.

She opened her eyes, and as she took in the furrow of his brow and the hard line of his mouth, Ara understood in a flash what he wanted.

"Take me to her."

"You don't have to do this." He let go of one of her arms and captured her chin between two of his fingers. The pressure of his touch felt oddly comforting. It centered her.

"We can take fingerprints," he said, tilting her face up to his.

Ara took a deep breath, the acrid scent of smoke burning her nostrils. "No. Fingerprints take time. I might be able to do this in a matter of moments. If it isn't Sam in there, then every second counts."

"Ara." His voice lowered to a soft whisper, his face reflecting a pity that nearly broke her in two. "It's probably her."

She fought past the lump in her throat. "I know."

* * *

The warehouse was cool, and Ara shuddered a little inside her leather jacket. The tear gas had dispersed, but the space remained surprisingly empty. She supposed Luke had kept most of the agents back, and the forensic crew, who would tear the place apart looking for DNA and fingerprints, hadn't arrived yet.

He held her hand in his own, a firm grasp of callused palm and warm fingers, and led the way farther inside. Her gaze skipped over the interior, her mind taking snapshots of the space.

A workbench with painting supplies in the far corner. Half-done paintings stacked against the walls along with several fresh canvases and easels. Trash piled up in the opposite corner, mostly beer cans and pizza boxes. Oil stains from some kind of vehicle marred the floor. Near the side door, there was a spattering of blood drops.

And in the center, surrounded by a few FBI agents, was a sheet-covered form.

Ara held her breath and nearly tripped over her own feet. She silently cursed herself, ignoring Luke's concerned glance. This wouldn't be the first time she'd viewed a body. She'd lost members of her team before, seen death up close.

Yet this one hit far closer to home. The faces of other teenagers, girls Ara hadn't been able to save, flashed across her mind. She remembered every one, could picture them as easily as if they were standing in front of her now. And it squeezed her heart so much she thought it would burst, the pain of her own failures like a vice on her chest.

Those girls had died in a flophouse in Russia. And this one in a warehouse in New York. But the grief and guilt Ara felt was the same. She had survived; they had not. And both situations were her fault.

"Guys, clear back and give us a little space." Luke's order had the other agents drifting away. They knew exactly why she was there.

He waited until everyone was out of earshot. "Are you sure about this? She won't be a pretty sight."

"I've seen gunshot victims before," Ara snapped, suddenly furious with him. "You don't need to tell me."

He didn't react to her outburst. At least not in the way she expected. Luke gently squeezed her hand. Immediately, her anger lost its edge. Getting upset with Luke was pointless. The person she was truly angry at was herself. But she did no one any good like this—not Luke, not the investigation, and definitely not Sam.

When he crouched down next to the sheet, Ara tensed in preparation and gave a hard nod.

"Do it."

He pulled the sheet back, revealing what was left of the poor girl's face, topped with fragments of hair that might have been blonde at some point but were now stained dark with blood. Ara's stomach jumped at the sight of the carnage, but she swallowed hard, forcing the bile back down. She stepped closer to the body.

"Pull the sheet off all the way."

Luke silently complied with her request. The woman was definitely Sam's height and build. Full breasts, slender hips, long legs. She was wearing a pair of skin-tight jeans, a coral-colored blouse, and cheap wedges.

"Those aren't the clothes Sam was wearing when she was kidnapped." Ara's voice came out flat, without a hint of the swirling emotions inside her.

"They may have made her change. That's not enough."

Ara nodded. Luke was right. It would've been smart for the kidnappers to have Sam change into different clothing. Especially if they hoped to move her at some point.

She sucked in a breath and forced her mind to clear of everything except the matter at hand. Ara bent down close to the body. She could smell the cloying scent of blood and . . . something else. Her heart picked up as she leaned down closer still, so close her lips nearly brushed the corpse's shirt.

Lavender. The scent of lavender.

"What?" Luke broke through her thoughts. "What is it?"

"Perfume. A scent Sam would never wear. She hates lavender."

Ara slowly tracked down the body. It wasn't until she got to the left foot that she found the proof of her suspicions.

"This isn't Sam." She pointed a finger at the barely visible curve of ankle just below the cuff of the blue jeans. "This girl has a tattoo on her leg."

She wanted to hoot with joy and relief, but her gaze caught sight of what was left of the woman's face, and the sound died in her throat. Luke leaned down, checking to see the tattoo for himself. When he looked up, confusion played across his features.

"If this isn't Sam, who the hell is she?"

CHAPTER NINETEEN

She kept replaying the details in her mind. They appeared in slow motion, like in a movie, almost as if it'd happened to someone else. Yet the rusty scent of blood coming from her skin was a constant reminder. It'd been all too real.

The escape plan had been half-witted to begin with. If she'd been thinking clearly, Sam would've realized they were no match for professionally trained killers, but she was desperate and she'd panicked.

It was only a short distance to the door, to freedom. At the time, it'd seemed possible.

The rapid beat of her heart, the sound of pounding feet against concrete, the nearly silent whistle of the gun and then . . . the blood and brain matter splattered her, shockingly warm. She'd been unable to stop herself, and she'd tripped over the body, sliding across the floor, scraping her skin raw.

She clambered to her feet and turned around. Sam could hear the scream building inside of herself, but it got caught in her throat, never clawing its way out of her open mouth.

Instead, she gaped, staring down at the body on the floor in front of her. The woman who had been, less than a second ago, alive and running for her life. Now she was dead, unrecognizable.

And Sasha, his gun pointed straight at Sam, had laughed.

It was the most terrifying thing she'd ever heard. That rumbling, deep-throated, full-scale laugh. Like he'd been told the funniest joke, the most delicious punch line.

Thinking of it now, hearing the echo of that laugh in her mind, fear curled in her belly and tightened her throat.

Sam had no idea where she was. Maksim and Sasha had bound and blindfolded the group of them and driven them here. She'd tried to keep track of the turns, but sheer terror had crept over her and she'd lost count.

She'd thought they were being driven to their death.

Instead, Maksim and Sasha had brought them here. A cold, dark place with a dripping faucet that was about to drive her insane. A basement, maybe? It smelled damp and faintly like mildew, and they had been forced down a staircase before being chained.

At least she wasn't alone. Sam stretched out her foot, and the chain holding her to the floor rattled. It was heavy and thick, no chance of ever breaking, but it was long enough that she could touch Nick.

He pressed back. She couldn't see him or talk to him through the duct tape, but his presence was reassuring. If she'd been left entirely alone, Sam wasn't sure she would survive it.

Selfish.

The thought ran through her head, the guilt like a hot blade in her gut. She was selfish, more selfish than she'd ever realized. If she truly loved Nick, she would never want him to be down here chained up with her. His words played in her head, over and over again.

This isn't going to work. You're playing with things you can't understand.

Oh, how she wished she'd heeded his warning. She had been playing with things she didn't understand. She'd been angry—about her father's and brother's deaths, about her mother's remarriage, about the restrictions Oliver placed on her. She'd been so filled with hatred, so desperate for attention that she'd foolishly believed faking her own kidnapping would solve her problems. Her mother would finally come to her senses and realize Sam needed her. She would understand that her daughter was more important than the charity events and social lunches.

How many times had Sam played the reunion in her mind? A hundred. A thousand. It would happen in the police station. Her mother would fling open the door and pause, searching the room for her. Sam would call out, and her mother's gaze would fly to her face. Tears would gather, spilling over onto her pale cheeks, and her mother would race to her. She would gather Sam into her arms, rocking her as she had when she was little and muttering all the words Sam desperately needed to hear.

I was so worried.

I love you.

I'm sorry.

It would change their relationship. Her mother would be so grateful that she would never take Sam for granted again.

A foolish dream. No, not just foolish. Stupid. Downright stupid.

And with every hour that passed, Sam had less and less confidence she would get out of this alive. Ara hadn't come. The message Sam had given her had been too cryptic, the trail too hard to follow. And now, next to impossible, since Maksim and Sasha had been smart enough to move them from the warehouse to this new location. Even if Ara could figure it out, there was no way to trace Sam here. For all she knew, Ara and the rest of her family had given up on her. They'd found out she'd planned the kidnapping and they'd stopped there.

They may have no idea about the trouble she was in now.

No, Sam was going to die. She would never see her mother again, never be able to tell her all the things she needed to say. She said them now, silently, in her head, praying her mother would somehow feel them and know.

I love you.

I'm sorry.

CHAPTER TWENTY

"**G**ina Antonova."

Thomas handed a manila folder to Luke, who opened it. Leaning over his shoulder, Ara got her first good look at Gina, staring back at her from a DMV photo. Flawless skin hidden behind heavy makeup and lots of eyeliner, large, dollar-store earrings, and crooked front teeth.

Thomas reached out and flipped the picture to another. This time of a woman behind the wheel of a van. "This is the cleaned up photograph we pulled from a camera near the restaurant."

"She was the getaway driver," Luke said.

"Yes, sir."

"What do we know about her?"

"Twenty-three," Thomas answered, efficiently giving the most important facts. "Small record for shoplifting and minor drug possession. Dad's dead. Mom's doing a stint in county at the moment for prostitution and drug possession. No siblings. I got forensics doing a sweep of the house, but it doesn't look like she's been there for a while. No food in the fridge. Smelled real stale. Neighbors haven't seen her for more than a week."

"So where has she been all this time?" Luke flipped to the next page. "Where does she work?"

"Officially, nowhere, although her neighbor said he's seen her down at a nightclub called Mist." He pushed his glasses up on his nose. "It's a nasty place. Supposedly owned by the Russian mafia."

Ara's heart skipped a beat. Luke passed a glance at her, almost as if he'd heard the flutter. She carefully schooled her features, but worry and fear left a metallic taste in her mouth.

"This doesn't look like a mob job."

The striking sound of a metal gurney snapping into place seemed to punctuate his sentence. Ara's gaze was drawn to the body, now wrapped in a shroud of black plastic, as the coroner's aide pushed it past them.

"The mob is usually cleaner than this," Luke continued, oblivious to the commotion happening behind him. "They wouldn't have left Gina here for us to find. Or they would have removed her fingers along with shooting her in the face, in order to prevent identification."

"Maybe they never expected us to find the warehouse," Thomas suggested. "Nick's record is squeaky clean. Without Ara, we never would've made it this far."

She appreciated the compliment, but it felt like a sword in her stomach. This was no real victory. A woman was dead, and if they'd been faster, if she'd been smarter, it might've been prevented.

Ara couldn't pull her attention away from the large blood pool on the concrete. She was jittery and upset, but cutting through all that chaos was the whisper that things were not as simple as she'd thought they were. Something was happening, something beyond a simple kidnapping and ransom request.

"Maybe," Luke went on, "but the whole job would have to be mafia related, and this is a bit too high profile for them. They're cockroaches mostly, making their money by human trafficking, drugs. Dealing in the unwanted and the unnoticeable. They don't like media." He frowned. "It doesn't make sense to me."

"Both Gina and Nick are small fish, though. Two people with very little criminal history, and they're jumping right into kidnapping. And now murder." Ara shook her head. "I don't think they're acting on their own."

Luke tilted his head. "It's improbable but not impossible."

"This doesn't feel right . . ." She felt cold. Her hands were like ice. She shoved them into her pockets and crossed the room toward the workshop. The brushes, the paintings, the half-done canvases. One caught her eye, and the piece of a puzzle clicked into place.

She felt Luke's solid presence come up behind her.

"He's the one making the copies." She pointed to the familiar, horrible gray painting. "This painting was in the gallery the night of the kidnapping. Holly purchased it for Oliver's office. It was supposed to be delivered today." Her voice dropped. "Delivered by Nick."

"He's switching them. Keeping the originals and delivering the fakes." Luke rocked back on his heels. "It makes sense. The gallery hangs the originals in their space. The buyer makes a purchase. Then Nick makes a copy. When he delivers the painting to the buyer, he gives them the forgery. The original gets sold on the black market."

"Right." Ara frowned. Something tugged at her, but she couldn't figure out what. She knew the dramatic escalation of the crimes was part of it. Painting forgeries was a far cry from kidnapping and murder. If Nick was acting alone, he'd jumped into far more violent territory than his record would reflect. As Luke pointed out, it wasn't completely out of the realm of possibility, but Ara just couldn't shake the feeling that she was missing something. Something vitally important.

"Sir." An agent waved Luke over from the center of the warehouse room. Ara tagged along with him, wanting as much information she could get.

"What is it, Vicki?"

"It looks like they had a car in here. Recently." She pointed to a stain on the concrete.

"You're right. This oil stain is fresh. The van, probably. Do we have someone retrieving the video surveillance?" Luke asked.

"Already working on it."

"Put out an APB on the vehicle. If we're lucky, they might still be driving to their new location. An officer might spot them."

Vicki's eyebrows creased. "Sir, there are a lot of white, unmarked vans out there."

"At this point, I'm willing to have officers stop every damn one of them if it gives us a bit of an advantage." He jerked a thumb toward a single room in the back of the warehouse. It was the only enclosed space, probably meant to be an office. "What's in there?"

"Not much. Agents have cleared it, but we haven't fully searched it yet."

Ara was already moving in the direction of the office. She felt, rather than saw, Luke and Vicki following along behind her. The light inside the room was already on and revealed a battered desk, a broken, wobbly chair, and several finished canvases.

Luke moved to the desk and began opening the first drawer. A few pens, some paperclips, and a stapler rattled against the metal edges. "What are the chances they left us a memo telling us where they are now?"

Ara snorted. "Not good, I'd say."

"Sir, we have several sets of fingerprints." Thomas appeared in the doorway of the office. "I've got them running through AFIS now."

"How many different sets?" Luke asked, opening the next drawer. Vicki selected one of the paintings and lifted it from the wall to look behind it.

"Four."

Luke straightened up from the desk. "Four?"

"We know Sam, Nick, and Gina," Ara said. "We're missing someone. Another accomplice, maybe?"

"Hold on." Luke frowned. "We can't jump to conclusions. Those fingerprints may have been here long before Sam. It's not necessarily connected to the kidnapping."

He was right. It was extremely possible none of the fingerprints they'd recovered would come back to the kidnappers.

She spun in a small circle in the room as her mind worked over the puzzle. Her gaze fell on the furthest corner of the room. A space slightly in shadow, almost covered by the corner of the desk. Was there something back there?

"I want to know the minute we get a hit," Luke said to Thomas. "Even if they aren't connected to the kidnapping, these people are connected to Nick and this warehouse. I'd like to talk to them immediately."

Ara moved around the desk, dread pooling in her stomach as she got closer to the item crumpled on the floor. She reached down to pick it up, already knowing what it was before she stretched the fabric between her hands.

Sam's dress.

The clinging, white dress Sam had been wearing at the gallery. It had been cut down the center, the edges jagged, and it was stained with dirt. And blood.

Ara couldn't help it—her mind began running through all the ways it could have gotten there. A shudder ran up her spine, and despite herself, she trembled, slamming her eyes shut. But the visions only become brighter in the darkness, more frantic and quick.

"Are her shoes there, too?" Luke's question cut through the images, and Ara forced herself to look back at the space.

"No shoes." Her voice cracked. "And no undergarments."

She had no idea what to think of the fact that Sam's bra and panties weren't with the dress. Was it a good sign or not? Desperate for something to hang onto, some positivity, she reasoned that it was good. It had to be good.

She laid the dress down on top of the desk, carefully arranging the jagged edges together to give the garment its original shape.

"That's blood spatter." Luke tilted his head, studying the expensive fabric.

"That kind of spatter wouldn't have come from a wound on Sam," Ara reasoned. "There would be an area of high concentration, like a solid mass of blood. It's almost as if she was . . ."

Her voice trailed off as the thought fixed in her mind. She glanced out the window of the office, toward the place where Gina's body had been left.

"She was standing next to her. Sam was right there when Gina was shot."

Luke nodded and turned to stare out the window. Ara followed the line of his body, the broad shoulders that narrowed to a trim waist, and then looked beyond, to the far wall of the warehouse.

To a door.

"They were trying to escape. To get out."

"It would explain why Nick shot Gina," Luke said. "Maybe she had a change of heart."

"Or Sam did," Ara offered, knowing full well it was just like Sam. She would do something impetuous, something stupid, and then, given half a minute to think about it, would realize it wasn't such a good idea after all. She'd backpedaled out of a few situations that would've been far more serious had she not realized the folly of her own thinking.

"How's your Russian?" Luke's question broke through her thoughts.

She hesitated. Could she really do this? The memories of her past were already threatening to overwhelm her.

Did she have a choice? Sam could still be alive. There was a chance to bring her home, and Ara wouldn't allow her fears to get in the way. "It's perfect," she said.

"Good." He smiled grimly. "I think it's time we paid a visit to Mist, and I might need someone to translate."

Thomas interjected from the doorway. "Sir, you need to tread lightly here. Dmitri Grishnokov is the owner of Mist, and he's extremely dangerous. He was busted for drugs and weapons running. Did ten years. Since then, he's been more careful. Mist is one of his legitimate businesses, but the agents I spoke to suspect he's laundering money through it."

"Is there a team inside Mist? Do we have undercover agents I might be putting at risk?"

"No, sir. There have been investigations off and on, but nothing currently."

Luke paused. "We'll be careful, but I need to take a look at the club. Right now, it's the only good lead we have." He gave Thomas a reassuring smile. "Besides, we're looking for a kidnapped girl. Not something Dmitri is likely to care too much about."

"Not unless he's involved," Ara said. She pointed to the forgeries, the frames, and half-painted canvases waiting against the far wall for delivery. "We don't know how all these people are connected. Nor do we know who they answer to."

"Agreed. But for right now, I think it's safe to assume Nick is working on his own."

Preposterous. Nick was clearly working with Kat at the gallery. Ara opened her mouth to say so, but Luke held up a hand to fend her off. "Until we have evidence linking Sam to the forgeries, I'm keeping them as separate cases. Right now, all I have is evidence that shows Nick started dating Sam, probably with the intention to convince her to go along with his kidnapping scheme. He saw a way to make a lot of money quickly and took advantage of that."

"And Gina?"

"Helped him. Obviously something went wrong between the three of them, and Gina tried to escape with Sam. Nick killed her and has moved Sam to an unknown location."

It all made sense. His reasoning was sound, but the lack of priors on Nick's record bugged Ara.

Still, she'd keep her doubts to herself. Without evidence, they were nothing more than suspicions and supposition. She could be wrong. Following the chain of evidence, as Luke was doing, would either support her or not.

And Mist seemed like the best place to start.

CHAPTER TWENTY-ONE

From the outside, Mist didn't look like a nightclub. The building was drab, with no design forethought and peeling paint. Only a small sign on the upper floor identified the club by its name. That and the line of scantily clad young people standing outside, waiting to get in.

Luke whistled. "Popular place."

"We can't get in like this." Ara unbuttoned two buttons on her blouse and separated the shirt, flashing a bit of her lacy bra underneath. From the pocket of her pants, she pulled out a knife and flipped the blade open. Carefully, she sliced her jeans along the upper thighs, giving them an edgier appearance. Luke stood silently beside her, but she was aware of him watching, his gaze like a physical touch.

She fluffed her hair and pinched her cheeks. She didn't have any makeup with her, which would have helped, but she hadn't counted on visiting a nightclub.

She eyed Luke in his sharp suit and frowned. "You look too . . . official."

He arched his eyebrows. "I'm an FBI agent. I'm supposed to look official."

"Not if you want these girls to talk to you. Flashing your badge at them won't get you anything."

"So what would you recommend?"

"Let me take the lead." She looped her arm through his. "And don't look so damn square. Loosen up a bit."

They got in the back of the line, which thankfully moved quickly. As they approached, Ara hung more and more on Luke until she was practically plastered to his clothes. The suit fabric underneath her fingertips was thick.

At the front of the line, she pushed Luke behind her. The bouncer looked her over, a gleam of appreciation flashing in his eyes. She gave him a knowing smile and flipped her hair.

As she'd hoped, he barely gave Luke a passing glance.

The inside of the club was a blend of crushed velvet, mirrors, and leather. A long bar stacked with every kind of liquor sparkled in the mood lighting. The music was pulse pounding and only served to increase Ara's already existing headache. She rubbed her forehead and leaned in toward Luke.

"Let's split up. We can cover more ground that way."

"No." He grabbed her arm. "We stick together."

She wasn't sure if he wanted to stay with her because he didn't trust her, or because he was worried for her safety. Surprisingly, she wanted to know which it was. It made a difference.

"There are too many employees," she said. "We can't possibly question all of them together."

Luke frowned. His mouth moved to her ear. His breath was warm on the curve of her neck. "Fine, we'll split up. But you stay within my sight at all times."

She felt a shiver race down her spine. She turned her head. His mouth was so close to hers, just a breath away.

"What's your plan?"

He gave her a crooked smile. "You're not the only one who can blend in."

With those words, he moved off, finding an empty table. When the waitress approached, Luke turned on the charm. He said something that had the waitress busting out in a laugh. She leaned in closer to him, her hands on the table, her shirt widening to give him a view of impressive breasts.

Ara fought back the sudden wave of jealousy. He was only doing his job. She needed to do hers.

Heading to the bar, she set her sights on the bartender. He was young, and sexy enough to be a Calvin Klein model. The area around the bar was surprisingly empty, most of the customers spending their time in the darkened areas of the tables and couches that lined the lower part of the club. She found a spot easily but didn't fully sit on the stool. Instead, she cocked a hip on it and leaned against the wooden bar, her unbuttoned shirt displaying her cleavage to its absolute advantage.

It only took a moment for him to notice her, and he closed the distance between them quickly.

"What can I get you, honey?"

He had a southern drawl that seemed out of place some-how. Like he belonged on a ranch, riding a horse, wearing a cowboy hat.

"Vodka with a splash of cranberry." She winked at him. "Very little cranberry."

His grin widened, revealing perfectly straight teeth. "You got it."

She watched as he whipped up the drink in record time, placing it in front of her and adding a short, red straw.

"Try it," he said. "Tell me if I got it right."

Ara hadn't actually intended to drink the beverage, but with him standing over her, she didn't have much of a choice. Taking a dainty sip, she set the drink back down and gave him a winning smile.

"It's perfect." She leaned in a bit closer. "You must be new. I haven't seen you around here before."

"Not so new. I've been bartending here for more than a year." He wagged a finger at her. "You obviously haven't been here in a while."

"Guilty. I just broke up with my boyfriend not too long ago and . . . well, a friend of mine suggested I come back here. She said it's still the best place."

"Well, your friend is right."

"Actually, maybe you know her. She works here. Her name is Gina. Gina Antonova."

The smile slipped from his face, and his friendly expression turned just a touch hostile.

"We don't use names here."

"Oh, I'm sorry." Warning bells went off in Ara's head. "Silly me, I forgot about that."

"You would be wise to remember. I wouldn't want to see your pretty little ass in trouble."

She gave a stuttering laugh. "Right. Well, still, maybe you know how I could find her."

He leaned over onto the bar, getting close to her face, and his voice lowered threateningly. "I don't know who you are or what you're doing, but if this girl is really your friend, she would've warned you about what not to do in this club. If you don't stop asking me these questions, I'm going to have to report you."

"Okay." She met his gaze and held up her hands. "No need for that. I'll back off."

She left the bar and her drink behind, weaving through the crowd toward a table in the far corner. Maybe the other waitresses were the way to go.

Twenty minutes later, Ara still had nothing. None of the employees were willing to talk to her. They were friendly enough, until she mentioned she was looking for someone. The minute they got a hint that she needed inside information, they closed up. After trying with more than six employees, Ara could no longer believe it was just a bad case of nerves. The employees were afraid and had been trained not to talk.

Which meant getting any information about Gina would be next to impossible.

She sighed and moved into a new corner on the upper level. Luke was down below, talking to a dark-haired woman wearing a sparkly bra top and the tiniest pair of shorts Ara had ever seen. When she strolled away, Luke glanced up and caught her eye. The nearly indecipherable shake of his head sent the message loud and clear.

He wasn't having any luck, either.

Ara gritted her teeth. It was time to stop messing around.
The waitress approached with a sway of her hips. She was young—barely eighteen if Ara had to guess. Thick eyeliner overshadowed small eyes, and bright-red lipstick made the most of her full lips. She had the narrow, small-framed look of a young boy except for the overlarge breasts, which were obviously implants.

"What can I get you to drink?"

Ara pulled some money from her pocket and flashed a bill at the woman. Her name tag read Michelle. No doubt it was a fake name.

"I need information."

Michelle's gaze darted over her shoulder. When she looked back at Ara, her friendly expression was locked behind one of determination. "I can't help you."

Ara slid the money across the table toward her. Then she added another bill. "I only want to talk."

Michelle didn't answer, but she also didn't walk away. Ara took that as a sign to continue and pulled out Gina's DMV photo and placed it on the table. "Do you know her?"

Michelle grabbed up the money and tucked it into her bra with one swift move. "Yes."

Ara pulled out more cash and passed it over. "Does she work here?"

The waitress didn't answer, but the tightening of her mouth gave her away. Gina had worked here. "She needs your help."

Michelle's smoky eyes widened. "Are you a cop?"

"No."

She pushed the photograph back across the table. "Put that damn thing away, then, before you get yourself in a whole shitload of trouble." She started to walk away, but Ara grabbed her wrist.

"Please," Ara whispered. "She's been murdered."

Her words shook Michelle. There was no change in her expression. It remained shuttered behind a look of indifference. But the woman's arm trembled slightly under Ara's fingers. It was only for a moment, but it was enough.

Michelle broke free of Ara's hold and lifted her chin. "I can't help you." The words sounded like they had been choked out. She spun on her heel, and on wavering steps, hurried away.

Ara quickly got up and followed. She'd heard the emotion in the waitress's voice. Michelle knew something, and damn it, Ara was going to find out what it was.

She followed the woman into the ladies' room. Michelle was trying to fight back tears, her face turning red with the effort.

The bathroom was occupied by several chatty women who fortunately left together in a cloud of perfume. Ara locked the door behind them.

She and Michelle eyed each other in the mirror, each wary of the other.

"I don't want to cause trouble for you." Ara kept her tone low and even, as if she were approaching a frightened animal. "I only want to find out some information."

"I can't help you."

Michelle tried to pass by her to leave, but Ara blocked the way. "You know something." She quickly pulled out another picture from her jacket pocket. This time it was of Gina's dead body. "Look. Look at what happened to her."

The waitress didn't even blink at the image. She was obviously no virgin to blood and gore. She shoved Ara backward. "What the hell is wrong with you?"

"She was shot in the head and left in a warehouse. Like she was a piece of trash."

"That has nothing to do with me."

"You knew her. You can help me find her killer." Michelle hesitated, and Ara pounced on that. "Please. I can't do this without information."

Her jaw tightened, and she gave Ara another shove. "You'll have to get it from somewhere else."

A pounding started on the door. The noise had Michelle's face turning deathly pale. "God damn you," she hissed at Ara before moving past her to quickly open the door. Luke stood on the other side, fists clenched and spine tense. He passed a confused glance between the two women.

"Wait," Ara said, but it was too late. Michelle breezed past Luke and disappeared into the crowd.

"Couldn't you have given me another two fucking minutes?" Ara snapped.

"I told you to stay within eyesight." Luke glared at her.

"What's the matter? You don't trust me?"

He stepped closer. "I don't want you to end up dead."

Ara fought against the rush of pleasure she felt. Luke cared about her. He also didn't think she was capable, and that was beyond irritating.

"I don't need you to protect me. I've been taking care of myself for a long time. Besides, you just lost me the opportunity to find the information we need. She was the only one willing to tell me something."

He ignored most of her statement. "What did she say?"

"Gina did work here." Ara sighed. "But Thomas is right. This place is locked down tight. No one's talking because they're too scared." She scanned the room, the dancing bodies twisting on the lower level.

Out of the corner of her eye, she caught sight of two bulky men approaching them. They moved with the thunderous grace of giants, and people quickly created a path for them in order to avoid being pushed out of the way. She recognized them for exactly what they were.

Security.

"Damn," Ara whispered. "We have company."

CHAPTER TWENTY-TWO

The security guards were dressed identically in dark suits with crisp white shirts and black ties. A wire extended from their earpieces and disappeared into the lapel of their jackets. Both were muscular and broad-shouldered with meaty hands. They moved together like a well-oiled machine, trapping Luke and Ara between their wall of muscles and an actual concrete wall. It was clear they'd done this a time or two.

The one closest to Ara had shrewd eyes and pockmarked cheeks. He towered over her. Each of his thighs was bigger than her waist, and although she was well trained in several martial arts, one punch from him and she'd be picking her teeth up from the floor for a week.

Not a pleasant thought at all.

His companion had a nasty scar that extended down the side of his face. It looked like someone had tried to cut off his right ear.

"You two need to come with me," Scar Face said.

No introductions, no questions. Just orders. They didn't show any visible weapons, but Ara had no doubt that there were several underneath their jackets.

"I'm FBI Special Agent Luke Patrick." Luke moved his jacket just enough to reveal the badge clipped to his waist.

Scar Face's expression didn't lose its menacing edge, although he did do the courtesy of leaning back a bit.

"You've been asking questions of our staff."

"We're trying to gather some information about a girl who works here."

"Then you should've come to us directly and asked to speak with the manager." Scar Face pursed his lips and jerked his head at his coworker. "Watch them for a moment."

He stepped to the side and whispered something into the wrist of his jacket. A moment later he returned. "Follow me."

Luke passed a glance to Ara, and she nodded discreetly. They'd come to the club for answers and they weren't having much luck with the staff. Might as well try the manager.

Of course, that was assuming they were actually being taken to the manager, and not to someone more dangerous. Ara shook the thought from her head. If this was owned by the mafia, they wouldn't be stupid enough to kill an FBI agent. Particularly one whose team members knew where he was. No, she thought, they would hire a hit on them later if they felt Luke and Ara knew too much. Yet another pleasant thought.

The two men flanked them as they crossed the upper floor of the club, Scar Face leading the way. Again, the crowd dispersed ahead of them, as though they were Moses crossing the Red Sea. At the back, opposite from the bathrooms, was a doorway labeled "Staff Only." Scar Face opened it, and they followed him over the threshold. When the door slammed shut, the music level immediately dropped to a dull thud.

Oh shit. Soundproofing.

The realization had Ara's heart pounding, and she silently gave thanks for the gun she had tucked under her jacket as well as the clutch piece in her boot. These guys might be bigger than her, but they were also probably slower, and guns were the ultimate equalizer.

They moved down a long hallway, all sounds from the club nearly indecipherable now.

Ara's hands grew sweaty. She wiped them on her pants.

Scar Face stopped in front of a closed door. Using a key from his pocket, he opened it and gestured for Luke and Ara to go inside.

It was empty save for one scarred wooden table. The walls were concrete, no windows.

"Please set any weapons you are carrying down on the table," Scar Face ordered.

"Not a chance." Luke's answer came easily, his tone deceptively calm. Ara could sense the tension in him. It flowed off like waves, feeding her own uncertainty about what they were doing.

Scar Face smiled, his eyes crinkling at the corners. "We cannot allow you to meet Mr. Grishnokov armed. It is against our policy."

"Seems to me, I'm the one at a disadvantage," Luke replied. "And it is against FBI policy to hand over my service weapon to anyone."

Scar Face jerked his head toward his comrade, who spoke into a microphone in his hand. A moment later, he gave Luke a nod. "You may keep your service weapon, but only if you empty and disarm it. In addition, we must insist you remove your jackets, along with any other weapons."

Luke unholstered his gun and removed the clip, leaving it on the table. Ara let go of the breath she was holding. She pulled off her jacket, belatedly realizing when the air hit her arms, her hasty wardrobe choice had been a significant error. The sleeveless, button-up blouse was meant to be worn under suit jackets. Now she was being made to strip off all her outer layers, and the scars crisscrossing the backs of her arms were exposed in a way she never let them be.

It was stupid, she knew, but she was humiliated by it.

Luke's gaze dropped to her arms and then rose again briefly to her face. His iron expression didn't change, his lips didn't even twitch, but she knew there would be questions later. Questions she would not, could not, answer.

"Your weapon," Scar Face gestured to her holster, snapping her back to the task at hand.

Ara hesitated for a moment but then undid the clasp and placed the gun on the table. She felt naked without it.

Scar Face stepped forward, efficiently doing a pat down, his massive hands covering every inch of her body. He quickly located and removed the knife from her pocket. She was upset with its removal but breathed a sigh of relief when he didn't find the second gun in her boot.

After Luke's pat down, Scar Face escorted them through another hallway into a back room. Ara stepped over the threshold behind Luke. The office was large, with dark-paneled wood and floor-to-ceiling windows with an impressive display of the city beyond. Plush visitors' chairs faced a desk. The man behind it rose as they entered. His dark hair curled over his collar and framed a clean-shaven face. He had a strong jaw and a nose that had been broken at least once.

His jet-black eyes locked on her, and Ara's breath hitched. A tingle of apprehension crept down her spine.

"Please, come in." He smiled, but it did not soften his features. If anything, it made him look more predatory, more frightening. His gaze was still locked on her, following her progression forward. It was as if Luke was not in the room. As if he was speaking directly and only to her.

The door clicked behind them, and Ara turned her head enough to see both bodyguards were flanking either side of the frame.

"Luke Patrick, FBI."

The man barely acknowledged him, his gaze darting briefly in Luke's direction. "I know who you are." He cocked his head slightly. "But you . . . I don't think my men caught your name."

"Ara."

His mouth twitched. "Ara. Lovely. Do you have a last name?"

"Yes."

Now he chuckled, clearly amused by their battle of wills. She was not. Whatever game he was playing, she wasn't interested in it.

"I hear a hint of my mother tongue in your voice." He came around the desk and approached her. As he grew closer, Luke stepped forward and there was a sudden rustle of movement.

Ara didn't have to turn around to know the bodyguards had drawn their weapons. Luke's gaze darted toward the door, his mouth drawn tight.

The man never paused in his movements. He continued forward, reaching out to take her hand. Drawing it to his mouth, he whispered, in Russian, "Lovely to meet you, Ara."

She held his gaze, not backing off or allowing even the slightest trace of fear to enter her expression. This was a game of intimidation. She could not allow him to see how much he rattled her.

"You too . . ." Her voice trailed off and she raised her eyebrows, sending the message that she was waiting expectantly.

"Dmitri, my dear. Dmitri Grishnokov."

He stared at her for several beats, and something hummed between them. His smooth words and gentle touch were in direct contrast to the uneasiness he created within her. She'd never seen him before—of that she was sure—and yet she felt an instinctive urge to get away from him.

"We need to speak with you about one of your employees," said Luke.

"Of course." Dmitri released her hand and walked back to his desk. "I didn't imagine a visit from the FBI was purely for pleasure." He waved a hand in the direction of the visitors' chairs. "Please sit down. Would either of you care for a drink?"

"No." Luke stayed standing, and Ara followed his lead. Behind her, the guards still had their weapons drawn. It was impossible to relax with a 9mm pointed at your back.

"I think you can call off your boys, don't you?" Ara jerked a thumb toward the bodyguards.

"Forgive me." Dmitri barked out an order that had the two men immediately standing down. "Your colleague was making them nervous."

He opened a decanter and poured himself a generous glass of vodka. "How can I help you, Agent Patrick?"

"Gina Antonova."

"I'm not familiar with that name."

"She's one of your employees here in the club."

"Forgive me, Agent, but I have so many." He replaced the decanter's lid with a clink of glass against glass. "I truly cannot keep track of all of them."

"Perhaps this photo will help." Luke placed the DMV picture of Gina onto the desk.

Dmitri crossed over, and taking a sip of his vodka, studied it. "She's beautiful. Ivan, does this woman work for me?"

"She does, sir. As a bottle girl."

Dmitri smiled and pushed the photograph away with one finger. "There you are, Agent. Question answered."

Luke's jaw tightened. "When did you last see her?"

A smirk played on Dmitri's lips. "As I have already shared, I don't keep track of all my employees. I'm sure the last time she worked is on the schedule."

"I would like to see the schedule."

"Why?"

"Because your bottle girl was murdered."

If Dmitri was surprised or shocked by the news, it wasn't apparent. His expression remained placid. Yet the fingers holding his glass tightened slightly. Just enough that Ara caught it before they relaxed again.

"That's a shame."

Luke arched his eyebrows. "A shame? It sure is. Her head was blown off."

"Tragic." Dmitri calmly took another sip of vodka. "But that has nothing to do with me."

"Great. Then you won't mind providing her schedule. In addition, I'd like to conduct employee interviews and search the club premises."

"I'm afraid I would mind." Dmitri leaned against the desk. It should have weakened him, the slightly shirking stance, and yet it didn't. He oozed power and control from every pore of his body. It took all of Ara's self-control not to repeatedly glance between Dmitri and Luke. Both of them seemed to have the same temperament, the same cool exterior. And both of them had a world of emotions hidden within those shells.

She knew Luke's.

She didn't know Dmitri's. And it worried her.

"If you would like such information, then you must provide me with a warrant." He smiled graciously. "I'm sure, as an FBI agent, you will have no trouble obtaining one."

"Correct. So let's just cut through all the red tape and allow me the access now."

"Impossible, Agent. You have people you answer to, but so do I. I cannot allow a search of the premises without a warrant. Come back with one and you will have my full and utter cooperation."

Dmitri waved a hand, and the two bodyguards stepped forward. Scar Face took Ara's arm and tugged her toward the door. Obviously, the meeting was over.

Luke jerked out of the other bodyguard's grasp. "No need to manhandle me."

"It was wonderful to meet you, Ara." Dmitri called out in Russian, before the door shut behind them. "I hope to see you again soon."

* * *

"Do you know him?" Luke demanded once they were outside.

"Dmitri?" Ara shrugged into her jacket. "No. Never met the man before."

"Well, he certainly liked you." Luke moved toward the car with a furious stride. "What did he say as we were leaving?"

"That it was—"

"Wait!" A woman called out, and Ara turned to see Michelle jogging toward them. Her breasts bounced against the neckline of her tight T-shirt, her curly hair keeping their rhythm.

Ara placed a hand on Luke's arm and passed a glance to him. He read her expression and inched behind her. A silent assent, allowing her to take the lead.

When Michelle reached them, she was slightly out of breath. A slim hand fluttered to her throat. "I need—I need to tell you something."

The woman glanced behind her, nervously. Ara followed the direction of her gaze. No one, it seemed, was watching them. Still, she placed a hand on Michelle's elbow and led her deeper into the shadows, away from the main street and the lights.

"Okay."

"It's about . . ." Michelle's eyes narrowed as Luke stepped closer.

"He's with me." Ara squeezed Michelle's elbow before dropping her hand. "FBI."

Michelle hesitated, suspicion and fear evident in the stress lines around her mouth and eyes. Ara understood her worries, could read them as easily as if they were flitting through her own mind.

"You have nothing to fear from us." She locked gazes with the woman. "I promise."

Michelle licked her lips. "I shouldn't even be talking to you." Another glance over her shoulder. "If I got found out . . ."

She didn't have to finish the sentence. Ara already knew what Dmitri would do to her.

"Gina was my friend." She angrily wiped away the tears forming in the corners of her eyes. "She didn't deserve to die that way."

"No," Ara agreed. "She didn't."

"You should look into her boyfriend, Eddie. Eddie Flores. He's probably the one who killed her."

Luke stiffened, and Ara knew he'd caught it, too. Eddie's last name was the same as Nick's. They couldn't be brothers, since their background check on Nick proved he didn't have any. But they could be relatives of some kind.

"Why are you so sure Eddie had something to do with it?"

"Because Gina was spying on him. For Dmitri." Michelle's mouth thinned. "Eddie didn't know she was watching him, reporting his movements to the boss. If he found out somehow, if she made a mistake, it's possible he would've killed her for it."

"What does Eddie do for Dmitri?"

Michelle laughed grimly. "What doesn't he do? He'd lick Dmitri's ass if he had to."

"Where can we find Eddie?"

"I don't know where he lives. Eddie was smart enough to keep quiet about that. I did go with him and Gina one time to this guy's house. Payment for some work the guy was doing for Dmitri."

By payment, she didn't mean the passing of money. She meant an exchange of flesh. The delivery of his own personal prostitute.

"Payment for what?"

"I don't know exactly, but the guy was into art. Had done something with some paintings Dmitri had."

Ara's pulse picked up speed. Someone in the art world. Again, they were back to paintings. She didn't know how the kidnapping fit into this whole scheme Nick had going, but it was becoming clear he might not have been working for the art gallery after all.

Maybe he was working for Dmitri.

But how did Sam fit into all of this? And Eddie? What was their tie to Nick and his paintings?

"I don't know anything more than that." Michelle waved her hands. "I didn't really pay attention to all the details. It was a quick job, in and out, if you know what I mean."

"I do."

"But they talked like they knew each other, Eddie and this guy." She reached into her bra and came out with a folded piece of paper. She handed it to Ara. It was still warm from the heat of her skin. "I wrote down the address for you. Maybe he can help."

"Thank you." Ara held up the paper. "Truly."

"Find Eddie." Michelle's expression darkened. "And when you do, I hope you cut off his balls and feed them to the dogs."

She turned to leave, but Ara caught her arm. "Wait." She took the folder from Luke and opened it up to the image of Nick. "Ever seen this guy before?"

Michelle peered at the picture and then shook her head. "No. I have no idea who that is."

"We think he might be involved in Gina's death."

The other woman shrugged. "If I was looking for the person who murdered Gina, I'd start with Eddie. Gina wasn't stupid. She was street smart and tough, but spying on Eddie was a big mistake and one that he would've killed her over."

"What about Dmitri?" Luke interjected. "How do you know he didn't kill her?"

Michelle glared at him.

"Because if Dmitri had killed her, we wouldn't be talking right now. Dmitri doesn't leave behind bodies." Michelle's voice was cold and matter-of-fact, certainty bleeding into every word. "The guy you're looking for is Eddie. At least, that's where I'd start."

CHAPTER TWENTY-THREE

Ara turned over the conversation with Michelle in her mind. Eddie, Sam, Gina, Nick. Somehow all these people were connected, and at least three of them—Nick, Eddie, and Gina—were connected to Dmitri.

Dmitri. In the car, in the dark, Ara allowed herself to shudder. He was one terrifying son of a bitch, and she had no doubt he would be ruthless with whoever dared to cross him. Michelle had done a really brave thing by providing them with information, and already Ara was regretting leaving her there. She'd tried to get Michelle to come with them, promised her protection, but the girl was having none of it. Still, she took the card with Ara's cell phone on it. Maybe she would call.

Ara was so deep in her thoughts, it wasn't until Luke stopped at a light in Midtown that she realized he was going in the wrong direction.

"Where are you going?" she demanded. "The address Michelle gave us—"

"We're going back to Boones' house."

"We can't. This guy may be involved. He may know exactly where Sam is."

Luke passed her a look filled with exasperation. "We don't even have a name for this guy. I am not walking into this blind, not with this much on the line. We need to do a background check on Eddie and figure out who lives at the address Michelle gave us. I'd also like to know how Eddie and Nick are connected. All of that will take time."

"You mean you need sleep," she said.

The judgment was clear in her voice, and Luke's face flushed. He pulled the car over to the side of the road with a jerk and slammed it into park. He didn't even look at her before exiting the car, slamming the door shut so hard it rocked the sedan.

Ara glared at his back through the windshield. He was pissed with her, and the sudden wave of his temper was both unexpected and refreshing. She never thought she'd see the cool, controlled Luke lose it.

Obviously she'd hit a very sensitive nerve, and a small part of her felt bad about it. Still, she climbed out of the car, ready to do battle.

His back to her, he shot out, "Are you questioning my commitment to this case?"

"I'm questioning your judgment," she retorted. "Sam doesn't have time. This case is finally getting some traction and you are going to slow it down by doing background checks and playing it safe."

"I will not risk the lives of my team, of any law enforcement officer, because I didn't do my job."

She crossed her arms over her chest. "But you'll risk Sam's."

"I could *kill* Sam if I go into this blind." He spun around to face her, and Ara was tempted to take a step away from him. Luke's blue eyes were like ice. "Don't you get that? If she's messed up with these mafia people, I have to tread carefully. And I need to know a lot more than I do, because right now," he said, spreading his hands wide, "we know jack shit. We don't even know if we're on the right path."

"We are." Ara could feel it in her bones. "You know we are."

He exhaled slowly, a long sigh that seemed to take the anger out of him as quickly as it had come. He ran a hand over his face, and Ara couldn't help but notice he seemed ragged. Deep circles, so dark they looked like bruises, shadowed the skin under his eyes.

"I want to find her, Ara. As much as you do. But I don't want to kill anyone else in the process."

There was a note of something in his voice. Not fear, but something sorrowful. Ara wondered if he was speaking from experience. She drew in her own breath and let it out. It was one thing to risk her own life, to hurtle toward something without caution. It was quite another to ask others to follow her. She had to remember Luke had people who took orders from him. People who would risk their lives to save his, and he owned them some measure of responsibility.

He was right. Whoever had Sam knew what they were doing. Going in blind might do more harm than good.

"I'm sorry. I—"

He held up a hand. "No, it's okay. I get it."

Maybe he did, but she still plowed ahead anyway. "When I worked on the force, there were guys who were there just to punch a clock. It didn't matter what was happening. If their shift was over, they left."

"And I strike you as one of those guys?"

"No." She smiled weakly at him. "But old prejudices die hard, I guess."

He approached, stopping only when he was close enough for her to touch. "Believe it or not, I'm not a machine. I've been going for more than thirty-six hours straight. I can barely see, let alone drive." He sighed. "Five hours. While my team is running down this guy Eddie and the address Michelle has given us, we'll take five hours." He put his hands on her shoulders. "And when I say we, that means you, too."

"I can't—"

"You will, or I'll pull you off this case. If we get into a situation and my life is in danger, you have to be able to shoot straight."

He was right, of course. She was so tired that her legs were trembling. Still, she poked at him. "It's all about you, isn't it?"

Luke's lips turned up in amusement. "Always."

Her breath caught as their eyes met. Warmth seemed to creep across her skin from where his hands rested on her shoulders. A sharp blade of desire sliced through her, sudden in its intensity.

"Ara . . ." Luke's gaze dropped her to mouth.

She pulled away from him, stumbling back. "We should get going."

A flash of something crossed his face, but he was too deep in the shadows, and she was too far away to read what it was.

"Right."

They rode together in silence, gliding through the dark streets of the city quickly. Ara rested her head against the cool window and tried not to think of Sam—where she was or what was happening to her.

Luke's voice startled her from her thoughts, so much that she jumped when he spoke. "Where did you get the scars?"

Despite herself, she stiffened. "An accident."

"When?"

"Why do you want to know?" Her tone was hostile, far more than she intended. The peaceful understanding they'd had for the last twenty minutes melted away in an instant.

"Because you're hiding them." He glanced at her before returning his attention to the road. "And you were upset when I saw them."

"I don't like them. They're ugly." The words were out of her mouth before she even knew what she was saying. God, she was more tired than she thought. Her face flushed with embarrassment. "I'm allowed to keep some things to myself, aren't I? Or do you force all the members of your team to share every piece of their past with you?"

"No." He paused for a moment. "I'm sorry. I shouldn't have asked."

The apology shocked her, and her anger ebbed away. He took the exit ramp off the highway, the streetlights casting him in a weird yellow glow that came and went as they passed them.

"Dmitri acted like he knew you."

"So you said." She yawned.

"Ever crossed paths with him? Maybe as a police officer?"

"No." Ara shook her head. "Not that I know of. If I'd seen him before, I would've told you."

He arched his brows slightly.

"What, you don't believe me?"

"I believe you want Sam back, so yes, I believe you. But I also believe you have secrets, Ara. And that makes me nervous."

The sudden and overwhelming urge to tell him washed over her. She opened her mouth, but the words got caught in her throat.

It would change everything. It would change the way Luke thought of her.

Ara closed her mouth and turned toward the window. She couldn't do it. Some secrets were meant to be kept.

CHAPTER TWENTY-FOUR

*T*he neon light blinks, barely visible between the crack of the blackout curtains. Red. Black. Red. Black. She watches it, counting the flickers, passing the time. In the bed across from her, Nadia whimpers, her beautiful face contorted in a painful grimace. She's having a nightmare again. Ara reaches out but stops before waking her. Whatever dream she is having cannot be worse than reality.

Instead, Ara simply runs a hand down her best friend's arm, murmuring words of a Russian lullaby that makes her think of her mother. As Ara's eyes tear up, Nadia quiets, breathing out a soft sigh before rolling away, leaving Ara with the sight of her back. Her blonde hair is filthy, knotted, and tangled. The metal bunk bed has no sheets, the mattress old and stained with God-knows-what. The room itself is pitiful, a crumbling structure with concrete walls and a rank smell she can't get used to.

At least she isn't still handcuffed to the bed. For some reason, today they've been given that small freedom.

She gets up, crosses to the only window. She parts the curtains, a forbidden activity, and stares down at the alley below. They are up high, at least several stories, the narrow buildings seeming to close in around them. A sudden need for fresh air, frantic and painful in its urgency, overtakes Ara, and she struggles with the latch on the window. It has been painted over many times, rust breaking through in thick, flaky layers. She strains, her muscles weakened, but is rewarded with a small movement. Using all her strength, she yanks, and the latch comes free.

Ara draws in a quick breath, straining her ears, listening for any movement beyond the locked door.

Quiet. Only the whimper of Nadia and the snoring of the girl on the top bunk, one of the many others, their bodies shrunken down from weeks of captivity.

Ara's hands shake as she pulls the window up and a sweet breeze blows in, running along her flushed face, cooling her skin with a kiss, and lifting loose strands of her hair. She gulps in the scent of it. Draws it into her lungs and holds it there before letting it back out again. She imagines she can smell sweet rolls, fresh grass, sunbaked hay.

It's heaven.

They are several stories up, and Ara forces her attention away from the fresh air to study the building. At first glance, it seems there is no way to escape the room, but she's determined. They have to get out. It's either that or die.

Their kidnappers are going to kill them. Ara is certain of it. She might only be thirteen, but she's heard the stories. She's been warned by her mother. There will be no good end to their captivity, even if Nadia's father pays the ransom.

There. The scaffolding. It's rusted and ancient, probably never used. It's also a bit of a jump. She and Nadia could make it with ease. Their gymnastics training has taught them to stretch and fly. But the other girls . . . Ara bites her lip.

She will have to teach them. They will have to try. It's their only chance.

"Ara?" Nadia's voice is sleepy and she blinks rapidly, pushing away her dreams. "What are you doing?"

Ara moves away from the window, dropping down next to her best friend on the mattress.

She can't keep the smile off her face.

"I found a way for us to escape."

Ara jolted awake, the image of Nadia's face fading, replaced by the semilit room. Her bedroom. In the Boones' house.

She sat up in her bed, swinging her legs over the side. Her arms ached down the entire length of her scars. She had the overwhelming urge to cry, as she often did when she dreamed of Nadia and the other girls. The well of hope the dream ended on was the worst part because the minute Ara opened her eyes, she was forced back into reality. Back into an existence in which she had not saved her best friend. Or the others. And the crushing weight of her failure made it hard to breathe.

Nadia, I'm so sorry.

Ara rubbed a hand over her face, forcing back her emotions. She could do nothing for Nadia now. She hadn't had a dream like this in months. It was this case. Sam's kidnapping had brought it all back up.

Ara glanced at the clock. Six o'clock. She'd slept for four hours. The briefing was scheduled for thirty minutes from now. She needed to move.

Urgency and a sense of purpose carried her through a quick morning routine. A cold shower to help her wake up.

Clean clothes. Soft socks and her trustworthy boots. She left her short hair wet and didn't bother with makeup or jewelry.

The house was still and quiet as she made her way to the dining room. The Boones had forced a vacation on most of the staff, leaving only the security team and a few trusted housekeepers. So far, the media didn't know about Sam's kidnapping, and if they were lucky, it would stay that way. Keeping staff to a minimum was one way to ensure that.

The strong scent of fresh coffee and a murmuring of noise preceded Ara's entrance into the dining room. The door was cracked, and as she opened it to step through, the noise level increased.

So many people.

The glossy wooden table, able to accommodate fifteen, was nearly full. Laptops, papers, and file folders covered it from one end to the other. There was a projector screen hung at the far end with the FBI symbol flashing across it. The room hummed with activity as agents helped themselves to coffee and an array of breakfast foods set up on the buffet.

"Good. You're here." Luke came up behind her. He had showered as well, his dark hair still damp, a few droplets staining the shoulders of his crisp white shirt. Dark circles still shadowed the skin under his eyes, but they weren't as deep as before.

"You can sit next to me. At the front." He gestured to the last two available seats. "After you get some breakfast."

It wasn't a request but an order, and Ara immediately bristled. Taking a deep breath, she bit back the retort at the tip of her tongue. She hadn't eaten . . . Hell, she couldn't remember the last time she'd eaten. He was right. She needed food.

More importantly, she needed coffee. Her plate loaded, she sat at the table in the chair he'd designated for her and took the first sip of the rich, black brew.

Oh, it was good.

"Everyone take a seat. We need to get started." Luke, with his own plate of breakfast and cup of coffee, took his place at the head of the table. With his orders, there was a shift in the room. All socialization stopped immediately, and the rest of the team found their places quickly.

Once everyone was settled, Luke gave a nod to the only person left standing. The woman was petite, her black heels barely making up for her short stature.

Ara clicked through the names in her head until she found it: Vicki. She'd been at the warehouse yesterday.

"Okay, people, I'll do a brief run-through to make sure everyone is on the same page, and then I'll get to the information that's been gathered about the relevant parties."

An image of Sam appeared on the projector screen. Ara didn't recognize the photograph and wondered if it had been taken from Sam's Facebook account. In it, she was smiling broadly, her head tilted, a long spill of blonde hair trailing to her shoulder.

"Samantha Harper, stepdaughter to Oliver Boone, was kidnapped outside of the restaurant Phillips two nights ago." Sam's image was replaced by a variety of images from the inside of the restaurant as well as the back alley. "She was nabbed through the back door, placed into a plain white van, and driven off. Through the search of her phone records and texts, we have learned Sam herself arranged for the kidnapping."

"Why?" a dark-haired man with a mustache asked from the middle of the table.

Vicki gave a half shrug. "The only thing we have at this point is speculation."

"Sam lost her father and brother in a plane accident two years ago," Luke said. "She's unhappy with her mother's recent marriage and probably wanted to kill two birds with one stone. Make her stepfather pay and make her mother sorry for ignoring her." He leaned back in his chair. "She may also have been manipulated and encouraged to believe the kidnapping was the answer to her problems."

He nodded at Vicki, silently passing the ball back to her, which she took gracefully.

"Sometime after the kidnapping, we believe Sam lost control of the situation and is currently in danger." A DMV photo of Nick filled the projector screen. "This is Nick Flores, age twenty-one. Several months ago, he delivered a painting to the Boone residence and met Sam. We believe this was their first contact, and through phone records and e-mails, we know Nick and Sam started dating. Nick has no priors on his record, but we traced him to a warehouse where we found evidence that Nick has been painting forgeries. He uses his job as a delivery driver to take the forgeries to clients who think they are getting the original paintings. We believe the gallery Nick works for is selling the original paintings on the black market. For his part in this scheme, Nick is getting paid well. His bank records indicate he's getting regular transactions from an offshore account we can't trace."

Another image appeared on the projector, next to Nick. An image Ara had seen before, and her stomach clenched just a little.

"Also, when we raided the warehouse, along with the paintings, we discovered the body of Gina Antonova. She'd been shot in the head. Clothes recovered from the scene, along with trace evidence, prove that Sam was in the warehouse at the time of the shooting."

Ara didn't want to think about that moment. Sheltered and protected all her life, Sam must've been out of her mind.

"From the direction of Gina's body, it appears the woman— perhaps along with Sam—was attempting to escape. That may have been why she was shot," Vicki continued. "Blood at the scene tests only to Gina. So far, we haven't found anything to indicate Sam is dead."

Vicki paused to sip water from the glass sitting at the edge of table. "Gina worked as a bottle girl at a club called Mist. This club is owned and operated by one Dmitri Grishnokov, an extremely dangerous individual with ties to the Russian mafia."

Vicki took another sip of water.

"An informant at the club confirmed Gina worked there. In addition, she gave us the name of Gina's boyfriend."

An older man, late twenties, with sleek black hair and a large nose appeared on-screen. "Meet Eddie Flores. Eddie is a small fish with a few priors for drug dealing, robbery, and domestic violence. He also works at Mist as a bouncer. More importantly, Eddie is Nick's first cousin."

One of the agents whistled. Inwardly, Ara felt a jump of excitement. Cousins? Beside her, Luke leaned forward in his chair. Breakfast and coffee forgotten, his sole attention was on the screen in front of him.

"We have contacted their families, along with friends and coworkers. No one has seen Eddie or Nick within the last two days. At this point, it's safe to say that Eddie and Nick are persons of interest in this case, wanted for questioning regarding the murder of Gina Antonova and the kidnapping of Samantha Harper."

"Are they working with Dmitri? Or for him?" Luke asked.

"We can't tie them together," Vicki answered. "Yes, Eddie works in the club, as did Gina. But other than that, we can't find any further connection. There's no indication, either from their arrests or from the people we've interviewed, that Eddie and Gina were in deeper with Dmitri or the mafia." She arched her eyebrows. "We can, however, tie them to the art gallery. Nick worked as a delivery driver for the owner, Katherine Carmichael, and we have evidence linking the painting forgery scheme to Kat. Eddie also worked at the gallery part time, doing odd jobs as needed."

Ara sucked in a sharp breath. Beside her, Luke held up a hand. "Hold on, Eddie also worked for the art gallery?"

Vicki nodded. "We have several witnesses, including former employees, who all agree that Eddie worked periodically for the gallery."

"And Eddie also worked for Dmitri. Can we tie Dmitri to the gallery?"

"No." Vicki pushed a button on the projector, and several investigative pages appeared on the screen, some highlighted. "And this scheme would be way outside of the realm of things he's suspected of. His most profitable businesses involve drugs and the sex trade."

"And yet," Luke interrupted, "if Dmitri is invested in the forgeries coming out of the gallery, it would be difficult to trace that connection. I think we need to keep him in play."

Several heads nodded in agreement around the table. Vicki's mouth pursed slightly. "In all honesty, sir, I can't understand why Dmitri would bother. The kidnapping would give him money, of course, but it's a huge risk to have kidnapped the stepdaughter of someone as well-known as Oliver Boone."

Ara raised her eyebrows at Vicki's argument. Part of her wanted to reject it. Dmitri was tied to several of the individuals involved, and Luke was right—it would be difficult to tie him to the forgery scheme if he was behind it. And yet, she had to admit that Vicki's point was spot-on. Dmitri's goal was to remain in the shadows, out of the direct sight of law enforcement and the FBI. Like a snake slithering through the woods, one they knew was there but could never quite catch. Kidnapping Sam would change the rules of the game, upping the attention on him dramatically. The amount of ransom requested didn't seem big enough for such a risk.

From the tightening of Luke's mouth and the tapping of his thumb, he was also considering Vicki's argument. Whether he agreed with her or not wasn't clear, and before Ara could ask, Vicki spoke again.

"We received an address from our informant at Mist. A house she went to with Eddie and Gina. This residence is owned by Marcus Jackson, an art restorer and appraiser."

The name rang a distant bell for Ara. She'd heard of him before. As she tried to place it, his image came on the projector. A sharp, handsome man with edged cheekbones and perfect, white teeth.

Ara gasped.

Luke looked over at her. "You know him?"

"Not personally. But Holly has used him, on occasion." The edge of her excitement wedged deeper, and she spoke faster. "He was recommended to her by Kat."

"We just keep coming back to the gallery, don't we?" Luke turned to Thomas. "I want Kat Carmichael picked up right now."

"If she refuses to come?" Thomas asked.

"Then put some men on her, watching her. I want to know where she is." He turned his attention back to Vicki. "Does Marcus have any priors?"

"Clean as a whistle." She lifted her chin a bit. "I took the liberty of having some officers patrol past his house last night when I learned of the connection. It's been quiet."

Luke flashed a quick smile that didn't reach his eyes. "Not for long. Good work, Vicki. I want the entire team digging into the art gallery and Kat Carmichael. I want money trails, I want evidence. I want to know if she's behind this kidnapping, if it's Dmitri Grishnokov pulling the strings, or if Nick and Eddie are working alone."

His voice hardened. "And I want every single place connected to Eddie, Nick, and Gina searched. They've moved Sam to a new location. We need to find it, people. And we need to find it *now*. Time's running out."

CHAPTER TWENTY-FIVE

The neighborhood was quiet and quaint in its simple touches. A child's bike lying across a driveway, a yellow ribbon tied around a tree, the bright, colorful cushions decorating front porch swings. Suburban America, complete with postage-stamp-sized yards and cookie-cutter houses.

Marcus Jackson's house was a small, one-story ranch style. The front porch was littered with dead plants, and the yard needed resodding. His roof was faded, and a broken gutter hung precariously, filled to the brim with leaves and dirt.

"The Homeowners' Association must hate him," Ara remarked as she climbed out of the car.

Luke frowned as he slammed his own door shut. "Does Oliver do background checks on people he uses?"

She gave a half shrug. "I would expect so, although you'd have to ask him for sure. Why?"

"This place is a far cry from the Boone mansion, that's all."

Ara followed him up the walkway but then took a detour to the garage. She borrowed a cement brick from the pile nearby.

Standing on top of it on her tiptoes, she looked through the tiny windows at the top of the door and whistled.

"What?" Luke asked.

"A Ferrari." She hopped down and replaced the brick before swiping her hands together to remove the dust her fingertips had picked up. "Candy-red and tricked out. He's getting some serious money from somewhere."

Luke nodded and continued up the porch. Ara followed, the rickety stairs creaking with her weight. The swift knock Luke gave the door sounded extremely loud to her ears.

No answer.

She reached out and rang the doorbell a few times. The chiming bells echoed through the house, but nothing stirred.

"I don't think anyone's home," Luke declared, leaning over the railing to look through the closest window. "I can't see a damn thing through the curtains."

"He could be inside but avoiding us." Ara pounded on the door with her fist.

"Come on." Luke spun on his heel, his long strides taking the creaky stairs with ease.

"Where are you going?"

"I'm calling it in. We'll get a team out here for surveillance." He cast a glance over his shoulder. "He's got to come home sometime, but I don't have the luxury of waiting around for him."

"Hold on." She bounded down after him. "He has to be home. His car's in the garage."

Luke shook his head. "He could have caught a ride with a friend. He could've taken a taxi."

"But we can't just leave without making sure." She tugged on his arm, and he stopped midstep. "This guy is the best lead we have at the moment."

"I'll get a warrant for the house."

"That'll take time." Ara glanced down at her watch. "We don't have it."

"Perhaps, but I don't have legal grounds to enter."

"That only means that *you* can't go in."

His eyes widened with understanding. "I'm a federal agent. I can't just stand by and watch you break into someone's house."

"Then close your eyes."

She marched up the driveway, circling to the back gate entrance. She rose on her tiptoes, peering over the fence and scanning the yard for any potential guard dogs.

It was quiet.

She pulled her gun from the holster before flicking the gate latch open and slipping inside. The grass was ragged with light-brown patches of dirt peeking through. The back patio concrete was cracked. A rusting BBQ sat in a corner offset by two large potted plants with sagging leaves and wilted flowers. Ara tried lifting the pane of the nearest window, but it was locked. The blinds were shut, preventing her from catching a glimpse of what lay inside.

Silently, she crept up to the back door. The top half was clear glass, the bottom wooden. No shades.

Her heart beat faster as the destruction inside the house slowly become visible. The kitchen's tile flooring was littered with trash, pots and pans, food from the fridge.

Cabinet doors hung open, forgotten. Drawers half cocked, their contents spilling out. She paused outside the door, straining to hear anything coming from inside. Dread twisted her stomach.

Using the tail of her shirt to prevent fingerprints, she gripped the knob on the door.

Please don't be locked. Please.

With a hard twist and a push, the door swung open. The small measure of relief was overshadowed by the smell that smacked her in the face. A scent she would know anywhere.

Death.

Ara hesitated. A quick flash of faces crossed her mind, the echoes of screams painfully loud, and she took a step backward. She sucked in a sharp breath and shook her head, clearing the thoughts.

With silent footsteps, she carefully traversed the kitchen, clearing the rooms as she passed. Each one was empty, each worse than the last. Papers, clothes, books, knickknacks. All of them had been thrown down, torn apart, smashed into pieces. The place had been completely trashed.

The smell grew stronger the closer she got to the front door. Keeping her back to the hallway wall, she slid up to the open door frame leading to what was probably the living room. A light, the only one on in the darkened house, was shining out into the entryway. With a final deep breath, Ara pivoted into the room, gun raised.

And came face-to-face with the source of that horrific smell.

Marcus Jackson was duct-taped to a chair wearing nothing but a pair of pajama bottoms. His feet were bare, the toes curled grotesquely into the carpet, the ankles bound with more tape. The dark sprinkling of hair on his chest could barely been seen through a thick layer of dried blood. His head was thrown back, his face damaged from the beating he'd received before his executioner had slit his neck from ear to ear.

Ara could see the white bone of his spine.

"Fuck," she whispered, lowering her weapon. "We're too late."

* * *

Luke's face reflected a hard coldness as he stared down at the dead man in the living room.

"Someone knew we were coming," she said, stating the obvious.

"Yes." He spit out the answer through clenched teeth. "But how?"

"Maybe Kat?" Ara suggested. "By asking Thomas to have her picked up, she may have figured out what was going on."

Luke shook his head. "No. This took time. The bastards were here last night." He didn't say it, but she heard it anyway. *While we were sleeping.*

The guilt raged through her until her muscles were so tight, she thought they would snap. Another death on her conscience. Another connection to Sam lost.

"It could've been Michelle," he said aloud, almost to himself.

"Our informant? Why would she tell us about Marcus and then have him killed?"

"She wouldn't have. But Dmitri may have figured out she spoke to us."

"So you do think he's involved," she said.

"It's still on the table."

A thought struck Ara with such force that she sucked in a sharp breath. "Oh God, it could have been us."

"What do you mean?"

"Dmitri was surprised by Gina's death. We caught him off guard, just for a moment, with the news. Maybe Nick and Eddie messed up by killing her, or maybe Dmitri didn't know about the kidnapping until we told him. Afterward—"

"He could've started a cleanup." Luke finished the thought for her. "Killing everyone who could connect him to Eddie and Nick."

"And the paintings," she added.

Luke grabbed his phone out of his pocket and dialed. Ara half listened as he spoke to Thomas in rough, clipped words. Kat hadn't wanted to come in for questioning. Luke ordered her immediate arrest.

As he continued with Thomas, Ara surveyed the room. The couch cushions were ripped apart, the stuffing pulled out to litter the floor. The television was smashed, statues cracked in two, bookshelves stripped bare.

"What were they looking for?" She brushed aside a novel split along its spine to reveal the papers lying underneath. Yesterday's mail. A flyer from a local grocery store, a cable bill, a notice from the Homeowners' Association.

"Something important to them." Luke snapped his phone closed and slowly circled the room. "Something valuable enough to beat and terrorize Marcus for."

"Or . . ." Ara bit her lip. "It's for show."

"To make us think they were looking for something," Luke added. He paused at the torn-up couch, his forehead creased. "To slow us down."

"Or to keep us from finding something that would really help us." Ara approached the desk. "If Marcus was involved in the forgery scheme, then he may also have been involved in the kidnapping. He may have written down where they're keeping Sam."

"I'll have forensics go through everything immediately."

"There's too much." Ara opened her hands, encompassing the entire mess. "If there is something in all of this to help us, Sam will be dead by the time we find it."

"Yes, but we have someone Dmitri hasn't managed to kill yet." His expression darkened. "And I'm going to make her tell me what the hell is going on."

CHAPTER TWENTY-SIX

"**A**re you ready for this?" Luke asked.

Ara watched through the observation window as Kat paced the tiny interrogation room. She was muttering to herself, arms crossed over her chest, face tilted to the floor. Nervous. Very nervous.

"I'm ready." Ara surprised herself by placing a hand on Luke's arm before he could open the door. "Thank you. For letting me in the room with you."

He could've easily kept her out. She wasn't a police officer or a federal agent. She'd been ready to fight to be in the observation room next door, at least, where she could see and hear Luke's interrogation. But before she could even ask, he'd shocked her with the news that she could be involved in the questioning.

At her thanks, the mask he wore dropped for just a moment. A breath. But it was enough to see the mixture of emotions crossing his face. Surprise. Pleasure. Then his jaw tightened, and his face smoothed into its normal, placid expression.

"You're a member of the team. And you know more about Sam than anyone. It's important you're in the room."

Those were all good reasons, but it was more than that. He trusted her.

Kat paled when Luke and Ara entered the interrogation room. She paused midstride, her gaze moving from his face to hers. The air in the room smelled sickly-sweet, like a mixture of sweat and fragrant body wash.

"What is the meaning of this? You promised to leave me alone if I gave you what you wanted."

"The situation has changed." Luke gestured to the closest chair. "Please sit down."

Her hands tightened on her arms, wrinkling the silky fabric of her blouse. "I don't want to sit down. I want to know why you've arrested me like some kind of common criminal."

"Maybe because you are a common criminal," Ara offered wryly.

Kat's cheeks flushed. "How dare you—"

"Oh, give up the victim act." The other woman's haughty tone was more than Ara could stomach. "You've been selling forged paintings for God knows how long. It's a wonder you haven't been arrested before now."

"You can't prove anything." Kat lifted her chin. "I had no idea Nick was delivering forgeries to my customers. It's shameful and embarrassing, but I'm not the criminal here."

She'd obviously been thinking about this, coming up with a reasonable explanation for the fake paintings hanging in the Boones' house, an explanation that would keep her innocent and pin all the criminal activity on someone else.

"Perhaps," Luke responded. "But, as I've said, the situation has changed. Arresting you was the only way I could ensure your protection."

"My protection?" Her voice rose to a screech. "How exactly is dragging me out of my gallery in handcuffs ensuring my protection?"

"I'm protecting you," Luke said, opening a folder and throwing down an autopsy photograph of Marcus, "from this."

All of the color drained from Kat's cheeks as her gaze dropped to the image before her. She swayed, her knees bending. She would've dropped to the floor had Luke not reached out to grip her arm.

"Marcus. Oh my God, Marcus."

Luke steered her into the closest chair. "We found him this morning. In his home. He'd been beaten, his neck slashed."

Tears flooded Kat's eyes, and she brought a trembling hand to her face. "And you've arrested me . . ." Panic made her eyes widen, her nostrils flare. "There's no way I can hide from him."

"From who?" Ara stepped closer to the table, placing her hands flat on its cold surface. "Who do you need to hide from?"

Kat's gaze remained glued on Marcus's face. She shook her head violently.

"I can help you," Luke's tone was a soothing whisper, a calm promise in the face of Kat's desperate panic. "I can protect you."

She let out a burst of laughter. "You can't protect me. I'm a dead woman walking. There isn't any place you can put me to protect me from him."

"Bullshit." Luke leaned in closer, dipping his head so that he could look her in the face. "I have the resources of the FBI at my fingertips. You tell me who you're afraid of, and we can make you disappear." He snapped his fingers and Kat jumped. "Just like that. It can happen in as few as four hours. He'll never be able to find you. I'll turn you into a ghost."

Ara could see Kat wanted to believe him. The desperation wavered, the panic losing its edge.

Suspicion took its place.

"Why should I trust you?"

Luke pulled out a new photograph from his folder. This one was of Sam, her sweetheart face lit up with a beautiful smile. "Because I want to save her life. And I need your help to do it. If you answer our questions, if you help me get her home, then I will help you out of the mess you're in."

Ara didn't like it. For all they knew, Kat had been in on the plan to kidnap Sam. She might've known where Sam was this whole time and never said anything. If nothing else, she knew more about Nick than she'd told them. The thought of it, of her watching them chase their tails while she held back critical information, made Ara's blood boil.

And now Luke was offering Kat a new life, a clean slate. *Focus on Sam. On the big picture.*

It was down to the wire now. The kidnappers would be calling within the hour to arrange the drop-off. They needed information, and as much of it as they could get. Which was exactly why Luke was willing to give Kat a second chance, despite her indiscretions. When looking at the big picture, it made sense. But it still didn't feel good.

Maybe after they got Sam back, it would.

"I want the deal in writing." Chin trembling, Kat lifted her face to look at Luke. "I'll tell you everything I know, but I won't do it unless the deal is in writing."

"Awfully demanding, aren't you?" The words popped out of her mouth before Ara could stop them.

Luke's mouth twitched. He didn't want to be doing this any more than she did, and Ara was making it worse. Kat glared at her and snapped, "Do you want the information or not?"

"We want it." Luke pulled out a premade contract. He reached inside his jacket pocket for a pen. "This contract states that the FBI will provide you with a new life, new identification, and immediate protection. In exchange, you will tell me everything you know, right down to your bra size, should I require it. If you hold anything back—and I mean anything—I will find out. And then the deal will be null and void."

"Understood."

When Kat reached for the pen, he smoothly moved it slightly out of her reach. "I don't have time for games. Don't test me, Kat. Lie to me and you really will be a dead woman walking. I'll turn you out without a second glance."

She hesitated, and Ara bit back a curse. They didn't have time for this.

The moments passed, long and uninterrupted. Luke barely blinked, and his gaze never moved from Kat's face. She looked away, studying the grain in the wooden table, weighing her options. Not that she had that many.

Then her gaze fell on the image of Marcus, and with a well-manicured finger, she pulled it out from underneath the one of Sam. Her mouth hardened at the sight of his battered and broken face, the visible slit along his throat. She dropped the picture and reached for the pen in Luke's outstretched hand.

She scrawled her name along the dotted line and pushed the paper back toward him. "I wear a size 34D. What else do you want to know?"

CHAPTER TWENTY-SEVEN

"**W**here is Sam?" Ara asked immediately.

"I don't know," Kat replied. She gathered up the photographs, placing the one of Marcus behind the smiling Sam, and gave them a tap on the table to line them up. She passed them over to Luke. "Put these away, please. I don't think we need them any longer."

Ara grabbed them from her outstretched hand before Luke could and threw them across the room. "Where is Sam?"

Kat blinked. "I told you, I don't know."

Luke passed a glance of warning toward Ara before turning to Kat. "You knew about the kidnapping?"

"Only after the fact. I knew he would do something about her because she'd figured out what we were up to but . . . I didn't know about the kidnapping plan until later."

"Back up," Luke cautioned. "Start from the beginning. You say you knew he would do something. Who is he?"

"Dmitri Grishnokov."

"The owner of Mist," Ara said, thinking aloud.

"He owns a lot of things," Kat replied. "A lot of people. And he doesn't take betrayal well. If he finds out I spoke to you about any of this, well, what they did to Marcus will look merciful."

"How did Sam get involved with him?"

"She didn't. Sam was just too damn smart for her own good." Kat sighed. "She had no idea, the poor girl."

"The art scheme," Ara said. "She figured out how the art scheme worked." The pieces began fitting into place, sending Ara's mind whirling. "You sold the paintings out of the gallery, but Nick was delivering the forgeries he painted."

Kat nodded. "Exactly. Then his cousin Eddie would take the original painting to Dmitri, who used it as currency."

"And if you ran into a problem, if a customer suspected or asked for an evaluation," Ara said, "you would send them Marcus."

"He would assure them that the painting they had was not only authentic but worth more than they'd paid for it."

"That's risky," Luke noted. "What if the customer didn't use Marcus?"

Kat smirked. "Dmitri's smart. He found one of the best evaluators, one of the most reputable, and put him on the payroll. Anyone who did a search on Marcus would find it difficult to justify not using him."

"How did Sam figure out what you were doing?"

"I'm not sure, exactly. Nick and Sam started dating, and it's possible Nick let too much slip. Or maybe Sam realized the painting in her room was a fake and told Nick about it. She'd obviously put two and two together."

"So you kidnapped her?" Ara asked. "How would that fix the problem?"

"Eddie was in a lot of trouble with Dmitri. He'd lost him a lot of money in a deal that went badly." Kat waved her hand dismissively in the air. "He came up with this idea to kidnap Sam, get the money he'd lost, and then hand her and the money over to Dmitri as payment for his mistakes. That way, Eddie killed two birds with one stone. He got Dmitri the money and he got rid of the one outsider who knew about our scheme."

"He convinced Sam to kidnap herself," Ara said.

"Yes," said Kat. "She had no idea he was planning to turn her over to Dmitri. She thought it was just a game to get back at the Boones."

"Eddie got Nick to help him. And Gina, his girlfriend."

Kat nodded. "They all had a vested interest in keeping Dmitri happy. They also knew that once he figured out Sam knew about the paintings, they were all dead. Better to sacrifice Sam and save their own necks."

"They took her to the warehouse," Luke said. "And when they handed her over to Dmitri's men, something went wrong. Gina ended up dead."

"Gina's dead?" Shock rippled across Kat's face. "What about Nick? And Eddie?"

"We only found Gina," Ara replied.

"You were probably next on his list. I saved your life by having you arrested." Luke stared at her. "They tore Marcus's house apart looking for something. What did he have that Dmitri wanted?"

"The warehouse code," Kat replied. "He had changed the password a while ago, hoping that it would give him some leverage with Dmitri. Idiot. It only got the shit beaten out of him before he died."

"What warehouse?"

"It's in a shipyard. It's what Dmitri uses to hold the originals before he has them crated and shipped out of the country."

"She's there," Ara said to Luke. "It's isolated, quiet, and they would be able to dump her body in the water. They took Sam there."

"Where is it? What shipyard?"

Kat shook her head. "I don't know exactly. I was never privy to that information. I just know it exists."

Luke's cell phone beeped and he pulled it from his jacket pocket. Scanning the screen, he cursed. "The kidnappers have made contact." He rose to his feet and quickly gathered his papers. "Ara, we have to go. Now."

"What about me?" Kat asked.

"Wait here." He was already halfway to the door. "I may need more information."

"Luke, one more question," Ara turned back toward Kat. "Why? Why did you get involved in the scheme?"

Kat's mouth twisted into a smile. "Money, of course."

"You couldn't have earned it?"

The other woman snorted. "Not the kind of money Dmitri was paying me. When he found me, I was in over my head in debt, about to lose everything I had. He gave me the kind of life I could only dream about."

Ara shook her head. "I hope it was worth it. Because it's cost at least two people their lives."

"They knew the risk," Kat said coldly. "We all did."

CHAPTER TWENTY-EIGHT

Sam jerked awake, her heart racing. Her eyes blinked several times, but they didn't adjust to the dark. It took her a moment to remember. She was wearing a blindfold. Tape over her mouth. Chains.

Oh God. She was still here. Her heart fluttered faster as the memories flooded over her. Sleep, evasive and fitful, had at least given her one gift—the ability to forget.

Faced with harsh reality, Sam breathed through the overwhelming emotions. The strong, acrid scent of body odor mingled with the coppery smell of dried blood. The hard floor beneath her was painful to her sore muscles, and they screamed in protest as she tried to move.

There. There it was again. The noise that had woken her. Someone was moaning.

Her heart stopped. Had something happened to Nick? She ignored her achy muscles and stretched out a foot, searching. It hit rubber, and the person jolted, startled by her sudden touch, before pushing against her.

Another moan.

She ducked her head. Clumps of tangled hair swung next to her cheeks. Her hands were bound in front of her, the chains just long enough that if she . . . Yes. Her fingers found the smooth cloth of the blindfold.

She hesitated.

If Maksim or Sasha caught her with the blindfold down, she couldn't begin to imagine what they would do to her. And if Nick was hurt, there was nothing she could do for him. She was still chained to the floor.

If he's hurt, it's because of you. It's all your fault.

The painful whimper drifting across the room made her decision. Sam pulled down the blindfold.

She squinted, her eyes struggling to adjust to their sudden sight. The room came into focus bit by bit. A concrete floor and walls. A water heater. Wooden staircase. The sole light came from a weak bulb hanging from a rafter in the ceiling.

A basement. Just as she had suspected.

The chains holding her arms and legs were thick, the interconnecting loops reaching down to a metal circle bolted to the floor. Blood spatter still stained her arms, and the image of Gina's head exploding flashed in her mind.

"Sam."

The whispered sound of her name pulled her out of the flashback. She followed it, past the chains holding her down, to another set just out of her reach. Her heart leapt as her gaze traveled over his body, unmarked and blissfully whole. Nick.

Thank God.

He was still wearing the ripped jeans and black T-shirt from two days ago. His normally tan skin looked pale in the light, his face gaunt and drawn.

Their eyes met, and Nick gave her a weak smile.

It took her a moment to realize his blindfold was down around his neck. He'd also removed the tape from his mouth. It hung, by a small section, to the side of his cheek.

The urge to speak to him was overwhelming. It took over, frantic and needy, and she tugged at her own tape, wincing as she peeled it away.

Oh . . . Sudden tears filled her eyes as she licked her cracked lips. It was painful. It was freeing. She never thought she'd be so happy to do such a simple thing as licking her lips.

Another moan reached her ears. She peered into the darkness, saw a lump huddled two arms' length away from Nick. She could only make out the curve of a back, the tangle of chains also holding the person down.

"It's Eddie," Nick whispered. "They fucked him up pretty bad."

Sam closed her eyes briefly. Despite herself, she felt pity for Eddie. But more than that, she felt awful for Nick. The pained expression on his face, the wince he didn't try to hide as his cousin moaned again—they were terrible for Sam to watch. Nick and Eddie were as close as brothers, and she knew that with every bit of pain Eddie felt, Nick felt it, too.

"I'm sorry." Her voice cracked. Her throat was dry and it was painful to speak, but Sam had to say it. "I'm so sorry."

"Don't," Nick whispered. "Don't apologize. I knew Eddie was in with some bad people. I've been trying to get us out of the forgeries for a long time."

"I should've told you what we were planning. Maybe . . ."

"I could've stopped you." Nick's gaze swept over her. "It's not all your fault. Eddie gave you this idiot idea. You didn't know enough not to go along with it."

But Nick would've. Sam knew enough to know that. It was part of the reason she'd kept him in the dark about the plan until it was already under way. Although Eddie was the older of the two, Nick was far smarter. He'd been taking care of his cousin, trying to keep him out of trouble, for most of his life. He felt responsible for Eddie.

He'd also felt responsible to her.

You have no idea what you're dealing with.

"You tried to warn me." Sam's voice caught on the words. "Even after you agreed to help. I should've listened—"

The jingling of keys struck terror and panic in Sam's veins. Nick held up his finger to his lips before placing the tape back over his mouth. She did the same and quickly lifted the blindfold.

The lock clicked open.

The cloth over her eyes was a little loose, and Sam could still see out of a small sliver. The blood rushed in her ears, and she swallowed hard against the terror biting its way through her stomach. Expensive, suede dress shoes came down the stairs and the jingling of keys grew louder. Sam ducked her head, afraid Maksim would notice her blindfold had slipped.

He stopped in front of her. She flinched as he touched her hair, his fingers tangling in the strands.

"Okay, little one—show time."

CHAPTER TWENTY-NINE

The Boone mansion was quiet when Ara and Luke walked through the front door, but the dining room, in contrast to the rest of the house, was controlled chaos. A few agents were on their phones, several on their computers. Oliver sat in a corner of the room, his face lined with exhaustion, dark circles shadowing the pale skin under his eyes. When he spotted them, he jumped to his feet and headed in their direction.

"Any news?"

"We have some leads."

Thomas approached and didn't even pause to greet them. "You made it just in time. We should all move to Oliver's office."

He led the group out of the room and down the hall. "They contacted us an hour ago and said they would call at four o'clock to provide us with drop-off instructions."

He twisted the knob on the heavy wooden door and pushed it open. Inside were two more agents, along with the equipment necessary for tracing and recording phone calls.

"Have we found the cargo ship warehouse yet?" Luke asked, sweeping into the office.

"No." Thomas ran a hand through his short hair. "I've got every man on it, but there are a lot of commercial warehouses around the port. Going through each of them, following the paper trails—that takes time. It would be better if we had boots on the ground."

Luke shook his head. "Don't have the manpower for all of them. Besides, we can't run the risk. Sam might not even be held there, and I don't want to tip our hand. So far, Dmitri has no idea we've connected him to the kidnapping."

"So you're more interested in catching the kidnapper than in getting Sam back." Oliver crossed his arms over his chest and bounced on the balls of his feet. "How quickly the story changes."

"No," Luke said, glaring at him. "If Dmitri knows we've discovered him, then he will kill Sam and disappear into the wind. We'll have no chance to get her back alive."

"The best case scenario," Ara explained gently, "is to find the specific warehouse and send in a small team."

"But we're running out of time." Luke glanced at his watch. "The kidnappers won't give us much more. Damn it, we're so close."

His frustration fed Ara's own. Given another few hours, things could be different.

The phone rang, cutting off her thoughts. The room flew into frantic activity. Ara and Luke pulled on headsets, which would allow them to listen in on the conversation. The agent manning the computer sat at attention. Luke jerked his thumb, clearing the room of unnecessary people.

Oliver sucked in a breath and then reached for phone as it gave the third shrill ring.

"Hello?"

"Do you have the money?" The same distorted voice as before.

"It's ready to go," Oliver answered. "I want to talk to Sam."

"No." The answer was firm and without hesitation. "You'll see her soon. The exchange will happen on the west side of the Bethesda Terrace in two hours."

"What about Sam?"

"Follow our instructions exactly and she'll be fine." A slight pause. "Ara is the only one we will allow to recover Sam. She is to come to the meeting point alone."

She froze in surprise, her hands tightening on the ears of the headset. Why did they want her?

Luke's jaw tightened, and he glanced in her direction. The same question was in his eyes, along with a whisper of mistrust.

"Why Ara?" Oliver asked. "I'll do it."

"You will follow my instructions or we will kill Sam. Ara, and only Ara, is to come to do the exchange. You have two hours."

The kidnapper slammed the phone down, the silence deafening.

Oliver hung up the phone, spinning to face Ara. "Why are they asking for you to do it?"

"I don't know." She removed her headset slowly, confusion muddling her brain. "Maybe because Sam asked for me in the last phone call."

Oliver nodded, appeased by her answer. Luke, on the other hand, was studying her with quiet consideration. Something was working in his mind, and Ara felt the bite of his silent questions. The trust she'd worked so hard to gain with him seemed, with a single phone call, to have disappeared.

Ara stood and waited for him to start asking more questions, to push further than Oliver had. To her utter surprise, he gave a nearly indiscernible nod and directed his attention to Oliver.

"We need your permission to use the funds we've set up for this."

Oliver drew himself up, straightened his shoulders, and set the line of his jaw. He looked ready to do battle. "Can you guarantee Sam will be returned safely?"

"Of course not," Luke replied. "But I can guarantee that we will do everything possible to make that happen."

"Which means nothing, since the kidnappers didn't even allow me to speak with her this time. You may arrive to the pickup point, transfer the money, and find out afterward Sam's already dead."

"True." Luke met his steely gaze with one of his own. "But there's also an equal chance she's alive and well."

"By not providing the ransom, you may be signing her death sentence," Ara added.

"Or we can negotiate," Oliver countered. "Right now they believe they have all the power. We have to take it back."

"This isn't a game." Ara couldn't believe what she was hearing. The money the kidnappers wanted was nothing but a drop in the bucket to Oliver. This wasn't about the cash.

This was about ego. "This isn't some boardroom deal you are trying to make. Sam's life is on the line here."

"You think I don't know that?" he shot back. "I don't care about the money. I do care about getting Sam back home alive, and right now, they are holding all the cards. If we ignore this demand, they'll call us back. And in the next conversation, they'll be far more willing to discuss the terms in order to get their money."

"Ignore the demand?"

The question came from the doorway, the voice incredulous. Ara turned to see Holly standing there, a horrified expression on her face. Her gaze was locked on Oliver, and she stared at him for a moment, clarity shimmering in those wide blue eyes. "Are you actually suggesting we should ignore the demand?"

Color rose on Oliver's cheeks. "Holly, it's not what you think—"

"Enough!" The word came like a blast from her chest, and she sliced the air with her hand.

She turned to Luke. "Is my daughter still alive?"

He hesitated a moment. "I don't know."

"If we pay the ransom, is there a chance we'll get her back?"

"Yes. There is."

She jutted her chin out. "Then I'll pay it. What do I need to do?"

"The money has to be prepared, set up in a special account so we can track it." Luke looked from Holly to Oliver and back again. "We don't have time to set up new funds before drop-off."

Her gaze narrowed. "You've already set up the account. The money is ready to go."

"We arranged it with your husband hours ago since we knew this was a possibility."

Holly spun around and jabbed a finger at her husband. "Transfer the money, Oliver. Give it to them."

He hesitated for a moment, and tears flooded Holly's eyes. "Who are you? Where is the man I married, the man who promised to take care of me and my daughter? If Sam dies because of your inaction, I'll never be able to forgive you."

He walked over to her, placed his hands on her arms. "That's what I'm trying to explain to you. I am trying to take care of Sam. If we give the kidnappers the money, we've lost any leverage we have in getting Sam back alive. By holding back, we may be able to force their hand."

"Or they may kill her," Holly whispered. "Isn't that right, Agent?"

Luke closed his eyes briefly and then opened them. "Ma'am, to be honest, I can't guarantee Sam's safe return. We're doing everything we can, but there are variables that can't be predicted."

Holly's gaze landed on Ara. "What do you think?"

The weight of the question drew down Ara's shoulders. She didn't want to be responsible for this, but it seemed there was no choice. "Pay the ransom and let me bring her back."

Holly nodded slowly and then turned back to Oliver. "I trust the FBI. And Ara. Give them the money."

Oliver sighed, low and long. Then he kissed Holly's forehead and drew her into his arms. He met Luke's gaze. "You have my permission to use the money."

Luke started for the door. "Ara, with me."

She followed behind him, pausing only long enough to glance over her shoulder at Oliver and Holly. Holly had started crying, her shoulders shaking with the strain. Oliver murmured words of comfort Ara couldn't make out. Their grief and fear pulled at her heart. She could not fail. Not just for Sam's sake. For Holly's and Oliver's as well.

She had to bring Sam home. No matter the cost.

CHAPTER THIRTY

"I'm not wearing the vest," Ara declared. "I've let you hook me up with a microphone and an earpiece, not to mention enough wires to electrocute myself with. But the vest . . . that's where I draw the line."

Thomas took a deep breath, his features struggling to remain passive. "Department regulations require it."

"I'm not an officer. I'm a civilian."

He snorted and waved the bulletproof vest in front of her. "Even more reason for you to be wearing it."

Ara glared at him. "Ha, you're so funny. It doesn't matter what your regulations say, I'm not party to them."

"Weren't you a cop, for crying out loud? Surely you've had to wear vests before!"

"I never liked them. They slow me down, and in this case, every second could count."

Thomas's tone lost some of its edge. "I get it. But look, these are Luke's orders, not mine, okay? So stop being a pain in my ass, put the damn vest on, and take it up with him, all right?"

She hesitated for a moment and then jerked the vest from his outstretched hands. She wasn't going to wear it, but Thomas was only following orders. Better to save the real fight for the man in charge.

She'd only just had the thought when the dining room door swung open and Luke walked through. Before he could open his mouth or get distracted by one of his FBI cronies, she went for the attack.

"I have a bone to pick with you." She lifted the vest and waved it at him. "I'm not wearing this. It'll slow down my response time and make it difficult—"

"Everyone clear the room. Now." Luke's order cut her off, and it was only then that she paid closer attention to the strain around his mouth, the tightness in his shoulders. She'd passed them off as tension due to the upcoming recovery, but his tone was harsher and colder than she'd ever heard from him when talking to his team. He hadn't even said please.

There was a rush of activity as the small FBI army cleared the room. Thomas was the last one left with them.

"She still needs to do a voice check on the microphone with the audio guy," he advised Luke. "We don't have long."

Luke gave a sharp nod of acknowledgment, and Thomas shut the door behind him.

The silence left in the room was unnerving and unexpected. After the last thirty minutes of flurried activity, it seemed wrong.

"What's going on?" Ara asked.

"I'm calling off the drop."

"What? You can't do that."

He moved to the long windows across the room. The late-afternoon sunlight flitted across his features, playing along his strong jawline, the curve of his cheek. "Who is Dmitri Grishnokov?"

Damn it. Anger overtook the shock, flooding her veins with heat. "I already told you. I don't know Dmitri. I had never met him before the night you and I interviewed him at Mist."

She'd seen the hint of mistrust in his face when the kidnappers asked her to do the exchange. Ara had hoped it would be dismissed, that her actions over the last few days might quickly dissolve whatever suspicions had crept back up.

Obviously, it was still an issue.

Hurt mingled with the anger. She walked toward him, her strides purposeful and efficient. "I thought we were past all this. I thought you believed me when I said I had nothing to do with Sam's kidnapping."

He didn't answer her, nor did he turn in her direction. Recklessly, she punched him in the arm. "I'm talking to you, damn it. There's only one hour till the drop-off. We don't have time for this crap now."

He spun, grabbing her upper arms, holding her in place. "This has nothing to do with trusting you. If I didn't believe you, trust you . . . Ara, you wouldn't be here." He scanned her face. "I'm trying to save your life."

"What the hell are you talking about?" She tried to break free of his hold, but he only tightened his grip.

"Dmitri Grishnokov knows you."

"That's impossible."

"Is it? Come on, Ara, you saw it as well as I did when we were at Mist. The way he reacted to you. The interest he showed in you."

She sucked in a breath. "What are you saying, Luke?"

"We missed it." He loosened his grip on her arms but didn't release her. "At Jackson's house. We didn't see it because his mouth had been taped shut, but they found it during the autopsy." He locked gazes with her, the force of those sharp blue eyes almost more than she could take. "Ara, his tongue had been cut out."

The weight of what he was saying slammed into her.

"The trafficking ring," she whispered. "From Austin."

"Yes."

"I don't understand . . ."

"Dmitri recognized you. When we interviewed him at Mist. He must've put two and two together and placed you as one of the cops from that day. It's why the kidnappers are asking for you to do the drop-off."

She frowned, her eyebrows creasing together. "Why would he want to come after me?"

"Because," he said softly, "a trafficker died that day."

"Viktor." She shook her head. "But he was a low-level player. Nothing a boss like Dmitri would lose sleep over."

"Maybe he wasn't as low-level as you thought. How much information did the Austin Police Department have on him?"

"Not much. He hadn't been in the game that long."

Luke nodded. "Exactly."

Ara again tried to break Luke's hold, and this time he let her. On shaking legs, she turned away, resting her head against the cool windowpane. A thousand questions rolled through her mind, but she forced herself to focus on that day in Austin. The scent of smoke and burning wood. The oppressive heat from the fire barely tempered by the cool breeze rushing along her bare scars. The shouts of her fellow officers, of her captain. The painful squeezing of her chest as she tried to pull air into her lungs. The feeling of being watched.

Ara jolted upright as the memory hit her.

"What is it?" Luke asked.

"A car. A town car passed by the house after I'd been pulled out. It was moving slowly, the window partially rolled down. It didn't belong there. The house was in a deserted area, no reason for someone to be going there unless . . ."

"They were there to meet with the traffickers."

She nodded. "I sent some men after it, but they lost it on the highway. The license plate was covered in mud, so we never had a shot at tracing it."

"Dmitri?"

"Or someone working for him."

"It's a trap, Ara. He's going to kill two birds with one stone. You and Sam." He came up, so close she could feel the heat of him, but he didn't touch her. "He has no intention of letting Sam live. Not with the knowledge she has of his organization. And by having you do the drop-off, he can exact whatever revenge he feels is necessary for Viktor's death."

"But why go through this charade? Why not just kill Sam now and take me out some other way?"

"Because this way he gets the money, too."

Now he did touch her, his hands tracing the lines of her arms, up to her shoulders. Strong, soothing.

Ara lifted her head from the cool glass, allowed herself one moment to lean against him.

"If I don't go, he'll kill her."

"Ara, she's dead anyway."

"She's not dead yet." Ara spun to face him. "I can save her."

"Didn't you hear anything I just told you? It's a trap."

"I don't care. I won't abandon her." She tilted her chin until she was looking him in the eyes. She wanted him to see her determination, to understand the price she was willing to pay. "I'm doing this, with or without you."

He scanned her face, taking in the set of her jaw. Luke hesitated only a moment.

"All right. You're doing this with me."

He reached into his pocket and pulled out a hair clip. Gently, he smoothed her hair back from her face and used the pin to secure it. "This is a GPS tracker. I'll be following your movements every step of the way."

His fingers brushed along her ear, where an earpiece was tucked inside, invisible to the naked eye. "I'll be able to talk to you, and you can speak to me through the microphone."

He palmed her cheek, his thumb fluttered across her lips. "Even with all this, even with a team of FBI agents, I can't guarantee your protection."

"I know," she whispered. Her heart pummeled against her chest.

"He'll do his damnedest to kill you."

"Then I guess I'd better make sure we get to him first."

CHAPTER THIRTY-ONE

Bethesda Terrace was bustling with people. Couples holding hands, moms with strollers, children running across the square. All Ara saw were potential victims, innocent people who she would have to protect just as much as Sam.

Her stomach twisted, and she resisted the urge to rub it. She wouldn't have been able to reach it anyway. Luke had won the argument over the bulletproof vest.

Ara scanned the area around the central fountain, narrowing her focus on the west side. No sign of Sam, although she did spot three undercover FBI officers. One reading a newspaper on the bench. Another two drinking coffee as they strolled along the path.

"Ara, we're ready." Luke's steady voice in her ear broke through her thoughts. She felt a sudden calmness come over her, a singular focus.

Get Sam out.

"Snipers are set up around the perimeter," he continued. "You won't be able to see us, but we're here."

"Roger that," she whispered, just loud enough for the microphone to pick up. Unless absolutely necessary, Ara would maintain radio silence with Luke. She couldn't know who was watching or where they were, and she didn't want to run the risk that the kidnappers would realize the FBI was in extremely close proximity.

She walked toward the fountain with long, steady strides. Once on the west side, she started pacing slowly. Staying clear of the crowds, working to make herself visible. Five minutes went by. Ten. Sweat trickled down her back despite the cooler temperatures the setting sun was ushering in. Where in the hell was Sam?

Her cell phone rang, vibrating in her jacket. She pulled it out and glanced at the caller ID.

Unknown. Her breath tight in her chest, she answered. "You made it."

The voice on the other end came through clear, smooth and silky, with the touch of an accent. He wasn't using a voice distorter.

That couldn't be good.

She turned slightly and scanned the area again. Out in the open like this, Ara was an easy target. She might as well have drawn a bull's-eye on her back. Fear made her palms sweaty, slick against the phone. They could be anywhere, watching, taking aim right this moment.

Stop. Stay calm.

She tilted the phone as close as she could toward the microphone on her lapel and said, "I see we've decided to drop all pretenses."

He chuckled. Deep and low. "There's no need to keep secrets between the two of us anymore."

"Do we know each other?" she asked, no hint of her fear in her voice. "Because, if so, you must not be that damn memorable. I don't recognize your voice at all."

"Trust me, Ara, if we'd met before now, you'd remember."

Cocky, confident bastard. This man wasn't Dmitri, that much she was sure of, which made him one of his henchmen.

"Now," he went on. "Let's get right to business. I'm sure you would like to know how to get your beloved Sam back."

"Where is she?"

"Are you always this impatient?" There was more than a hint of amusement in his voice. Having the power, playing with her—it was fun for him. She stayed silent, not rising to the bait.

He sighed heavily. "Look toward the trees on your left-hand side."

She spun, holding her breath. There was a teenager standing next to a group of trees. A ball cap obscured her features from Ara's view, but the body size and shape matched Sam's.

She took one step forward, and the kidnapper tsked in her ear. "Don't move."

Ara froze. Her feet itched to cross the distance between her and Sam.

"If you take one more step in her direction, I will kill her." The kidnapper's voice was blunt and matter-of-fact.

"Ara, we're going to see if we can get close enough," Luke whispered in her earpiece. "It's okay."

Even as he spoke, the undercover agents having coffee started up the path, chatting.

"I won't move until you tell me to," Ara said.

"Good girl. Now then, on to the money transfer. I'm going to hang up now and send you a text with the account number on it. You're going to send the money. The moment it appears, I'll let Sam go."

"It sounds simple."

"It is."

"Yeah, except how can I be sure you won't shoot Sam anyway, even after you get the money?"

"Well . . . бабушка надвое сказала."

He was playing with her, using an old Russian proverb. The literal translation was "Granny said two things." In English, "We'll see what we'll see; maybe rain or maybe snow, maybe yes, maybe no."

There was no way for her to be sure. But she didn't have a choice in the matter.

She would just have to do what he said and hope he followed through with his end of the bargain.

"And Ara." He paused, the amusement leaving his voice, replaced by cold, lethal steel. "I'm watching. If anyone—and I mean anyone else—approaches Sam, I start shooting."

He hung up before she could respond. Silently, she cursed.

"We heard it, Ara." Luke's voice was tense, and she knew he'd been thinking the same thing she was. They couldn't save Sam any other way. They had to transfer the money and hope their mysterious henchman would follow through with his end of the bargain.

Her phone beeped with the text message. She pretended to dial the phone and lifted it to her ear. Keeping her eyes glued on Sam, she read the numbers off for Luke's benefit.

"Okay, Ara," Luke said. "We're doing the transfer now. It's confirmed that the girl standing at the perimeter is Sam."

A tinge of relief cut through the tension, but Ara wouldn't allow herself to revel in it. Sam wasn't safe yet.

"We can't tell if there's someone with her," Luke continued. "Hidden in the trees. There might also be a sniper we're not aware of, so we're doing another check."

But those checks took time. And that's something they didn't have.

"The money transfer's done."

As soon as Luke's words finished, Sam started running across the grass. Ara sprinted toward her. Her pulse pounded against her sternum, her single focus on getting to Sam.

She jumped over the low gate and nearly slipped on the wet grass. She righted herself and kept going.

Closer. Just a little closer.

Sam stumbled. Had she been shot? Panic and urgency fueled Ara's last steps, and she flung herself around Sam, trying to block as much of her body as she could. The teenager was trembling violently, and Ara clutched her closer. She kept her moving toward a secure location. The agent from the bench caught up with them, flanking Sam with his body as well.

Relief washed over Ara as they stepped into the protected area. She registered the thin frame, the wholeness of the girl in her arms. "Sam, it's okay. It's over."

Luke came running up the pathway, followed by Thomas and several other agents.

"Sam, are you hurt?" Ara ran her hands over the girl's torso, but there was no blood, no wounds. "Are you all right?"

Sam said nothing, and Ara lifted the ball cap off of her head, desperate to make sure there were no injuries. A waterfall of long blonde hair spilled out.

The wrong shade.

The ball cap tumbled from Ara's fingers, and she took a step back. Dread washed over her like a wave of sudden sickness. Luke drew up short and sucked in a sharp breath.

The girl lifted her face, confusion etched on her features. "Who's Sam?"

* * *

Ara's body felt like ice. Her hands were shaking so hard, she had to ball them into fists to stop it. They'd fucked up. Big time.

"God damn it!" Luke cheeks were flushed, and he turned on one of the agents who'd been a part of the takedown team. "You told me it was her. You said you saw her face."

She blinked. "I . . . I thought . . ."

Luke cut off the stuttering agent with a swipe of his hand. "Who are you?" he demanded of the teenager.

"J-J-Jane Johnson." Her green eyes were wide and darted from face to face. "What's going on?"

"That's exactly what the hell I would like to know. How did you get here?"

"Some guy hired me for a hundred and fifty bucks to stand at the clearing edge, wearing these clothes, and then run toward her," she pointed at Ara, "when he gave me the okay."

"They set us up," Ara said.

"Yes, but he had to physically be in the area in order to pull this off." He narrowed in on Jane again. "The guy you arranged this with. What did he look like?"

"Dark hair. Brown eyes." She pointed to a spot on her right cheek. "He had a mole right here."

"How tall was he?"

"I don't know."

Luke jabbed a finger at himself. "Taller than me? Shorter?"

Jane eyed him. "About your height."

He pointed at several agents. "Make the rounds of the perimeter again. Use this description and find him. Now."

He pointed to several more. "Stop anyone you've seen in the last twenty minutes passing through the square and question them. Ask them if they've seen the guy."

There was a flurry of activity as the agents moved off.

"Thomas," Luke continued. "Take Jane and see if you can get a composite of the guy we are looking for."

They were left alone on the pathway. "Ara . . ."

He reached for her, but she moved out of range. If he touched her, she would fall apart. She shook her head. "No, don't. I know. I already know."

Luke's cell phone rang, and with a growl, he unclipped it from his belt and glanced at the number. "Oliver. Shit."

He moved off to take the call.

She held it together long enough to turn away and take a few strides toward the fountain. Tears stung the backs of her eyelids, and the tightness in her chest burned like acid.

Sam was dead. There was no doubt in Ara's mind.

She'd failed. Again.

For a moment, she was back in that dirty room in Russia. Nadia's warm body next to hers. If she closed her eyes, she could hear her voice.

"I'm scared."

The commotion outside the door increased in intensity. Shouting. Footsteps on the stairs. A couple of the girls screamed. One was crying.

"I'll go first. Then you can follow me once you see how I do it."

The night was so dark, the only light coming from that red sign. The feel of the metal scaffolding under her hands. Her grip was tight, the years of gymnastics training giving her the upper-body strength to hang on.

"Come on, Nadia! Hurry!"

The bang of a door answered her. Screams. Gunshots. Nadia's face froze, and a dark spot bloomed across her chest.

The wind blew, and some droplets of water from the fountain sprayed her face. Ara opened her eyes and wiped her cheeks with a shaking hand. She hadn't been able to save Nadia or any of the other girls.

And now, she'd failed Sam, too. The pain coursing through her was crippling. There was so much blood on her hands.

Her cell phone rang. Ara yanked it out of her pocket, and her body grew rigid when she saw the caller ID.

Unknown.

She answered.

"I knew you wouldn't listen. You broke our agreement and brought your FBI friends to the party." He tsked. "I told you—no one but you. Although I must admit it was quite fun to see the look on your face when you realized the girl wasn't Sam."

He was here. In the park. Close enough to be watching. She started searching the perimeter. "Where's Sam?"

He laughed. "Do you really expect me to answer that?"

Ara spun around, her hand gripping her phone even tighter, and scanned the area again. Her gaze darted over the runner to her left, the couple kissing on the bench, the man in the trench coat walking away from her. "You bastard. If you've hurt her, I will hunt you down myself and you'll wish you'd never been born."

"Sam is perfectly fine, I assure you."

Was he lying? Or was there a chance she could get Sam back alive?

She took a deep breath and said, "You got your money, but that's not all you're after."

"It's not?"

"No. Let's end this game."

"And how do you propose we do that?"

"Easy. We'll make a trade. Me for her."

There. She caught sight of a man on the east side of the fountain, up on a hill under a grouping of trees. A cell phone in his left hand. Tan jacket, blue jeans, dark hair.

His mouth started moving just as the voice came through on the phone. "That's an interesting proposition."

He looked in her direction and their eyes met, just for a moment across the distance. He froze like a deer, registering the fact that he'd been made.

She stepped forward. He took off running.

Ara sprinted across the square and dove through the trees after him. Her heart pounded in her chest as she jumped the small fence enclosing the area and spotted him several yards away. The bastard was fast.

She kept her eyes locked on his tan jacket as she barreled down the path. He glanced over his shoulder. He veered to the left onto a dirt path, and she felt a surge of adrenaline.

Wrong way, buddy.

His panicked decision forced him to climb a hill and traverse a rock formation. He clamored over the boulders. Ara gave a last burst of speed. He came flying down toward the main path, and she sprang at him.

They landed in a tangled heap on the leaf-covered grass. The kidnapper jutted up with his elbow, and Ara moved her head just in time to avoid having her nose broken. She fought to grab his hands, but he rolled and managed to get back on his feet. She grabbed his jacket. He twisted, his arms sliding out of the garment, and took off down the pathway again.

Son of a bitch.

Ara took off behind him. The bulletproof vest felt like a vice, and mentally she cursed it. They ran through the park. With every footfall, she managed to close the distance between them, but it wasn't enough. He darted out onto Fifth Avenue and took a left. She used the last of her resources and put a final burst of power into her legs. In the hustle of New York, she could easily lose him.

Bursting onto the street, she was slammed from behind. Her hands shot out in front of her, just in time to prevent her face from connecting with the concrete. The squeal of tires barely registered as she jabbed an elbow into the man on top of her. He grunted and punched the side of her head hard enough to have her vision blurring.

He took advantage of the moment and secured her hands behind her. She caught a glimpse of tennis shoes, the metallic inside of a van before everything went black as a hood was placed over her head and she was lifted into the vehicle.

Before the door slammed shut behind her, she heard one voice, calling out her name.

Luke.

CHAPTER THIRTY-TWO

Luke saw everything in quick flashes.

The van with the muddy license plates. The huge man hauling Ara inside. The squealing as it pulled away from the curb.

Thomas came crashing out of the trees behind him, but Luke didn't pause to speak to him. Instead, he bolted down the street, pulling his identification from his pocket.

"FBI. Give me your keys."

A man held his motorcycle helmet under one arm and gaped at him. Luke didn't bother to say it twice. Ripping the keys out of the man's hands, he mounted the bike and started it.

"Hey!" the man shouted.

Thomas caught up and physically held the man back. "FBI, sir."

"But that's my—"

Luke grabbed the helmet and shoved it onto his head. Heart racing, he peeled down the street. The van was weaving and bobbing ahead of him. Several blocks up, it took a left-hand turn.

They were heading for the tunnel. If he didn't move fast, he would lose them.

Luke pushed the bike to the limit, weaving through cars. His chest felt tight, the wind whipping around him. He took the turn a little too sharply and almost took out a street vendor.

Shit. He regained control and flew through a yellow light.

Faster. Faster.

It was a mantra in his head as he went through another yellow. Cars honked their horns in furious succession.

The light in front of him turned red. A truck pulled into the intersection. Pedestrians started crossing the street. Luke slammed on his brakes, and the motorcycle fishtailed. He tightened his grip on the handlebars and turned just slightly.

Everything moved in slow motion. The shock on people's faces as they threw themselves out of his way. The side of the truck looming in front of him. Luke fought the urge to close his eyes.

Please. Please.

The bike skidded to a stop. He could've reached out and touched the side of the truck. Luke blinked and took one deep breath. He was still alive, and so was everyone else.

Ara.

Cursing, he pulled his phone from his pocket and dialed. When Thomas answered, Luke bit out, "Tell me she's still wearing the GPS tracker."

"She is."

Relief flooded over him, sharp and strong.

"They're in the tunnel headed toward Brooklyn," Thomas continued. "Where in the hell are they going?"

Brooklyn. . . . There were so many potential hiding places, so many places they could . . . Luke gripped the phone tighter as the answer slammed into him.

"There's a commercial shipyard in Brooklyn," he said. "That's where they're going. Get the units and meet me there."

He hung up the phone and sped off. With any luck, he would only be a few moments behind them.

Luke didn't want to think about how a few moments could mean the difference between finding them alive and finding them dead.

* * *

For the first few minutes, sheer panic ruled. Being tied up, unable to see anything, and at the mercy of the men who'd taken her was enough to set loose every terrifying memory of the first time she'd been kidnapped.

Ara's heart pounded. It felt like she couldn't get enough air, the fabric covering her face pulling in tighter with every intake of breath. She screamed and kicked out, but all she got for her trouble was a solid rap to the head.

"Shut the fuck up. Do you want to get Sam back or not?"

Sam. The one word was enough to bring her back to herself. She was not a child any longer. This was not Russia. She was an ex-cop, and there was a teenager who was depending on her to keep it together.

Ara stilled and made a conscious effort to slow her breathing. She was still wearing her vest, and although her hands were tied, her gun was still in its holster. She couldn't use it now, but there may be a time . . . Ara titled her head against the floor and felt the clip in her hair dig into her scalp. She still had the GPS tracker on. Luke would be following. He would come.

Focus.

The van was flying now, which meant they had to be on a highway of some sort. Twenty minutes passed, and she counted every one of them, listened for surrounding sounds, kept up with the turns.

They slowed down, making one final left.

"I'm going to free you, but you are not going to kick me." His voice came from the direction of her feet. "You can't see it, but there's a gun pointed right at you. So much as twitch, and I will shoot you."

The slide of metal against metal and the faint rush of wind. The van door was open. The ties were clipped from around her feet and her hands. Before Ara could move, her hands and feet were instantly grabbed. She was lifted and thrown. The sensation of free-falling. Ara had just enough time to tuck herself into a roll before she slammed into the ground. Tires squealed.

She reached up and jerked the hood off of her head. The van peeled out of the parking lot, its taillights barely winking.

Ara didn't waste a moment. She pulled her gun from its holster and got to her feet. She ducked behind the nearest building, using it for cover. Where in the hell was she?

She peered around the corner and caught sight of the vessels at dock. The huge crane. The containers. They'd brought her to the shipyard. Her hands trembled just a bit and she willed them steady. Clearly, the kidnappers had delivered her here for a reason. Ara could only hope that reason was Sam.

Taking the comfortable, familiar stance of an investigating officer, she lifted her gun and moved away from the building wall she'd been using for cover. Her gaze swept across the parking lot as a quick wind fluttered through her hair. It carried the scents of gasoline and trash. The slap of waves breaking against the ships and docks echoed across the expansive, empty space. The shadows were darkening by the moment as the last streaks of sun faded in the sky.

There was no sign of Sam. Ara's heart was pounding as she reached the middle of the parking lot.

Where is she, damn it?

She sucked in a deep breath and lowered her gun. Ignoring every instinct telling her to run away, Ara closed her eyes. She strained to listen to the sounds around her.

The slap of the waves. A distant train whistle. The rushing from the highway.

"Help! Someone please!"

Her eyes flew open and Ara spun to her left. On the far side of the parking lot was a wooden dock. She sprinted toward it. Her tennis shoes slapped against the pavement, the sound turning to a thumping when she crossed over onto the wooden boards of the dock.

The end of the dock was cast in deep shadows. She peered forward, slowing long enough to draw up her weapon once again.

"Please. Is anyone there?"

Her heart skipped a beat. It sounded breathtakingly like Sam. Ara could barely make out a form at the end of the dock. It took her a moment to realize the person had been tied to one of the posts.

She moved forward, caution keeping her senses alert. As she drew closer, the familiar features of Sam's face appeared like a mirage in the desert.

Her long blonde hair was loose and tangled, hanging in clumps around her face. Dark circles seemed even starker against her pale skin, and she was dressed in only her undergarments. Relief, sharp and nearly painful in its intensity, rushed through her.

Ara knew the moment Sam recognized her because her eyes widened. "Ara! Oh my God, Ara!"

She pulled against her binds.

"It's okay, Sam. It's okay," Ara whispered. She wanted to reach out and touch her, to remove the loops of chains securing Sam to the post, but she didn't dare shift her protective stance.

Ara took a final scan of the area. Nothing moved except the water, swirling underneath them. She waited a beat, then another second more. She forced herself to lower her weapon and drew closer to Sam. Tears flooded the teenager's eyes, spilling over and streaking clear paths down her dirty cheeks. Ara's heart ached at the sight of those tears, at the obvious relief coming off of Sam's whole body. She couldn't, didn't know how to tell her that they weren't safe yet.

"Ara, they locked me up . . . they killed . . ." Sam was sputtering with relief, her frantic need to communicate interfering with her ability to talk.

"Everything is going to be okay." Ara placed a firm hand on Sam's shoulder. She kept her tone confident and reassuring. She didn't feel it. Inside, she was a bundle of nerves and half of her was waiting for the sound of a gunshot to ring out. "I promise."

Sam sucked in a breath, held Ara's gaze for a moment, and then let it out. The panic seemed to ease in her, disappearing with her breath into the cool night air.

Ara ran her hands along the chains securing Sam to the post. The darkness of the dock made it nearly impossible to see, even though her eyes had adjusted.

"We need to get you out of here." She frantically started unwrapping the chains holding Sam to the post.

"Hurry," Sam cried. "Hurry."

The roar of a motorcycle gave Ara pause. She spun around and saw it enter the parking lot. Placing her body in front of Sam's, she held her weapon out.

He disappeared behind a building. Ara's heart pounded in her chest. She waited. One beat. Two. When he appeared again, he stayed along the shadows. She tracked his movements and then, just for a moment, a faint light hit his face.

She let out the breath she'd been holding. "Luke! We're here!"

A sickening crack echoed across the shipyard, and Ara was jerked off her feet. Her gun flew out of her hand and skittered across the wooden dock as she slammed onto it, rapping her head hard enough to see stars. A thunderous roar broke through her haze. When her vision cleared, she watched in slow horror as the dock broke away from the mainland in a shower of splintering wood.

"Ara! The dock is being destroyed. Get off the dock."

Luke's urgent commands spurred her into action. On wobbly legs, she grabbed at Sam, pulling and tugging the chains off of her. She was so consumed with the need to free her that she didn't see the incoming boat until it was too late.

A container ship sliced through the end of the dock like a knife cutting through butter. The damaged wooden structure shuddered, but miraculously stayed afloat, and with a tug, it began to drift out to sea.

The last chain of Sam's makeshift prison fell away, dropping into the whirling sea. Sam clung to Ara, gripping her with painful desperation. The dock swayed and rocked violently, thrown against the waves caused by the container ship, as the propellers churned the water below. Jumping in now would probably kill them both, and it was the only reason Ara stayed on the dock, holding the post Sam had been chained to with all she had.

On the deck of the container ship stood several men. Two of them she recognized immediately as the men who'd cornered her and Luke at the club: Scar Face and Ivan. The last man, the one holding a gun, was tall and good looking.

And he pointed a weapon straight at them.

CHAPTER THIRTY-THREE

"**W**here is the damn coast guard?" Luke demanded. "We need them out on the water now!"

"They're on their way, but there are a lot of ships." Thomas advised. "It's going to take them time to navigate to the one she's on."

"God damn it. What about helicopters?"

"Twenty minutes out."

"They don't have twenty minutes."

Thomas leveled a look at him. "You couldn't have known they would tear a dock away with Sam and Ara on it. We planned for a foot attack, a potential sniper, not for a battle on a ship."

Luke shook his head. "It doesn't matter."

The entire operation had turned to shit. Any sense of control they'd had was gone. Luke had planned and strategized for what he thought was every potential scenario. But this . . . there had been no preparation for this, and his mistake would cost Ara her life.

"Do we still have a GPS location on her?" Luke asked.

"We do." Thomas showed him the tracker. "And I've forwarded the coordinates to the coast guard."

Another member of his team ran up. "She's still wearing her microphone." He handed Luke the communicator. The sound of Ara's breathing along with Sam's whimpers cut him straight to the bone. He felt helpless.

Taking a calming breath, careful to keep his voice steady, he clicked on the microphone that would transmit his instructions. "Ara, I'm here. Keep talking, if you can. Give me everything you know about your location. I'm sending help."

He waited, uncertain if she could still hear him. Nothing over the speakers. Just the sounds of water and wind.

"Three men on board."

Her voice came through clear and controlled. Luke swallowed hard. In clipped, cop tones, she described the setting. "Scar Face and Ivan from Mist. The other one is dark haired, five-nine, one-eighty. Dark hair has a handgun."

"Maksim." Sam's voice was muffled, but still Luke could make out the name.

"Dark-haired man is named Maksim," Ara confirmed. Beside him, Thomas flew to the computer balanced on a nearby car and began researching.

"I can't see the name of the container—" Ara stopped midsentence. It took everything Luke had not to get on the microphone and demand she keep talking.

"Don't shoot," she said loudly. "We'll get on the ship. There's no need to threaten the girl."

Damn it. Maksim knew exactly how to control Ara. She would do anything to protect Sam, and he would use that weakness against her to gain the upper hand.

"Let Sam go and you can take me."

A pause. Luke strained, desperate to hear if he could pick up anything else. The gunshot turned his blood cold.

* * *

In her arms, Sam jumped and screamed as the bullet whizzed past them, so close Ara swore she could feel the heat of it graze her.

"Ara!" Luke voice yelled in her ear. "Ara!"

"We're okay," she whispered, hiding her mouth from the men behind Sam's head. "No one's hurt."

"Climb up the ladder," Maksim ordered. "I won't say it again."

The water still churned underneath them, rocking what was left of the dock so violently Ara wouldn't have been able to stand upright if she hadn't been holding onto the post. Still, she glanced at the water, trying to calculate their chances.

"The propeller is running." Amusement made Maksim's accent richer and heavier. "You'll be sucked under the boat and killed nearly immediately. If you'd like to save me the trouble, though, by all means."

The other men laughed.

In her arms, Sam trembled, and tears silently streamed down her face. Another piece of the dock splintered, came off, and was quickly tugged underneath the ship, just as Maksim had promised.

There wasn't a choice.

Ara leaned closer to Sam, whispering in her ear. "Climb the ladder. Stay close to me."

"They're going to kill us."

"They haven't yet, which means they want something else."

The rungs of the metal ladder felt icy under her fingers. Above her, Sam wobbled, and Ara briefly placed a reassuring touch on her ankle.

"Hurry, Luke," she whispered into the microphone.

Despite her words, Ara was already considering alternative options. It was just her out here with these men, and she couldn't count on Luke being able to help her now. She needed to come up with some way of protecting Sam, of escaping.

Sam was jerked off the last rung by Maksim, who held his gun directly to her head. He flashed Ara a winning smile as she climbed over the lip of the ship and dropped to the deck. She raised her hands in surrender. The two other henchmen circled up behind her, close enough she could feel their breath on the back of her neck.

"Don't shoot her," she said to Maksim.

He smirked. "Don't make me. Take off all the wires you've been given."

Ara hesitated. Cutting radio contact with Luke was bad, but she'd still have the GPS tracker. He would still be able to find her.

She reached inside her shirt and pulled out the microphone. She also removed her earpiece. Scar Face snatched them from her hand with one meaty fist and tossed them overboard.

"Now," Maksim continued, "the GPS tracker please."

Her eyebrows creased in mock confusion, even as a cold feeling of dread washed over her skin. "I'm not wearing a GPS tracker."

"You're lying." His mouth twisted in anger, and he pushed his gun harder against Sam's temple. He crooked a finger at Scar Face, who approached Ara with a portable scanner.

Damn it.

She squelched any trembling through sheer force of will. The scanner quickly beeped, and Scar Face smirked, ripping the barrette from her hair.

"Do you think we're fools?" he asked her.

"Get him," Maksim ordered. Ivan moved quickly below deck, his wide shoulders barely able to fit through the space. Sam whimpered, and Ara met her frightened, wide-eyed gaze. She let her expression warm, keeping her back straight, conveying no possible hint of fear to the teenager. It didn't matter that they were trapped on a boat with three men who were going to kill them. What mattered was that Sam remained calm, kept her wits, and took the moment of opportunity when it came.

Ara couldn't be sure, but she thought a hardness entered Sam's gaze, an ever-so-slight lifting of her chin.

There was a clatter on the stairs, and moments later, Ivan returned with an unconscious figure thrown over his shoulder. He threw him down onto the deck at Ara's feet.

Eddie Flores. Ara winced to see his bloody and bruised face.

"Put the tracker on him," Maksim ordered. "Quickly."

The henchman moved faster than Ara would've thought for someone of his size. Clipping the barrette into Eddie's dark locks, he hauled the man up over his shoulder again.

What were they doing?

He walked to the far side of the boat and flung Eddie right over. Sam screamed.

"Don't worry, he isn't dead. Yet." Maksim passed a glance over to Ara. "Shall we go and see? Mark, take her."

Maksim shoved Sam toward Scar Face, whose real name was obviously Mark, before passing him the weapon as well. Mark promptly placed the gun at Sam's temple, holding a firm arm around her throat.

Maksim, his hands now free, grabbed Ara's upper arm and tugged her over to the side of the ship.

"Look," he ordered, pointing down below.

Eddie was on a small, motorized boat. Still unconscious, his arms and legs splayed out, lifeless as a doll.

Maksim stepped up closer to Ara. He smelled like rich cologne, and Ara knew, if she ever lived through this, she would never again be able to smell the scent without gagging. He bent down to whisper, his breath warm on the shell of her ear.

"You see, I've rigged the boat with some explosives. They're set to detonate soon."

The boat started moving, and Ara caught, out of the corner of her eye, Ivan using a remote control. Her eyes drifted back to the small vessel starting to make its way out to empty sea.

She couldn't save Eddie. That knowledge cut her to the core. Eddie was far from innocent, but he didn't deserve this.

An anger, deep and powerful, bloomed inside of her. If she survived, she would never stop until she'd hunted Maksim.

He'd threatened Sam and her. He'd played with Eddie's life. And now he'd put more lives at stake.

The FBI, Luke—they would believe it was her. They would think she was on that boat, and they might send agents after her. When the vessel exploded, it would kill them all.

Her heart sank to realize that Luke himself might try to come after her.

"How long?" she asked.

Maksim just chuckled in response. He grabbed her arm again, jerking his head toward the gunman holding Sam. "Let's take them below deck."

Ara sucked in a breath. It was now or never.

She swung around suddenly, her fist primed and ready. It connected with his chin and, to her extreme pleasure, Maksim's head flew back. Another well-placed jab to his stomach knocked all the wind from him, and he landed on the floor of the ship, whistling for air.

Without pausing, without even thinking, Ara lowered her head and ran toward the man holding Sam. A shot grazed her and heat flamed in her arm. She ignored it and kept pumping ahead, slamming into him with all her body weight.

Oh God, it was like hitting a concrete wall.

He stumbled back and his arms windmilled, trying to prevent the fall. Ara only took one second to push Sam out of the way before she slammed into him again.

He screamed as he flew off the side of the ship.

"Ara!" Sam's panicked cry gave her only a moment to turn and duck before the other henchman, Ivan, swung a fist at her head. It missed the main target and glanced off her shoulder.

Fuck!

He'd hit her gunshot wound, the screaming pain bringing a rush of tears to her eyes. She sidestepped the next blow and attempted one of her own, a well-placed jab in the kidney that would have him pissing blood for days. He howled with rage and swung around, catching her by the neck and tossing her to the ground like a rag doll. Dazed, she struggled to get to her feet.

Click.

"Don't move, or I will kill her."

Ara shut her eyes. Taking a deep breath, she tilted her head up, and through the strands of her hair, saw Maksim holding Sam, once again at gunpoint.

Sam's gaze was apologetic, but Ara could hardly blame her. She was not a trained officer. The only way off this ship was with Ara, and even she hadn't been sure how they would get away.

Maksim stepped forward and swiftly kicked Ara right in the stomach. All of her breath was stolen by the sharp point of his boot, and she collapsed again against the cold, hard floor of the main deck.

"You stupid bitch." He kicked her again and Ara gagged. The sickening crack of a rib or two was followed by a stabbing pain. "I liked Mark."

She felt a swell of pride at the anger in his voice. She'd surprised him, humiliated him, and there was almost nothing worse for a criminal of his nature.

There was no way she could overpower them, though. Not now. Her best bet would be to fake it, to pretend her injuries were worse than they were. Ivan's meaty hands closed around her arms, pulling her to her feet, and she played as though her legs would not cooperate. Blood from the gunshot wound ran down her arm, helping to give the impression that she was seriously wounded. In all truth, it was probably nothing more than a graze. It hurt like hell, but she'd been shot before and this wasn't nearly as bad.

"I've fucking had it," Maksim muttered as he jerked Sam's hands behind her back and secured them with a zip tie. As he approached her, Ivan pulled on Ara's wrists, and she winced. She let out a cry of pain. Maksim tightened the zip tie more than necessary around Ara's wrists, and the plastic cut into her skin.

Jerking his head at Ivan, Maksim once again claimed Sam's arm, and the group of them moved toward rickety stairs leading to the belly of the ship.

"There's no need," a voice said from the darkness. "I got tired of waiting. I'm coming up."

Instantly, the demeanor of the two men changed. They backed away from the stairs, taking Ara and Sam with them. Their shoulders straightened, their backs went rigid, their jaws tightened. All of the arrogance Maksim seemed to exude from his very skin washed away with those simple words.

Ara's gaze locked on the stairs to see what had caused such a transformation. As the man rose on the stairs, coming out from the darkness like the devil from hell, the light hit his face and Ara immediately recognized him.

Dmitri Grishnokov.

CHAPTER THIRTY-FOUR

"**H**ello, Ara. So nice to meet you again." Dmitri's voice reminded her of good Russian vodka. Smooth, powerful, but with the promise of a bite at the end.

Behind him, two men appeared. Ara instantly recognized one as Nick Flores. The young man had been beaten, much like his cousin. His face was a mass of bruises, one eye swollen shut, his nose most likely broken. He was pushed forward, at gunpoint, by another of Dmitri's henchmen.

Sam released a hushed sob at the sight of Nick.

"Sam," Nick whispered, and earned himself a solid punch to the stomach from his jailer. He hit the deck with a thud, gasping for air.

"Don't!" Sam screamed, fighting against the hands holding her. "Don't hurt him."

Dmitri chuckled, stepping closer to Ara. "Ah, young love. Isn't it a beautiful thing?"

His dark gaze took in everything, missing none of the details. The blood seeping out of the sleeve of Ara's jacket, the bruise appearing on Maksim's face.

"What happened?" Dmitri demanded. "Where is Mark?"

Maksim ducked his head. "There was some resistance."

"I warned you. She's not one to go down without a fight." Dmitri clapped a hand on the other man's shoulder. "You've disappointed me, cost me a good man. We'll deal with that later."

"Yes, sir. It won't happen again."

"Uh, I hate to break up this bonding moment the two of you have going on but," Ara said, lifting her chin and meeting Dmitri's gaze with a hard one of her own, "you have received the money as agreed. Your man can confirm it's in the bank account you provided. Now let us go."

"Not yet."

He began to circle around her, Ivan stepping back so that Dmitri could make a full round.

"What do you want?" she demanded.

The corners of Dmitri's mouth curled up in a cold imitation of a smile. "Don't you remember me?"

"We met at Mist."

"No, no, my dear Ara. We met long before that."

He was close to her now, his breath warm and minty on her face. She stared into his dark eyes. "You were in the town car. When the house in Austin was burning down, you drove by and then sped off."

Dmitri smiled, trailing a finger down the curve of her cheek. "Bravo. You found it." He gripped her chin forcefully. "But do you know why I was there?"

"Because it was your operation."

"No, no, no." He turned her head one way and then the other before squeezing even tighter. It was like being in a vice. He leaned closer. "It was my son you killed that day."

Her eyes widened with shock, and she sucked in a sharp breath.

"Yes, darling Ara, you murdered my son."

He backhanded her across the face so hard she flew to the cold metal deck. She was pulled back up by Ivan and turned to face Dmitri.

The murderous intent in his eyes froze her blood. He was not going to let them go. He'd been planning this for a long time. Dmitri wanted revenge, and he would take it, painfully.

"I didn't kill your son." Ara forced her voice to stay calm in spite of the rising panic within her. "He died in a fire he set himself."

"Do you think me some kind of fool?" Dmitri scoffed. "You handcuffed my son to the bed. You left him there to die."

Ara shook her head. "I tried to save him. I went back into the fire and nearly died myself. I tried to get him out."

"Lies!" Dmitri screamed, suddenly losing any sense of control. His face twisted, mouth contorting with rage. "You murdered him, you stupid bitch! He wasn't even supposed to be there. He'd gone to that miserable house in the middle of fucking nowhere to *prove* himself to me, to show he could take over our operations. He wanted to make me proud."

He drew closer to her, threateningly close, and Ara prepared herself for another blow.

It didn't come.

Dmitri sucked in a deep breath, and just as quickly as it had begun, his tirade was over. He smoothed down his tie, checked his hair.

"Now." He held out a hand, and Ivan reached into his jacket, producing a long, jagged knife. Ara's heart picked up speed and her mouth turned dry. What the hell was he going to do with that?

"Tell me, Ara, it's been hell for you these last few days, hasn't it?" Dmitri paused, a glint in his eyes. "I've taken great pleasure in knowing the pain you've been suffering."

She didn't answer. Dmitri didn't seem to expect her to. He moved toward Sam, and Ara struggled against the binds. Ivan simply tightened his hold.

Sam whimpered as Dmitri grew closer, her gaze fixed on the blade in his hand. Her fear fed Ara's own, and before she could stop herself she cried out, "Don't!"

Dmitri paused, and Ara forged ahead. "She has nothing to do with this. I'm the one you want."

He chuckled, long and low. A shiver raced down Ara's spine at the sound of his laugh.

"On the contrary." Dmitri turned toward her, his expression triumphant. "She has *everything* to do with this and always has. Right from the beginning."

His words hung in the air between them. The only sounds were the slapping of the waves against the boat and the hum of the engines. Realization slammed into her like a sledgehammer to the chest. She couldn't breathe.

He planned this. All of it.

Her mind flashed through the last couple of days, the clues they'd come across along the way. Sam's kidnapping was never about the money, or about Eddie paying off his debts. That was all a mask, a cover-up for Dmitri's real intentions. He used Eddie and Nick to get close to Sam so he could arrange her kidnapping, knowing that by taking her, Ara would feel responsible. Knowing she would join the investigation.

Everything had led them to this point, to this ship, to this confrontation.

To her.

Understanding must have shown in her expression because he laughed again. "Yes, Ara. This . . ." He waved the knife toward Sam, Eddie on the dinghy. "All of this was part of my revenge."

Ara's gaze darted to Sam, and guilt clawed at her. The whole reason Sam was standing on this boat, shivering in the cold wind, was because of her. Ara knew, better than anyone, the pain and terror of being kidnapped. The knowledge that her failures had caused Sam to go through the same horrifying experiences she had once endured was gut-wrenching.

"Aren't you curious about why I devised this particular method for you?" he asked, pulling her focus back to him. He was gloating now, his chest puffed out with pride, as he moved to stand in front of her.

Dmitri waved the knife in her face, and the blade caught the moonlight as he placed the point of it at her throat. She knew he could see the racing of her heart through the thin skin at her neck, but she would not give him the satisfaction of being openly terrified. She kept her face placid and met his gaze straight on.

He chuckled, amused by her challenge. "You, dear Ara, are a warrior. A survivor." The knife's edge trailed down her body, in between her breasts, across her navel. "And even though you are a murdering little bitch, I find some qualities in you to admire."

Dmitri gripped the bottom of her jacket and used the blade to slice through it, cutting it straight off her body. Ara closed her eyes as his hands ran along the outside of her thin, long-sleeve T-shirt, his fingers trailing the length of her arms.

The slicing of the fabric brought her back. Dmitri cut away her shirt, tearing it off her body. Her skin prickled from fear and the sudden rush of cold night air.

Dmitri passed the knife back to Ivan before once again circling around her. But this time, while standing behind her, he stopped. Ara craned her neck, desperate to see what he was doing. She had visions of being knifed or shot but quickly reminded herself that wasn't Dmitri's style. He didn't like making death easy for those who'd wronged him.

And Ara had wronged him. In the worst possible way. She jumped when she felt his fingers on her shoulders.

"These scars . . ." He traced the long, puckered scars down her arms to just past her elbows.

He leaned in closer. She could feel the thick wool of his suit jacket against her bare back, and she fought the urge to step away.

"It took me a long time to find out how you got these, Ara. But once I knew your name, and learned you had come to the United States at the tender age of fourteen, it was a simple matter of calling my Russian friends."

Her stomach twisted and churned. She was going to be sick. "It seems my son is not the only person you've murdered."

She was shaking violently now and couldn't bring herself to stop. "Your son was a piece of shit who trafficked and raped young women and children. It's not my fault he died."

Dmitri breathed out a sigh, nearly like a release. He seemed to absorb her pain, using it like a salve on his own wound.

"Ah, Ara, but what about those girls?" He touched her scars again, the constant reminders of the lives she hadn't saved. "Those girls you left behind in Russia. What do you think happened to them?"

She fought back the sudden rush of tears. She knew what had happened to them. Of course she did.

Dmitri gripped her shoulders and spun her around. "You see, Ara, I could torture your body. But once I'd learned what you had survived as a child, I knew that you would be able to withstand any physical pain."

His voice was low and smooth, like a snake. "No, what I needed to do was to hurt your soul. And so now, I'm going to have my men kill Eddie, Nick, and Sam before they kill you. That way you'll know, before you die, that there were three other people whose deaths you are responsible for."

His words cut through her.

"Fuck you." She spat in his face.

Ivan stepped forward, his fist already clenched, but Dmitri held up a hand to stop him.

"No, no. It's all right. It's merely a sign that I am correct." He removed a silk handkerchief from the front pocket of his suit and wiped his face. "Isn't that true, Ara?"

She glared at him, and a knowing smile stretched across Dmitri's face. He clapped his hands suddenly. "Maksim, Ivan. I leave you to carry out my orders."

"You'll never get away with it." She tossed the words at his retreating back. "The FBI knows about you, about your involvement in the forgery scheme. They'll catch you."

He half turned and chuckled, confident, controlled. "I don't think so, my dear. I hear Mexico is quite lovely this time of year."

She didn't have time to even give him a retort. Ivan scooped her up, carrying her toward the edge of the boat. From the pocket of his jacket, he pulled out a gun, cocked it, and held it to her temple.

Out of the corner of her eye, she saw Dmitri disappear on the far side, followed and protected by one of his henchmen. The vibrations of the ship ceased immediately, and Ara realized they'd stopped moving.

He was escaping.

She wanted to scream with fury and frustration. She wanted to kill him with her own bare hands. But she didn't have time to focus on Dmitri. She had much more immediate problems.

Sam, with her hands still zip-tied behind her back, was forced at gunpoint by Maksim to stand next to Ara. Her lips were turning blue and her teeth were chattering violently. Nick was shoved into place alongside her.

"Shoot me first." Nick's voice was hollow and flat, but when he met Ara's gaze with his one good eye, he tilted his head just slightly in Sam's direction.

Ara blinked, hoping he would understand that she had gotten his message. Loud and clear.

Sam, however, was pulling out of her glassy-eyed state. Nick's words seemed to have ignited her fear.

"No, no, no." Each word heightened her pitch until she was red in the face.

"Shut the fuck up." Maksim whacked her in the back of the head with his hand, and the words died on her lips. She sucked in breaths with great gulps, and Ara feared that if she didn't calm down, Sam would hyperventilate and pass out.

Maksim pointed the gun at Sam, and Nick moved suddenly, without warning. Ivan's head turned, momentarily distracted, and Ara took the opportunity.

She ducked and kicked, slamming her leg into Ivan's groin before ramming her shoulder into his stomach.

A gun went off. Faintly, as if from a faraway place, she could hear Sam screaming.

Ivan toppled over, his gun skittering away into the darkness. Ara gave him one swift kick to the face, hard enough to shatter his nose in a spray of blood. Before he had a chance to recover, she struck him again. His head slammed against the side of a container so hard it gave a sickening, egg-like crack. With one glance, she knew he was either dead or unconscious.

Nick and Maksim were wrestling a few feet away. Both of them were crouched over, each trying to gain control of the gun between them. Nick's hands were slick with blood, his face red with effort. Maksim bared all his teeth, kicking out with his feet. One of his hands hung loosely and unused next to his side, giving the beaten Nick a fighting chance.

Sam stood to one side, motionless and expressionless. Even the screaming had stopped.

"Sam!" Ara cried. "Move now!"

She shoved the girl, pushing her into the darkness with her shoulder. She had to get these damn binds off her hands. She couldn't help Nick without doing that first, and she needed Sam out of the way, hidden, and at least partially out of danger.

As they moved further into the ship, Ara scanned their surroundings. There was only a sliver of a moon, barely enough to see by, and it was difficult to make out anything distinctively.

She shoved Sam next to a container, into the shadows. "Are you hurt?"

"N-n-no," she stuttered. "Oh my God, Nick."

"I need something sharp. Something to cut the ties off with."

The request created a calm in Sam. Her shaking stopped, and she helped Ara look. A moment later, she whispered, "Here! I found something."

Ara closed the distance between them quickly. Sam jerked her head toward the jagged edge of a container that had been worn away by rust.

"Will that work?"

"It's perfect." Ara spun around and maneuvered her hands into position. Jerking her body back and forth, she sliced through the tie in three motions. The rusty metal had also cut her hands, but Ara barely felt the wounds.

"Now you," she ordered Sam, placing her into position. More carefully than she'd been with herself, she released the teenager's bonds.

The sound of a gunshot echoed across the distance, bouncing off of the metal. Sam sucked in a sharp breath, her eyes widening with terror. She gripped Ara's arm.

"Nick."

Ara reached down and pulled out her clutch piece from her boot. It was small, with a limited number of shots, but it was all she had.

They needed to get off this boat.

She grabbed Sam's hand and started leading her toward the front of the vessel.

"Where are you going?" Sam halted, drawing Ara to a stop. "Nick is the other way."

"I'm getting you somewhere safe."

"We can't just leave him." Sam threw away Ara's hand. "He needs our help."

"We don't—"

"No. I tricked him into this. He didn't know about the plan. He was furious when he found out. Nick tried to talk us out of it, but I wouldn't listen. Then these men came, and it all went to hell . . ." Tears welled in her eyes. "He risked his life to help us. We can't just leave him to die."

Ara looked into her face and saw the determination, the loyalty. Sam was right. He'd risked his life to help them escape. They couldn't leave Nick behind.

"Okay." Ara jabbed a finger at her. "But you stay behind me. Close."

"You got it."

CHAPTER THIRTY-FIVE

Ara hid with Sam behind a container, listening. There was nothing. No sounds, except for her own ragged breath and Sam's behind her.

Keeping to the darkness as much as possible, leading with her weapon, she crept toward the spot where she'd seen Maksim and Nick wrestling. Sam clung with both hands to the back of Ara's jeans, and while it made Ara's progression forward slightly awkward, she didn't complain.

They moved to the final container, then Ara slid up next to the smooth metal. Sucking in a breath, she peeked around the corner.

Nick lay still on the deck, his limbs splayed out. Underneath him was a dark pool of blood.

"Nick." Sam took one step toward him, but Ara stopped her, swinging an arm around her waist.

"Listen to me."

Sam struggled against her. "No, no, Nick."

"We can't help him now," Ara hissed. "And if we don't get off this boat, they are going to kill us, too. Do you want to die?"

Sam stopped, the question as effective as a slap to the face. "No, I don't want to die."

"Good. So help me get you out of here." Ara peered around the corner of the container again. Ivan was still right where she'd left him, in the same crumpled position, and she felt a brief sense of relief. But as she scanned the area further, she saw no sign of Maksim.

Damn it.

He was wounded and armed, which made him even more dangerous. And while she'd only seen Maksim, it was possible there were more men on board the ship than just him.

She hesitated. There had to be dinghies attached to some part of the ship. They'd placed Eddie on one. The poor bastard was still out there, drifting on the ocean with a ticking bomb underneath him. Dmitri had escaped on one, too. If she was lucky, there would be a third for Maksim and his men. She just had to find it first.

Dmitri had moved toward the back of the ship. It wasn't much, but it was the best clue she had. She took a quick look at the deck. They had to pass through the empty space—and a relatively well-lit empty space at that—in order to go in the direction of the dinghies. It was dangerous—Maksim could be hiding in any number of places, waiting for them to appear again. She could only hope he'd gone after them, or that he was lying somewhere in a pool of his own blood.

If they weren't lucky . . . Ara tightened her grip on her weapon. She would just have to be the better shot.

Ara grabbed Sam's hand. It was cool and small. "We're going to make a run for it. Don't look anywhere except down at your feet." She didn't want Sam seeing Nick's body more than she already had. "Do you understand?"

Sam gave a swift nod.

Still holding the teenager's hand, Ara bolted out from behind the container. She kept her focus on the red container opposite of them, the darkness beyond it. Safety was a mere 500 feet away.

400.

300.

The gunshot rang out, pinging off of the metal deck near Ara's feet. Maksim stepped out of the darkness right in front of her.

She screeched to a halt so fast Sam slammed into her back. They both nearly tumbled to the ground, with only Ara's firm footing preventing them from becoming a tangled heap.

Maksim grinned, the blood streak across his face making it macabre. "You cops are always so predictable." He stepped forward even more. His arm, covered in blood, hung loosely at his side. "So stupid. You can't help yourselves."

Ara hid the hand holding the gun carefully behind her, wedged between her and Sam. She needed to bring him a little closer. There would only be one shot, and she wasn't going to mess it up.

"How so?" she asked, allowing her voice to tremble with fear.

"You were trying to save poor Nicky-boy, weren't you? You always have to play the hero."

"You're injured," she said. "And at the rate that wound is bleeding, you're going to pass out soon."

He smirked at her, a twist of beautifully shaped lips, and raised his weapon. "Not soon enough for you."

With one hand, she shoved Sam down to the floor, simultaneously raising her own weapon.

The gunfire echoed off of the metal containers, reverberating in the air.

Something slammed into her vest just as Maksim's head exploded like a watermelon. The smell of gunpowder and blood filled her nostrils.

Then she heard the rush of pounding footsteps.

Pulling Sam up to her feet, Ara's breath felt like it was tearing through her chest. She was nauseous and cold. Blood ran in a river down her sleeve from her injured arm. From overhead came the *thump, thump, thump* of a familiar sound.

A helicopter.

It flew low and fast over them, heading out to sea where Eddie's boat sat waiting. Shoving and pushing Sam, hair flying from the high winds created by the helicopter's propeller, they managed to reach the side of the boat.

Several armed men came around the corner.

Ara thrust Sam overboard, and she hit the water with a splash. The sky lit up with a brilliant, white light as Eddie's boat exploded. A wave of heat rushed over her. Smoke, thick and viscous, immediately poured out from the remnants of the dinghy. The helicopter veered to the left, dangerously close to spiraling out of control.

Ara passed one glance behind her. The men, momentarily thrown by the explosion, were now closing in fast. She had no other option.

She tumbled into the sea. The sensation of icy cold water, and then blessed blackness.

CHAPTER THIRTY-SIX

Bright sunlight streamed into the hospital room, washing across her face. The view outside was beautiful, the fall colors of the trees in the courtyard vibrant. It would have been perfect if it weren't for the multiple tubes and machines she was currently attached to.

Ara tried to sit up higher in the bed, but even that simple movement made her wince as a sharp pain shot through her shoulder. With gentle fingers, she felt the bandage.

"I would leave that there. Otherwise the doctors are going to tie you to the bed." Luke strolled into the room, a half smile on his face.

Ara leaned back against the pillow and smirked. "I'd like to see them try."

He laughed, the smile widening. "How are you feeling?"

"Like I was shot and some sick, twisted doctor had the enjoyment of stitching me back together."

"And he'll demand payment to boot, believe it or not." He reached the side of her bed and took one of her hands in his.

His palm was calloused and warm. He smelled like fresh air and sunshine. "We caught him."

She blinked, thrown off by his sudden shift in conversation. Then her eyes widened, and her own smile tugged at her mouth. "Really?"

Luke nodded. "Just outside the Mexican border. Dmitri was a fool to think we wouldn't find him."

"He didn't expect me to survive long enough to tell anyone where he was going."

"I suppose not."

Ara patted the mattress, and Luke perched himself there. "There is something else I need to ask you about. I wanted to wait until you were stronger before—"

"The scars." Ara cut him off, knowing exactly which piece of the puzzle Luke still didn't have.

"Yes. How did he know so much about you, know that killing people in front of you was more damaging than physically harming you?"

Ara took a deep breath, letting it out slowly. She hadn't told this story to many people—the painfulness of it so embedded in her soul, it felt like a stone in her chest. Still, the burden, the secrets . . . they weren't helping her heal.

As she looked into Luke's gentle blue eyes, she wondered if changing her own way of coping would.

"When I was thirteen, my family lived in Russia. One night, coming out of gymnastics practice, my best friend Nadia and I were abducted."

He didn't say anything. He didn't even move. But Ara heard the nearly silent catch of his breath.

"I wasn't the intended target. That was Nadia. Her father was wealthy, and they wanted to ransom her off. I happened to be in the wrong place at the wrong time." She turned to look out the window, but she no longer saw the beautiful fall leaves. "They took us to an apartment, a place where they kept other girls they had kidnapped or kids they'd taken for sex trafficking purposes. At first, they handcuffed us to beds, kept us in the dark. As the days passed, they became less strict."

Her voice lowered, the words sounding hollow, even to her own ears. "One night, there was a commotion outside of the apartment. A lot of banging, screaming. Gunshots. The police had gotten a tip and were raiding the apartment, although we didn't know that at the time. I tried to convince a few girls to go out on the scaffolding, but they wouldn't do it. They were terrified."

She closed her eyes and could smell the scent of the tear gas, the sweat, her own fear.

"I went out onto the scaffolding, and I called out to Nadia but . . ."

Ara's throat closed up, the words so painful she didn't know if she could bear to hear them said aloud. "She died."

Luke said nothing, but he squeezed her hand gently. When she opened her eyes and looked at him, the understanding she saw there nearly ripped her heart in two. He reached out and wiped away the tear that had escaped.

"You survived."

"I did." She lifted her arm to reveal the scar. "The scaffolding tore up my hands and shoulders. I could never be a gymnast after that. My parents moved us to the U.S. and we started a new life."

"But you never really did, did you? Because you still blame yourself."

"I should have done more," she said with heavy conviction. "I should have saved her. All the girls in that room. It's why I became a police officer; it's why I went off the rails when it came to certain cases. It wasn't a job for me—"

"It was repentance."

"Yes." She breathed out the word. He got it. Although she supposed if anyone would, it was Luke.

"That's why you pushed so hard for Sam." His expression held both awe and, more importantly, respect. "Why you risked so much."

"Of course." Ara gave a half shrug. "She was me."

"I'm sorry I ever doubted you."

"Don't be." Now it was Ara's turn to squeeze his hand. "You were doing your job. I would've done exactly the same."

Their eyes met, and the tension in the room felt palpable. Luke licked his lips, and her breath hitched. For a moment, Ara swore he was going to lean down and kiss her, but a knock at the door interrupted them.

Ara peered around Luke to see Sam standing in the doorway. In her arms was a huge bouquet of flowers.

"I can come back later—"

"No, no." Ara waved her in. "Please."

Sam gingerly stepped inside. "I tried to visit you earlier, but they wouldn't let me into the ICU."

"It's okay. I probably wasn't much fun."

Luke chuckled. "She's not much fun now, to tell you the truth."

Ara glared at him and then watched as Sam set the vase down on the table next to the window. She was wearing a T-shirt and jeans, and her long, blonde hair was pulled back into a ponytail. Her naked face was pale, her already slender frame painfully thin.

But she was here. And whole.

"Those are beautiful." Ara smiled warmly at her. "Thank you."

"There's no need. It's the least I can do." Sam's gaze lifted to briefly meet Ara's before dropping back down again. "You did save my life and all. When I think of how I treated you, what I did . . . I still don't understand why you helped me."

Ara waved her closer, and Sam dutifully complied. "You saved my life, too. The way I see it, we're even."

After Ara had dived into the ocean, the blood loss coupled with too many knocks to the head had caused her to lose consciousness; Sam had kept Ara's head above water until help arrived. She'd saved them both.

Ara sucked in a deep breath, the guilt as sharply painful as her bullet wound. "I'm sorry about Nick."

Tears flooded Sam's eyes. "I should have . . ."

"There was nothing you could've done." Luke locked gazes with Sam before turning to Ara. "Either of you."

His words were logical and simple enough to hear, but Ara saw in the grief written across Sam's face that she didn't believe it. Ara didn't want Sam going through what she did. The guilt, the pain, the weight of the what-ifs.

If she could spare Sam even a little of that, she would.

Telling her story to Luke had freed a part of her. Maybe hearing it would help Sam heal. Help her forgive herself.

Ara smiled at her gently and said, "Sit down, Sam. I think there's something about me you need to hear."